I0629015

SARAH'S GONE MISSING

a novel

Jacki Bishop
Early Riser Publishing

Sarah's Gone Missing
by Jacki Bishop

ISBN: 978-0-9905315-3-1

Early Riser Publishing
P.O. Box 711
101 E. Baltimore Ave.
Media, PA 19063
www.JackiBishop.com
jaxstir@gmail.com

Disclaimer:
All of the towns mentioned including Media, PA, East Hampton, NY, Branford, CT, and New Haven, CT are portrayed authentically. The characters and situations, however, are fictional, a product of the writer's imagination.

Cover Artwork: Darkworx |Dreamstime.com

Cover Design: Rik Feeney / www.RickFeeney.com

DEDICATION

In Loving Memory

Leah Greene, mentor and friend

Michael Kennedy, loving husband, father and friend to all

Maria and Michael Tulli, Soulmates

Loving parents and grand-parents

Mitzi, the best cat ever

RIP

ACKNOWLEDGEMENTS

I would like to thank first my husband Hank, formerly my "tech guy," now my advisor, editor, and fact-checker. He has become almost as involved as I am in the whole process.

My sons Andrew, a budding writer himself, and Eric, along with his wife Emily (who helped market my first book on the West coast) have my gratitude and love. Thanks goes to my sisters, Marcia and Joyce, who enthusiastically support my writing endeavors.

Thanks to my cousin, Pam (and Herb, "The driver") and all of the Oklahoma cousins, for their support.

Many thanks to our "in-laws," Kathy and Joe, who introduced us to Branford, CT. and all of its charm, including the Thimble Island tour and The Kelsey House.

Thanks especially to our good friends Paula and Gary (the 'old clammer'), our East Hampton experts, who not only walked us through the EH sites in the book, but also answered questions by email and text during the writing process.

Thank you, Dorothea, for the beach pix, and for your support of my writing.

Thanks to Rob and Lisa (the real ones) for letting me use their names.

Thank you, Lyn, for promoting my first book and writing the best review on Amazon.

Once again, thanks to Mary, for laboriously checking my first copy and making appropriate suggestions, and her husband, Lance, who also supports my efforts.

Thanks also goes to Media, "everyone's home town," and my many friends in the area who give me encouragement.

To Rik Feeney, my editor, thanks for helping me through the process, and for allowing me my "tantrums," when we disagreed.

As always, it takes a whole community of friends and family to publish a book.

PROLOGUE

The darkly handsome young man sat staring fixedly at his computer. For months he'd been tracking Sarah Justice; he had hacked into her computer and knew more about her than anyone should, except maybe Sarah herself.

Now a huge smile spread across his face as he easily slipped into her Facebook account, using the name of one of Sarah's law school acquaintances. Sarah had immediately "friended" this young woman, though they weren't really friends.

He'd also found out that she had a good friend, Lisa, who was an assistant DA in New York City. He frowned. That was not so good. Sarah was going to visit Lisa and her husband, Rob at their "cottage" on Gardiner's Bay in East Hampton. Sam, Sarah's co-worker, probably her boyfriend, was not going with her; that was good. The man was surprised that someone as smart as Sarah would discuss her private life on a notoriously public site.

He sat in front of the brightly lit screen weighing the pros and cons. He had to go through with it. The plan had been in the works for quite a long time, and he had to make sure he succeeded. If he did, he would rise to the top of his organization. He focused on that, refusing to accept defeat. This operation would go forward.

CHAPTER 1

Daylight had begun to filter in through the blinds when the incessant buzzing of her cell phone awakened Rory Chandler. Reaching blindly for it, she nearly knocked it to the floor. Glancing at the clock she saw it was 6 a.m.; this could not be good news.

Taking a deep breath, she answered with an uncertain "Hello…"

"Rory, it's Sam. I'm sorry to call you so early, but I just couldn't wait any longer; it's Sarah—she's gone!"

Shaking her head, as if to clear her brain, Rory noticed that Marc was awake and looking at her quizzically. She gave a helpless shrug, and tried to concentrate on Sam.

"'Uh, Sam, I'm not sure I follow; you knew she was going to the Hamptons to visit friends, right?"

"Yes, yes, of course! She'd been there a few days; her friends just called me, well, that is they called around 3 a.m., to tell me Sarah went out for a walk along the beach, and she hasn't come back!"

She could feel Sam's pain through the phone; Rory tried to soothe him. "I'm sure there must be some mix-up; it's not like Sarah to go off and not tell anyone."

"I know, I know; that's the thing, it's not like her. She went out after dinner; Lisa and Rob went to bed early and left the light on for her. When Lisa woke up during the night, she noticed the light was still on and checked Sarah's room; she wasn't there!"

Marc was fully awake now and looking concerned. She handed him the phone and mouthed, "It's Sam, not good." Rory left the room to make coffee.

"Sam, this is Marc; I gather there's a problem with Sarah. Rory just handed me the phone and from what I heard, it sounds serious."

Sam sighed, "Yes, I'm afraid it is serious, you see Sarah was staying with friends in the Hamptons. She went out for a walk on the beach after dinner and never came back!"

"And did her friends go out searching for her?"

"They did, as soon as they realized she was missing, but that was in the middle of the night. It was dark out so they couldn't see much."

Rory walked into the room and told Marc that coffee was brewing. Marc spoke to Sam again. "Hang on, Sam, Rory is making coffee. Look, why not just come over here; it's best we talk in person and put our heads together, ok?"

"Sure, thanks so much, I'll be right there." Sam said.

"Hey, Sam, drive carefully." Marc advised, before he disconnected.

"He sounds bad!" Marc said.

"I know," Rory replied, sitting down on the bed close to Marc, "he's not at all himself."

Sorry I dumped the phone on you, but I just didn't know what to say. I'm glad you invited him over." Rory shuddered involuntarily, and a tear slipped down her face. "God, where could she be? She's become like a third daughter to me, and Sam, well, it's hard to imagine what he's going through." Standing up, Rory said, "Mind if I shower first? It helps to clear my mind."

Marc nodded. "No problem." His face was grim.

In the shower, Rory gave in to her tears, letting the warm water wash them away. She'd known Sarah for, what? Five months? Sarah and Sam had been interns in Rory's law office over the summer. Together, they'd solved a crime and saved an innocent man from a possible death sentence. They'd grown very close in a short period of time. Sam and Sarah had become an "item," and now they were living together, both in their last year of law school; Sarah was at Widener and Sam at the University of Pennsylvania. Although she no longer saw them every day at work, it felt like they were part of her family. She couldn't fathom losing Sarah.

Getting out of the shower, Rory mentally shook herself as she dried off. She was no good to Sam if she lost it; they had to find Sarah.

Reentering the bedroom, she found Marc sitting in the same spot; he seemed in a daze. "Your turn," Rory said, gesturing toward the bathroom, "It helped get the cobwebs out and now I need to get dressed before Sam gets here."

"Yeah, I hope…" Marc wandered into the bathroom, his sentence dangling.

Rory threw on some jeans and a tee shirt. They'd been enjoying beautiful fall weather; Rory loved October and typically felt invigorated by the cooler weather. Right now, it felt as if she was moving through heavy sand.

Without drying her hair or putting on makeup, Rory went down the back stairs to the kitchen. The sun was up now, lending a cheery note to her well-appointed kitchen. Sitting in the breakfast nook, her favorite spot in the house was comforting. She looked out the window and took in the gorgeous colors of fall foliage.

The knock on the front door sent a jolt of adrenaline through her; Rory hurried to let Sam in before her daughters awoke. It was Saturday, and still before seven.

Rory wasn't prepared for the Sam Logan who appeared at her door. He was unshaven and his longish brown hair was flopping in his face. Typically handsome with a boyish smile and warm brown eyes, he'd lost his best friend and his troubled visage reflected that.

She opened her arms to give him a hug. Sam clung to her like a child and began to quietly cry on her shoulder. Rory kept her own tears at bay as she patted him on the back and reassured him, "We'll find her, I know it!" She hoped her words, which sounded implausible to her ear, would comfort Sam.

Marc came down the front stairs as Sam was pulling away from Rory and wiping his face.

"Hey man," Marc clapped him on the shoulder, "rough situation; we need to talk and put our brain power to work. Come get some coffee."

Rory asked Sam and Marc, "You guys hungry? We should probably eat something…"

Marc answered for both of them, "Let's just have eggs and toast; give our brains a boost."

Sam nodded, as he took the cup of coffee Rory handed him.

Marc and Sam sat in the breakfast nook while Rory prepared breakfast.

She could hear Marc talking quietly to Sam. He was asking Sam to think back over the past week with Sarah, before she left to visit her friends. Marc wanted to know if he could think of anything unusual that might have happened. Was there anything atypical in Sarah's behavior? Why did she decide to visit her friends at this time, and why hadn't he gone with her?

Rory felt reassured by the questions Marc was asking. She was so glad to have him in her corner. Thinking back over the past, very difficult summer, when Marc had been angry with her much of the time—ostensibly for taking on a tough case that might interfere with their vacation plans—Rory was relieved that he was now fully supporting her. Of course, his anger had been just the tip of the iceberg, she found out as her criminal case was being resolved. Marc had cheated on her. Yes, it had been a difficult summer, but she and Marc were back on track. Her feelings of betrayal were there, beneath the surface, but she and Marc were in counseling and they had a good, solid history; quite simply, they loved each other. Recently, their communication had improved immensely, and in Rory's mind that was key.

Glancing at the nook where Marc and Sam were still deep in conversation, Rory noticed that Sam looked marginally better. Marc knew what he was doing. As a forensic psychologist, he was well equipped to ask the right questions. He had certainly put Sam at ease.

Rory brought the plates of food over and sat down to eat and join in the discussion.

Sam picked at his food as he talked. He'd listened to Marc's questions, and, after a bit of reflection, began to answer them.

"Sarah had seemed upset for the past few weeks. I pressed her on it, and she finally admitted that she was afraid a guy she'd dated her first year of law school was stalking her again. She had told me about Henrique Alvarez and how she'd ended the relationship, but he wouldn't let it go until she threatened legal action. When she got the invitation to visit Lisa and Rob, it seemed like a good idea for her to get away. I had planned on going with her, but I had some finals coming up...damn it!! Why didn't I go with her?" He slammed his fist on the table.

"Even if you'd been there; do you think you could've stopped it?

"I don't care! I should've been with her! I thought maybe I could be a decoy and try to catch the guy. But I never dreamed it would turn out like this!"

"Of course you didn't!" Marc reassured Sam. "Like Rory said, he'd have likely gotten Sarah, and God only knows what he might have done to you!'

"Did you ever see the guy, or feel as if you were followed?" Rory asked.

"No, but Sarah's fear was real; she's not the type to play things up. It never happened when I was with her," Sam said. "That's why I guess I believe if I'd been in East Hampton, she'd have been ok." Sam got up and began to pace. "I need to do something; I can't stand feeling useless!"

"Why don't you use my computer and see what you can find out about this Henrique guy? Then, if you get any Intel, we can talk about it," Marc suggested.

"Ok, I'll do that," Sam said as he left the room.

"This really sucks!" Rory said to Marc. "I feel helpless, too! What can we possibly do?"

They heard Sam's cell ring and soon he came into the room talking on his phone. He listened, nodding, then said, "Thanks, Lisa, appreciate it. I'll be in touch." The color had drained from his face.

Rory and Marc sat quietly, awaiting his response.

Finally, he turned to them and said, "They found Sarah's sandals at the end of the beach."

CHAPTER 2

Sarah awoke, her head pounding, mouth dry, tongue swollen. She looked around the unfamiliar, darkened space, hardly a room, and felt panic rise from her belly. Looking down, she saw that her hands were bound in front with duct tape and her wrists were rubbed raw, they were nearly numb. She was on a narrow bed, which took up most of the room; it was more like a berth. The smell of the sea was strong.

She struggled to get her mind to work and tried to remember. She first recalled dinner with Lisa and Rob, was it yesterday? Sarah remembered going out for a walk on Gardiner's Bay after dinner as the sun was setting. She pictured herself grabbing her small phone from the charger and heading out.

She'd been obsessed with gathering shells, jingles in particular. The jingles on this beach had a beautiful, tangerine hue, a color which she'd never found on any other beach. There were many shells scattered on the beach from a storm earlier in the day. Sarah had become hyper-focused on getting the best and biggest of the shells.

Wearing her cargo pants with many large and some small, hidden pockets had been a good idea; they were perfect for collecting her shells. She'd slipped her phone into a zippered pocket on the inside of her thigh to make room for an especially large haul of shells. Holding a handful of the fragile shells, she shook them, reveling in their signature jingling sound, like a pocket full of change. Then she'd placed them carefully in her large pockets. By the time she'd noticed that darkness was falling,

Sarah had walked nearly to the end of the beach, close to the parking lot. Standing up, she'd been massaging her lower back when… her brain didn't immediately kick in with what happened next. Then, in a painful rush, Sarah remembered being roughly grabbed from behind and struggling with her captors until she felt the sharp pinch of a needle. And then everything went black.

It was probably Rohypnol, or GHB, she thought; both strong anesthetics, also associated with the phenomenon known as "date rape." The reasoning part of her brain seemed intact and Sarah felt hopeful that her mind was slowly beginning to function. She knew she'd need all of her faculties to get out of this nightmare.

Sarah vaguely remembered hearing gruff, male voices, speaking rapidly in a foreign tongue. Then…nothing until this moment.

So, here she was, with no idea of who had captured her or where she was, but it was somewhere on the water. She was hurting all over, but her head was clearing. Looking over herself, trying to assess the damage, she noticed that her ankles were also bound and her feet were bare. Her large pockets were empty, shells gone.

Suddenly remembering her flip phone, Sarah felt for the hidden pocket. Oh my God, she thought, is it possible they didn't get my phone? With a mixture of hope and fear, she pushed and prodded to unzip the pocket. The small flip phone popped out and landed on the dirty mattress under her. Tears of joy flooded her eyes and she sent a small prayer of thanks. Her smart phone was back at the house; thank God she'd always brought the smaller one to the beach.

Maneuvering with bound hands was difficult, but doing it quietly was a greater challenge.

So far, she'd heard no voices since coming to, but had no doubt her captors were close by.

After nearly dropping the phone a few times, Sarah was able to secure it in her right hand. Flipping it open, she turned it on and noticed it was still on vibrate. She saw several missed calls from Lisa and Sam and thought, Oh, God, what must they be thinking? Sarah bit her lip to ward off the tears that threatened. Emotions were her enemy right now. What she needed was a cool head and logical thinking.

She focused on crafting a text for Sam. Holding the phone and typing with her thumb proved arduous, but she had no choice. She typed: "911 I was grbd @ bch dk whr I m but I m on water use trk app 2 fnd me xo"

Sarah sat back, exhausted, but hopeful. She'd started to doze when her phone vibrated.

The text was from Sam: "Thank God, Sarah; we've all been sick with worry! Marc's on the computer now, trying to find you. I love you, hang in there! Keep the phone on."

Tears of relief came, and she sobbed quietly, her chest heaving. Just to connect with Sam and to know he was looking for her elicited a flood of warmth throughout her body.

Forcing herself, she typed back a short response. "call lisa wl lv cel on if bad gys don't get it hnds r bnd cnt txt mch xoxo"

Another buzz came in; it was from Lisa. She texted that she and Rob had noticed some suspicious looking guys a few days earlier, appearing to do work on the abandoned house a few down from hers. Lisa felt sure they could identify them. She sent her love.

Sarah tried to respond to the text, but she was feeling dizzy and nauseous, as if she were seasick. I'm on a boat! That was her last, terrifying thought before drifting off, her phone cradled in her hand.

***

The tension in Marc's office was reflected in Rory's and Sam's faces as they watched Marc trying to get a fix on Sarah's location. The signal wasn't strong, and often he would lose it entirely. He was not altogether familiar with this software, having used it on only a few occasions. But he was determined; Sarah's life depended on this. So he soldiered on, praying for quick results and a successful rescue.

Suddenly, the screen went blank. "What the fuck?!" Marc blurted. "I was getting close, and then… nothing!" He slammed the desk with his fist.

"Maybe she turned it off so her captors couldn't find it; maybe they came in and she had to hide it!" Sam was grasping at straws.

Marc continued to try and coax the program back to life. The message on the screen read: "number unavailable."

"I'll keep trying. It's possible there's a glitch in the program." There was a false note of hope in his voice. "I think I'll call Roland; the state cops do this sort of thing…"

"Speaking of cops," Sam said, "I'll call Lisa and have her call the local police and maybe the coast guard. Sarah mentioned she was on water, but God, she's staying on Gardiner's Bay so she's surrounded by water." Sam stopped suddenly, thinking, and then said, "We have to consider that she may be on a boat, which opens up a whole new scenario."

Sam reached Lisa and repeated all he knew, asking her to contact the local authorities.

Almost as an afterthought Sam added, "Do you know how to reach her dad? He should probably be contacted."

Lisa answered, "Of course I'll do that. I just sent a short text to Sarah telling her that Rob and I noticed two guys working on the roof of the old cottage no one's been living in for years. We could give their description to the police."

"Ok, sounds good. Let me know if you hear anything." Sam said. Then he began pacing again.

"Sam," Rory said. "Come sit down, we have to look at all the facts and try to make sense of them."

Sam sat, looking devastated.

Rory reached across the table, putting her hand on Sam's while looking him in the eye and said, "I know things aren't looking great just now, but we don't have the luxury of letting our emotions run wild. We've solved some difficult problems in the past; this one's tougher because it's personal." There was a hitch in her voice. Rory cleared her throat and continued, "Our best assets here are our brains and our ability to process information logically. Sarah deserves nothing less."

Marc left his computer, finding Rory and Sam seated again in the breakfast nook.

"Roland said they usually hand these cases over to the FBI; they have much more sophisticated methods of tracking. But," Marc added, "Roland's more than happy to be part of our team and lend his expertise. And Sam, he said to tell you he's very sorry."

At that moment, Sam's cell trilled. Looking panicked, Sam picked up his phone and put it on speaker.

"Sam, hi, it's Lisa," she seemed reticent, speaking slowly. "I just spoke with Sarah's father…it was strange. I called him from Sarah's smart phone and when he answered, he sounded frantic. He said, "Sarah, my God, where are you?"

CHAPTER 3

Sarah had fallen into a deep sleep after the exertion of texting Sam. She had received, but not replied to, Lisa's text. The phone dropped from her grasp as the boat took a sudden turn and slid across the mattress, hitting the wall with a thud.

Almost immediately, the door burst open and Sarah was jolted awake, terrified to see a ski-masked face above her. Before she could react, her phone was snatched from where it lay. As he left, her captor backhanded her full in the face, displaying his AK 47 and slamming the door.

Sarah dissolved into a quaking mass of fear. She could hear two different voices screaming at each other, in a language which sounded vaguely familiar. A third voice, curiously calm and quiet belonged to a man who seemed to be in charge. There was something about his voice that held Sarah's attention.

Suddenly the engines roared to life and the boat took off, thrusting Sarah against the wall.

She had a sinking feeling that GPS tracking of her phone wouldn't work now. She hoped fervently that she'd given Sam enough information to begin the search. Sarah had a gut feeling that her best course of action was to stay calm, use her wits and somehow find a way to escape. She felt anger rising in her belly and vowed never to play victim.

***

Sam, Rory, and Marc sat in stunned silence following Lisa's phone call.

Sam was the first to speak, "Shit! This is suddenly getting bigger!"

"What do you mean, Sam? What are you thinking?" Rory inquired.

"Sarah's dad's a Federal judge! Think about it. Federal cases aren't peanuts; they involve some pretty bad dudes, and apparently he's known as a hard-assed judge. She's told me that much."

"Jeez..." Marc exhaled. "So, you think she's been grabbed by some bad actors to influence the judge's decision on a case he's hearing? That would take a set of brass ones, I mean, kidnapping the daughter of a Federal judge!"

"What else could it be?" Sam asked in desperation. "Her dad answers the phone, thinking it's Sarah, and then starts back-pedaling, saying to Lisa he hadn't heard from her for a while and was worried. That's bullshit! She seldom calls him. And then telling Lisa not to call the police, he'll 'handle it.' What the fuck does that mean?"

"Yeah," Rory replied, "that sort of puts us in a bind and well, it certainly puts Lisa and Rob in a bad situation, since they'd already called the police; they can't exactly say 'never mind, she's back.'"

"I'm sure they've no intention of doing that. I think they'll tell the police to keep it quiet, but there's only so much they can do; it's out now." Sam speculated, "Actually, I think the Feds should get involved. I know the locals don't always want to give over to them, but they also don't want to screw up a case potentially this big."

"Also, Sam, I think we have to consider that it may not be related to her father. You mentioned this Henrique guy; what about him? Certainly it looks like a high-level kidnapping, but we have to look at all possibilities."

21

"Henrique could definitely be a player; I need to get back to the computer, see if I can find out anything."

Before he could say more, Sam's cell rang. He glanced at the screen, saw a blocked number, and put the speaker on. The voice on the other end was distorted, "Stay out of this lover-boy if you want to see your pretty miss alive!"

CHAPTER 4

Rob Higgins, a tall, well-built black man with a chiseled face and a shaved head, answered the door, to meet two uniformed East Hampton police officers. They showed their badges and identified themselves as Lieutenant Hannigan and Officer Thatcher. Rob wondered why they hadn't sent a detective; surely this wasn't a routine investigation, so why hadn't they?

Lisa, equal in height to Rob with a mass of shiny black hair and piercing green eyes, introduced herself. "Hi, I'm Lisa Higgins, won't you come in?" Both men accepted and followed her to the small, cozy living room.

The lieutenant, a beefy man with a ruddy complexion and thinning reddish hair, was the senior officer. Thatcher, tall and lanky, probably in his 20's, appeared to be a rookie. Hannigan cleared his throat, and said authoritatively, "So, you've reported a possible kidnapping. Can you tell me what happened?" He looked toward the couple, and Lisa answered.

"First of all, Sarah is a friend of mine from way back. Secondly, her father is a Federal judge, which may be a possible motive for her disappearance. She was staying with us—she'd been here a few days. Sarah went out to walk on the beach after dinner last night, as she likes to do, to collect shells. Then she usually sits on the beach for a while. Anyway, we went to bed early and left the light on for her. When I awoke at about 3 a.m., the light was still on and she wasn't in her bed. I woke up Rob and we went out searching for her, calling her name. We couldn't see much, even with flashlights. When we searched this morning, we found these," Lisa said, holding up a pair of sandals. "We're pretty sure they are hers." Lisa's face fell.

Rob looked at her and picked up the tale. "Sarah evidently had her small flip phone with her and was able to put out a few texts; a friend of hers was attempting to track her, then he lost the signal. In her first text she said she'd been grabbed off the beach and that she was on water—well, look, that could mean anything out here, but it's possible she's on a boat. If that's the case, they could be out on the Atlantic, or the Sound, or in Connecticut, to mention the most obvious possibilities."

"Since she'd left her smart phone here, I had her father's number and called him from her phone," Lisa continued. "When he answered, he said, 'Sarah, my God, where are you?' When I told him who I was and what had happened, he didn't exactly sound surprised. He seemed sort of fake concerned, at least to me. Then he said that we shouldn't involve the police, he would 'handle it.' Well, I'd already called the police, but I didn't tell him that. And he really didn't ask any other questions. I thought that was strange."

"By the way, two days ago," Lisa continued, "we saw two swarthy looking men on the roof of the abandoned house a few houses over; they were hammering, but they didn't really have other tools with them. I'm sure we could describe them and maybe an artist could get it right."

"So, what we're saying is that this could be a very big case, and if Sarah's being held to try and influence a Federal judge, then probably the FBI should take over. Even so, she could be out of state by now. No offense, but we should talk to your Captain." Rob looked at the officers apologetically.

Lieutenant Hannigan looked perplexed, rubbing his chin, not speaking immediately.

Officer Thatcher looked like a deer in headlights.

"Well, it does sound like an involved case," Hannigan finally replied, "we should at least run it by the chief. Why don't you come down to the station, maybe around 10:30? You can see Chief Mayer."

Rob looked relieved. "Thanks, Lieutenant, we really appreciate this; we'll be there," he said, checking his watch, "about 10:30 then."

They ushered the officers to the front door, thanking them again for coming.

"Whew! I'm surprised; I thought they might push back." Rob said.

"I'm not surprised, frankly," Lisa said. "East Hampton is no bum-fuck town out in the sticks. After all, they have some of the richest and most famous people summering here, not in humble abodes like this one, but out on the ocean and of course in the village. They're used to accommodating the upper crust and would hate to have a scandal on their hands by botching a case."

"Whoa, I stand corrected," Rob said with an affectation and his nose in the air.

Lisa smiled for the first time since Sarah's disappearance. "I thought I'd told you all about East Hampton when I inherited this place from my great aunt. Too bad you never met Aunt Lilia, she was a hoot." Lisa smiled at the thought. "Don't get me wrong, I love it here."

"Well," Rob said, "I sort of remember what you'd told me, but this is the first time I've actually been here, so it may take a while to sink in."

"Getting back to Sarah," Lisa said with a worried frown, "I think we should get ready to go to the station."

Rob put his arm around Lisa; drawing her close, he gave her a quick kiss. "You know I'm here for you; we'll find her."

"I'm still put-off by her father's reaction." She looked up at Rob, "Aren't you?"

"Hey, I don't know the guy, but it does make you wonder…"

Lisa's phone rang. She glanced at the number, shooting a puzzled look at Rob.

Then she answered. Lisa held the phone out so she and Rob could both listen. It was an engineered voice that rasped: "You wanna' see your friend again, keep it to yourself, Lisa!"

CHAPTER 5

Rory, Marc, and Sam were blindsided. This phone call had obvious, sinister intent.

Silence reigned as each of them digested this new, unforeseen event with varying degrees of emotion.

Marc was the first to verbalize his feelings. "Ok, so we knew, or surmised that Sarah's captors had taken her cell phone. That means they have phone access to everyone in her contacts. Now Sam, she'd texted you, so they are aware of your relationship. Not surprising that they'd try to frighten you into keeping quiet. And any missed calls, from you, and...."

"Lisa! I know Lisa tried to call her several times, as did I. Lisa texted her, too. So, we should check with Lisa and see if they've gotten to her."

"It may be that they're just trying to make you think they're watching you, to keep you from involving the police." Rory weighed in. "It's already gone farther than they'd planned, because of Sarah's phone."

"We can't rule out the possibility that they have access to surveillance, but I would bet, Sam, that you went off their radar when she went to East Hampton," Marc reasoned.

"But, we've no idea how long they've been shadowing Sarah." Sam said with a shudder.

"I know she's suspected it for the last several weeks. She had told me about Henrique before, but until recently she thought the stalking had stopped."

Just then, Sam's cell rang. He looked at it in resignation and said, "I don't recognize this number," but picked up anyway.

Relief flooded his face and he put the phone on speaker. It was Lisa.

"Hope I didn't scare you, Sam, calling from Rob's phone, but I'm a little freaked out. Just after the police were here I got a call, with a phony voice warning me not to go to the police. Well, if they'd been watching the house, they'd have known that the police were here…We don't know what to do; we're supposed to meet with the chief in, like, a half-hour. And if they're watching…"

"They called me, too, with the same warning. We're not sure if they're just trying to intimidate us, or if we are actually being watched. I think we have to take some precautions, but I can't tell you what to do…" Sam's voice trailed off.

"Yeah, but I'm asking for advice; what do you think we should do?" Lisa sounded frantic.

"I don't know… maybe you can call the chief from Rob's phone and ask him to meet you somewhere, explain why? If you don't keep the appointment, they're bound to show up back at your place, and that's not good." Sam looked tentative.

"Actually, that sounds like a plan… what the hell; we have to do something, right? Rob and I will talk it over and get back to you later. Thanks, Sam, that's helpful. Bye for now."

"It's got to be fucking Alvarez! I'm going back to see what I can find out on the internet."

"I agree," Marc said. "I was thinking along the same lines myself. We need to decide what we're going to do." Marc paused. "I think our first move has to be to see Sarah's father, the judge."

"Hold on!" Sam spoke up. "For sure the judge is being watched, if this is going down the way it looks. I'm afraid doing that would tip our hand and put Sarah in more danger. Whatever we decide to do, it has to be on the down-low. But I'll be fucked if I know what that is!"

Rob and Lisa slipped out the back door of the cottage, trying to appear casual. Lisa purposely looked at Rob and initiated chatter, trying very hard not to look around for vehicles that could be involved in surveillance. But, since she was wearing sunglasses, she was able to use her peripheral vision without detection.

The shells on the driveway crunched underfoot as they made their way to their green VW Beetle. Lisa felt the sun on her face and noticed that it was a beautiful day; normally this would put her in a happy mood, but today, her heart was heavy. She got into the car and glanced around the area. Fewer people were here this time of year; she recognized the cars of a few of her neighbors, but there were no other vehicles that she could see.

Once they were in the car, Lisa spoke. "I didn't see anything out of the ordinary, only the neighbors' cars that were here before. I guess maybe we should take a roundabout way to Montauk. It's only about 20-minutes this time of year, so we can take our time. We agreed to meet Chief Mayer at about noon."

"Just direct me," Rob replied. "You know I have no sense of direction."

Lisa smiled, "I'm glad you can admit it. I'll pay attention and give you plenty of time."

She studied the road. "It's hard to see the signs with all the trees, but I know my way pretty well. OK, see where that car up ahead is turning? Make a right there. We should be on this road for a while."

"OK, boss, got it." Rob said with a smile. "Seriously, we should think about a GPS for the car, even though I've heard mixed reviews on them... What?"

Lisa was looking behind them with a worried expression. "Turn right at the next road!"

Rob executed the turn on short notice. "What's up?"

Lisa was looking out at the side mirror. She breathed a sigh of relief. "I guess I'm just jumpy, but that car, the black SUV, just sort of appeared out of nowhere. He's not behind us now, but we'll see. It's fine to stay on this road for a while; it parallels the road we were on. We can take a side-trip to Amagansett; it's pretty, you can see the ocean and lots of 'old time' beach houses, like ours.

She looked out the window at the old houses. She noticed they were casual, a little weather-worn and they really blended in with the beach. She'd had offers on her beach house, very high offers, from developers. But she knew their intent was to raze the house and put in an over-size house that would compete with the natural beauty of the place.

They drove in silence for a while, then Rob said, "Wow, there's the ocean; it's beautiful! You're right, these houses are about the same vintage as yours; the ocean is in their backyards."

"Right," Lisa agreed, "but they're worth at least twice what mine is, because it's oceanfront. I'm glad that most of them have stayed the same."

Looking in the side mirror, Lisa said, "I think we're alright to go back to the main road, so make a left on the third street to your left; it's a bit complicated since these roads meander so much.

After executing a few more turns as instructed, they were back on Montauk Highway.

"So this will take us into Montauk and I'll direct you. I know where we're going, but have to feel my way as we get closer. I'm really glad the chief agreed to meet us at the Montaukett for lunch." The weather-worn façade of the restaurant came into view; the parking lot was nearly full, attesting to its reputation for good local food. There were few of the fancy, expensive cars prevalent in East Hampton.

CHAPTER 6

Rob led the way into the Montaukett and Lisa followed, casually looking around for Chief Mayer, who'd been described to her. A middle-aged man, sporting a Yankees cap, jeans and a tee shirt, gave her a brief nod. He was sitting on one of the stools with views overlooking the water.

Lisa asked quietly if the two seats next to him were taken. He smiled and said, "Be my guest, Lisa?"

She smiled back, and said, "This is Rob." They nodded to each other.

"I hear the clam chowder is the best here, that true?" asked Rob.

"Only if you like clams," he answered with a smile.

Lisa asked quietly, "Can we talk here? We'll follow your lead."

"We'll talk after lunch; take a walk on the beach…" the Chief answered. "There are a few plain-clothes men scattered about, inside and out." He spoke without looking at her. "If one of my guys senses a trap, after I leave, he'll give you instructions. Otherwise, just follow me on the beach shortly after I leave."

Getting up to place the order, the chief asked, "Clam chowder all around?"

Rob and Lisa nodded.

As they waited for their lunches, the three discussed the view (spectacular), the weather (brilliant), and the Yankees. Lisa was a Yankee fan, so she had the most to say about that. Rob, a staunch

Phillies fan, despite their uneven performance, stayed out of that discussion.

The chowder arrived and conversation slowed down.

The Chief finished first, nodded as he left; he'd already paid the bill.

Rob and Lisa purposely dawdled, watching as Chief Mayer walked along the beach below them. Rob noticed that the Chief was trim and fit, probably a jogger, he thought.

Looking around the restaurant, it appeared to be filled with locals, mostly men, possibly fishermen. He also had the distinct impression that he and Lisa didn't fit here.

"Ready?" Rob asked Lisa.

She nodded, leaving a few bills in the tip jar as they left.

Once outside they discussed walking on the beach. The Chief was far down the beach at this point.

Lisa, wearing sandals, slid down the incline to the beach, Rob catching her before she fell. She smiled her thanks and said, "Well, I guess we'll just look for shells and keep the chief in our sights."

"Oh, I think he'll let us know when and where we can talk." Rob said looking around. "Don't look now, but one of the guys from the restaurant just came out; he's leaning against that beat-up Toyota in the parking lot."

Lisa didn't look around, but had a quizzical look on her face.

"He's probably one of the undercover guys," Rob concluded.

"Ohhh," Lisa answered, looking unobtrusively toward the Toyota; "Yeah, probably."

"Chief's out of sight, around the bend up there; let's pick up the pace, maybe jog." Rob suggested.

"You can jog, I'll power-walk. I just had lunch." She held her stomach as Rob jogged ahead.

Soon, he too had disappeared around the bend. Lisa took it up a notch and reached the bend in a few minutes. She looked around, seeing neither of them, confusion on her face.

A shrill whistle, Rob's, led her to a dune, on the other side of which she found the two, seated on a large driftwood log.

The Chief stood and held out his hand, "Chief Mayer, call me Thom," he said.

"Lisa Higgins," she answered as she shook his hand.

"I knew your aunt; everyone loved your Aunt Lilia."

"Thank you, Thom, I have some great memories of spending time with her here."

Seating herself in the sand across from the men, Lisa looked up expectantly.

Rob glanced at the Chief and said, "Just to fill you in, I've told Chief...er, Thom what's transpired so far. You can give your version, in case I've left anything out."

"Well, Rob tends to be pretty good at getting the main points," Lisa told the chief, "so you probably have a full picture. Also, since he hasn't known Sarah as long as I have, he's less emotional than me. But, I'm thinking the FBI should be in on this and whatever investigation takes place needs to be on the down-low. We don't know how big this is or who's even involved, but two of Sarah's best friends have been threatened and given explicit instructions to not seek police intervention."

"Yes, I gather it's a very sticky situation. And the supposition that Sarah's father has probably been threatened makes this whole thing take on a larger scope. This is no minor thug we're up against." Thom weighed in.

"Yes, but, we're dealing with, as you say Thom, suppositions. It seems to me we need to know the truth," Rob said. "How do we get to the judge and find out the real story?"

"I know the judge, not well, but we've met." Lisa said. "I mostly know of him from Sarah. They don't have the best relationship. Since his wife, Sarah's mother, died when Sarah was ten, the judge sort of shut down. That's when he sent Sarah to boarding school, where we met, so she had to sort of fend for herself. I'm not saying he doesn't love her, I'm sure he does. And he would definitely go to any length to keep her from harm."

"The thing is, where Federal judges are concerned," Thom interjected, "they have a ton of protection. I know for a fact that Federal marshals are in the same building where the judges hold court. I doubt, however, unless there's reason, that the marshals provide surveillance outside of the courthouse." He shook his head.

"But, this isn't an ordinary situation; don't you think they'd be on alert 24-7 now?" Lisa was biting her lip.

"That's hard to say, I mean yes, they probably are, but they'll have to tread lightly. They may be able to protect the judge, but that doesn't necessarily mean they will mount a search for Sarah." Thom answered.

Lisa gasped, "I just can't stand this; we're helpless to do anything to help her and we don't even know who the enemy is!" Her chin trembled as she fought back tears.

"But," Lisa said, as she remembered something she wanted to tell the chief, "we did see two guys on the roof of the abandoned house in our neighborhood the other day. They were certainly out of place, and if we could see a police artist, we might be able to get a good description."

Chief Mayer answered, "The problem will be finding a place where you can meet with the artist; we don't want to put you in any more jeopardy." He thought for a minute and said, "I'll send someone to your cottage after dark; he'll come in the back way, and I'll call you first. Otherwise, stay put. If you need groceries, get them on the way home."

The chief continued, "I have undercover cops with me today. They often help out in situations like this. And we can do some investigating, especially, as to establishing whether or not there was a boat involved; there are several marinas near here that would know about recent rentals."

Lisa sighed, "Thank you, I'm appreciative of anything you can do."

"Well," Thom said, "Just know that I will do anything in my power to help you out. I'll call you tonight and tell you when to expect the artist."

Just then the chief's cell went off, to the tune of the William Tell Overture. "Thom here," he answered. He frowned as he listened, then spoke urgently, "Well, get on it, don't be obvious, and keep me in the loop. I'm headed back to the office."

He looked at Lisa and Rob, as if weighing his thoughts. Then said, "My guy in the restaurant saw someone he thought was suspicious snooping around your car. Soon as he came out of the restaurant, the guy jumped in his car, a black Range Rover, and took off. Seems like every third car in East Hampton is a black Range Rover, so this will not make things easy."

CHAPTER 7

The trio in Rory's breakfast nook was still engaged in conversation, although sometimes it seemed to Rory that they were going in circles. A thought was flitting through her mind and she couldn't quite capture it. Then, in a flash, it came to her. She interrupted Marc and Sam.

"Sorry to butt in," Rory apologized, "but that Henrique guy, did you say he dropped out of school right after she dumped him?"

Sam didn't answer at once. He was probably thinking about it, Rory thought. Then, Sam said, "Yeah, I think she said he did drop out right away, at least she seemed to connect the two. I'm trying to remember what else she told me."

Rory waited again as Sam collected his thoughts.

"I did pay attention when she talked about the guy, because she was still somewhat afraid he might show up again. Sarah told me how they met," Sam continued. "She downplayed this, but I had the impression this guy was quite handsome and charming. His native tongue was Spanish, so he'd asked for her help in translation. After a while, she realized he was fluent in English, so she thought it'd been a pick-up line. By then, they were seeing each other all the time."

"So, how long do you think they were together? Did she say?" Marc asked.

Rubbing his chin, Sam said, "Couldn't have been more than a few months, because she said he'd left school before Christmas. I remember that because she told me he got her a gift which she refused. After that, he got angry, kept calling her until she had the number changed, and then he started showing up at school."

"So, he became your average stalker," Rory put in.

"Oh yeah, and Sarah was afraid of him. She got a roommate, tried to never be alone, and then she took the final step of threatening Court action, you know, getting a "Stay Away" order. That seemed to stop him, but she was always on the alert, making sure she wasn't followed, feeling a bit uneasy. It had quite an effect on her." Sam finished. "And now it looks like he's way worse than she thought."

"The reason I brought him up was I think we have to look at all angles of this kidnapping. Obviously, it's not one person, but we don't know what this guy's motive was for hooking up with her in the first place, and what connections he might have." Rory said.

"I don't like the way this is sounding, not at all! I think the fucker is up to his neck in this, and I shudder to think of who's backing him! I've gotta get back on the computer; too many interruptions," Sam said as he left the room.

Rory looked at the clock; it was nearly noon. She'd started hearing noises from upstairs, indicating that the twins were finally up. She was feeling ready for a nap, since she'd been up so early. But she knew she couldn't sleep, not with all the caffeine and the worry.

Marc seemed to read her thoughts. "God, this is awful; I feel as if it's happening to one of our own kids. I don't know how to deal with feeling helpless."

"True," Rory answered, "I think we need to find something we can focus on, like Sam is doing, something concrete that might yield results."

"Like, what did you have in mind?" Marc asked. His brow was furrowed and he looked worried.

"Well, right now, my mind is running full-speed and I can't keep up with my thoughts.

Too much coffee! I think I'm going for a jog to get rid of the excess energy and free my mind. How about you?"

"I don't know, I think I'll pass. Sam may need some support..."

CHAPTER 8

Judge Carson Hayes Justice sat in his office in the Federal Courthouse in New Haven. Two U.S. marshals were with him. Carla Nelson was the senior marshal and the judge's personal protector. She was in her mid-forties with fine features and a mid-length bob. Tall and muscular, she was both fragile and tough.

Andrew Milano, a marshal with eight years of experience was built like a wrestler, with a thick neck and torso. He was dark, almost swarthy, and had thick curly hair cropped close. He had an aura of strength and could be intimidating.

The judge knew he looked awful; he hadn't slept since he'd gotten the news last night. Whoever was behind this had called him at home in the wee hours of the morning, taking him completely unaware. He didn't normally come to his office on a Saturday, but the caller had told him he would contact him in his office.

His daughter, his pride and joy, the light of his life, had been kidnapped. And it was all because of him. Well, to be fair, because of what he did. He'd always known there were risks attached to his position, but he'd never, ever, believed it would put his daughter in danger. Anguish consumed him.

Carla broke into his thoughts, "Sir, Your Honor, what do you think of that?"

"I'm sorry, Carla, I must've drifted off. What were you saying? And from now on, please call me Carson. We'll be spending lots of time together, I think."

"What I was saying Your Honor….Carson, was that we may have to call in the FBI. They have more experience with this sort of crime. Our job is to protect you. Also, there might be another approach. What do you think about undercover operatives?" She looked to Milano, for support.

"Not a bad idea, Carla," Andrew spoke up, "about the undercover ops. You know as well as I do that it isn't always fun to involve the Bureau. It shouldn't be that way, but it is."

The judge looked up, fire in his eyes, "Well, for sure we need to do something and I think we need to start with our people. The more agencies involved, the more likely it is to get out, and then what?"

"Of course, we'll need to run it by the Chief," Carla said matter-of-factly. "I don't think he'll stand in the way. In fact, I think he'll be outraged at these brazen thugs who have the audacity to threaten a Federal Judge."

"I'm outraged," the judge said almost inaudibly, "but my first instinct is to save my child..."

The office grew quiet. Carla, who had a daughter, began to tear up. Andrew looked away.

The judge took a deep breath, then said, "There's really no time for sentimentality; the kidnappers have several hours on us. They're calling me here, but they didn't specify a time, all the better to knock me to my knees. I still don't know what the bastards want, but there are several cases coming up that could have major criminal organizations behind them. Hell, that's most of my cases!" He looked around as if he'd just taken in that fact. Then, he remembered something; he'd discussed one of his cases with Sarah—something he rarely did— because it was weighing on his mind.

"Carla, can you get me the case, I don't remember the name, of the drug cartel underling up for parole this month. There's something about that case..."

"Of course, I'm sure I can find it and I'll bring the others as well." Carla spoke quietly, "We'll have our experts go through them, the one you specified first, and look at all angles. We have to assume it's big, very big, to take on the Federal government. It sounds like the case you've described would meet those criteria. We'll start digging now."

"My guess is," Andrew weighed in, "they will start feeding you bits of information in their calls; get you ready to agree to anything. That's the kind of torture you'll need to prepare for, I think."

"I can't imagine the torture can get any worse," the judge said quietly, "but this is war and war is hell. You're right, Andrew, I'd best prepare myself. I had no idea how vulnerable I was…"

The judge shifted uncomfortably in his chair. Looking at Carla, he said, "You know, I feel bad at how I treated Sarah's friend, Lisa when she called. I don't want her messed up in this, but she must be really upset. I guess there's nothing I can do about that now. The best thing is to get Sarah back safely."

Carla's features softened as she looked at the judge. "What else could you do under the circumstances? I'll get the briefs on all of your upcoming cases."

"I know some of the undercover guys and I think they're getting tired of patrolling airports and flying all over the country," Andrew reflected. "If the chief gives us the go-ahead, I think they'd jump at the chance to do something more interesting."

Carson knew that Milano had done undercover work himself, as well as a variety of other cases, including kidnappings. He believed Andrew was well-suited to handle this situation.

"Why don't you approach him since you have some people in mind?" Carla suggested.

"And I'll get on with my part."

"What should I do when they call back?" the judge asked.

"I've called communications and they are sending someone over ASAP."

Andrew left while Carla waited for the communications expert.

Within a few minutes, a young woman, stick-thin with a head of tumbling dark curls that seemed heavy enough to knock her over came through the door. She looked around uncertainly saying, "I'm Anya Leskov, from communications?"

"Good timing," Carla commented. "Come right in; this is Judge Carson Justice. We need a hook-up on his phone to record and track. He's expecting a call at any time, so the sooner we get it hooked up, the better. And, you'll be here until the call comes in."

"Good to meet you, Your Honor, this won't take long," she said as she opened her equipment box and started.

Carla said, "I'll be off to see what I can find, should be back soon with some briefs for you." She nodded as she left.

The judge watched as Anya went quickly about her task. God, he thought, she looks younger than Sarah. He caught himself as a tear slipped out. What is wrong with me? He'd never seen himself as sentimental. When his wife had died, the sentimental part of him had seemed to die with her. Now he realized just how much of Sarah's life he'd missed out on. He prayed he could make up for lost time.

Anya finished making the necessary connections. The judge's phone was now hooked up to a small machine.

"You did that quickly Anya, have you been at this job long?" the judge asked.

She blushed, saying, with a trace of a Slavic accent, "I've been here for five years, but my training took four. Technology's so advanced now, that I need training on the latest innovations all the time. This machine," she said, pointing to what she'd just installed, "is the best we have. It can trace a call in the shortest time yet, under a minute, but doesn't leave a footprint. So, if you can keep your guy on the phone for a minute, we can get a fix."

"Amazing," the judge responded. "I'll do my best."

Anya and the judge conversed for a few minutes; the judge was curious about the new technology and Anya was very knowledgeable.

***

Carla returned with the briefs. "Here are the briefs for the next few weeks. The one on top sounds most like the case you described."

As Carla turned to leave, the phone rang.

The judge looked to Anya for direction and she nodded.

"Hello…" he started uncertainly.

The same computer synthesized voice he'd heard earlier said, "You need to cooperate, judge, if you want to see Sarah alive…"

"What do you want?" demanded the judge.

"You'll know in good time, just do as we say and don't tell anyone, don't be stupid, like Lisa was."

His heart sank, they knew about Lisa. Anger flooded through him as he pounded his fist on the desk, bellowing, "I want proof that Sarah's alive!" The line went dead.

CHAPTER 9

Sarah, with a bruised, swollen face, and renewed resolve to find a way to escape, sat on the filthy mattress and tried to eat the disgusting food the masked man had shoved at her. She wasn't hungry, still felt nauseous, but she knew she had to keep up her strength. What is this shit? She thought. Tentatively raising it to her lips, she realized it was chicken nuggets and mashed potatoes. She forced herself to eat it, though it wasn't the least bit appetizing. She was thirsty, very thirsty.

When her tormentor came back to get her half-empty plate, she asked, "Could I please have water? I'm very thirsty and I need to use the bathroom." He left, slamming the door, gun held at his side.

Within a few moments, he was back. He put the gun down long enough to tie a rag tightly over her eyes. Then he roughly pulled her up, prodding her in front of him. She heard a door open. Her captor then undid her pants and pulled them down, pushing her onto the toilet seat. She heard him chuckling as she urinated. She felt around for toilet paper, but her hand was knocked away and she was jerked to her feet, her pants pulled up.

When she was back in her cell, the rag was ripped off her face. Swallowing her growing anger, she asked again, "Could I please have some water?" He left without a word.

Sarah sat on the bed, trembling, not with fear, but rage. Things became crystal clear for her; she knew that her survival depended upon submission, or the appearance of it, as much as it went against her instincts. This was the key to lulling her captors into believing they had intimidated her. To be sure, she was intimidated, who wouldn't be with the AK47 being thrust in her face. Sarah would need her determination to act the victim, while planning her escape.

The same masked man, Sarah had committed his appearance to memory, came through the door with a glass of water.

She took it meekly, without looking up, and said "Thank you."

The water tasted dreadful; she was sure there was something in it, but she drank it anyway. Soon, she felt very sleepy, and was sure the water was spiked with some drug, as she drifted off.

***

Later, Sarah was dreaming; it was a wonderful dream. She and Sam were making love and she was so happy. Suddenly, a sharp pain brought her half-awake. Sarah felt a heavy weight on her, then a painful thrusting and she heard heavy breathing in her ear. This was not Sam and it was not a dream; with a cold clarity, she knew who it was. She was repulsed and it took every ounce of her control to play dead, unresponsive. Sarah bit back the gasp that almost escaped as the pumping increased and she felt as if she was being ripped open. She knew him; she knew he'd be done soon.

Before he finished, the door opened and she heard one of his thugs, probably the one who always dealt with her, come in and it sounded like he took a picture. Then, he laughed and said something in a foreign tongue, which Sarah now realized must be Spanish.

Blessedly, her captor—now she was sure it was Henrique— ejaculated with a loud grunt in Sarah's ear. Still, she gave no response. Removing himself, he pulled Sarah's pants up. She felt his hand brush her face where the bruise still bloomed and he said quietly, "My beautiful Sarah, what has happened to you? I warned you…" And he left.

His parting comment had removed any shred of doubt. Her rage at being raped had turned to a cold anger. How had she ever been attracted to Henrique? How had she allowed him into her bed?

Then, she thought, I was right, he was following me for the past few weeks. She now wished she had insisted Sam come with her to East Hampton, but at the time she thought she'd be safer out here.

Sarah realized although she despised Henrique, it was to her advantage that she knew who was in charge, the person who had pulled off this monstrous deed. But why? Her mind buzzed with thoughts of revenge until, finally, she felt herself pulled toward sleep with that thought in mind.

CHAPTER 10

It was Sunday morning and the judge was waking up as the sun came in his east window. He was feeling groggy, having seen the doctor and taken medication for sleep. He hated the idea of medicating himself, but knew he wouldn't survive this ordeal without it.

Two marshals were downstairs, where they'd spent the night. He heard them moving around, talking. Then he heard the front door open and close, and the sound of pounding feet running down the pavement. What the hell? Had something gone wrong already? He wondered.

Listening intently, the judge sensed that one of the marshals remained and he thought he heard pacing. Throwing the covers off, the judge dressed quickly and went downstairs to see what was going on. He proceeded cautiously, in case there was an intruder.

To his relief, he saw one marshal, Roger Land, standing at the front door, looking out. George Anderson, the other marshal, was nowhere to be seen.

"Roger," the judge called, "what happened? I heard some noise."

The marshal turned around, saying, "Good Morning, Your Honor, this envelope just came through the mail slot." He was holding it with two fingers at the edge and showed it to the judge. "George took off to try and catch the guy. I think he got him," he said, looking out the window. "And it looks like they're on the way back here. Jeez, it's just a kid."

The marshal, George, entered with a boy about eight-years-old, holding him by the arm. "Morning Judge, sorry if we woke you up. This kid just left the envelope and we need to find out who gave it to him."

The boy, whom the judge recognized now as a neighbor, looked terrified. The judge said, "Thanks, George, you can let the boy have a seat; he's a neighbor." He tried to smile at the boy to put him at ease.

Carson Justice sat across from the boy and asked in a calm voice, "What's your name? I'm sorry, I don't remember."

"I'm Billy Sommers. I live in that green house across the street. I, I didn't do anything wrong, Judge. I was riding my bike, like I told the guy," he indicated George, "and this car pulled up; it was a black SUV, with dark windows. This guy asked if I knew where the judge lived and I pointed to your house. He talked kind of funny, like foreign? And then he gave me twenty dollars for putting it through your mail slot. I said I would, took the money and he took off. That's it; you can have the money. I didn't mean any harm, honest."

"Do you mind, Judge, if I ask a few questions?" Roger, the senior marshal, asked.

"Not at all, go ahead Marshal."

"Ok, we have no reason to think you're lying, but we do need the money to check for finger prints." Billy handed over the money without hesitation. "Do you think you could describe the guy? Do you have any idea what model car it was?"

"The car was a Range Rover," Billy said with certainty, "just like my friend's mom's car. But the guy... like I said, the windows were dark. All I remember is that he was dark. He had on sunglasses, a cap, and had a black beard. But he was mostly in shadow, so I couldn't say any more for sure. Am I in trouble?"

"No, you're not in trouble and we appreciate your cooperation. We will have to speak with your parents, but not to get you in trouble," Roger answered.

"OK, George, you want to take Billy home and explain what happened. And tell them we'll put a marshal at their house." Roger said, looking at Billy, "so these bad guys don't come back to bother you."

"Right, Billy, let's go," George said.

When they'd left, Carson asked Roger, "May I see the envelope? I can't imagine what's so important…"

"Actually, no Sir, I don't want you to touch the envelope. Someone from forensics is on the way to test it for any poison, like ricin, or anthrax and to dust it for prints. Then, after you've seen the contents, we'll have to confiscate it for evidence. Sorry."

"No apology required; I know it's your job. How long will this take before I can see what's in the envelope?" The judge clasped his hands to keep them from shaking.

Roger, looking out the window, said, "Well the forensics person is arriving now, so it may take fifteen-minutes or so."

A moment later, a striking black woman entered. She was tall, slender and had almond-shaped, green eyes; she could've been a model, the judge thought.

"Hi Geneva, thanks for getting here so fast. This is Judge Carson Justice. Judge, this is Geneva Dawson."

They exchanged pleasantries and Geneva, pulling on latex gloves, took the envelope and got her kit out. "Do you mind if I work in the kitchen or laundry room if you have one?"

The judge directed Geneva to the laundry and then went into the kitchen. He called to Roger, "Would you like some coffee? I think I can manage that at least, until my housekeeper arrives."

"Sure, thanks," Roger answered. He was quiet for a moment and then said, "The housekeeper might complicate things…"

"How do you mean, Roger? I'm not sure I can survive without her."

"Well, anyone who has regular contact with you outside of the office will need protection, and that makes one more person who has some idea of what is going on."

"Oh, I see. Perhaps I should call Doreen and tell her I'm on vacation or called away on business; that would probably be more believable. I'd best call her now, before she leaves home. It looks like we'll have to find a decent place for takeout." The judge frowned at the thought.

Following up, Carson called his housekeeper and told her he'd be out of town on business, and he would call her upon his return. "But, Doreen," he added, "you'll be paid in full. That's only fair because I couldn't give you advance notice." This seemed to pacify her and, he thought, it was the right thing to do.

"Now," the judge said, "I think the coffee's ready."

As they headed for the kitchen, there was a knock at the door. Roger went to see who it was, and opened the door for George.

"So, you must've smelled the coffee from across the street," Roger joked with George.

"You make it?" George asked.

"No, the judge did," Roger answered.

"Good, then I guess it's safe." George chuckled.

Overhearing the banter, the judge joined in, "I can't vouch for it guys, but it should be ok."

Roger went to the laundry room and invited Geneva to join them for coffee. "I'm just finishing up here, if you don't mind saving me a cup?" Geneva answered.

"You got it, Gen."

"Forensics is almost done," Roger said to the judge. "So you'll be able to see what they sent you."

In a few moments Geneva joined the group in the kitchen. She appeared hesitant and guarded. "Your Honor, why don't we go into the living room…"

The judge knew this wasn't good, but then he'd known that all along. He steeled himself to expect the worst.

As they took seats in the living room, Geneva said, "There was no poison, nor prints.

This might be difficult to see…" she lowered her voice and her face was grim.

Taking the envelope, the judge removed what turned out to be a picture, a picture of Sarah being raped by a man whose face was turned away from the camera. Scrawled across the front was written, here's your proof.

With a howl of pain, the judge yelled, "Fucking bastards!"

CHAPTER 11

Trying to return to quasi-normalcy at the Chandler home, Marc and Rory had made a big Sunday breakfast, served later, so the twins could join them. It had been a rough night for Marc and Rory, and certainly for Sam, who'd been up late at the computer and had stayed over in the guest room.

Marc and Rory were sitting in the alcove. The family cat, Peaches, was curled up in Rory's lap. "Glad you came out of hiding," she crooned to the cat, which disappeared whenever there was commotion in the house.

Soon Kate straggled in and asked, "Can we eat now or do we have to wait for Sam? I think he's up."

"Well, if he's up, he should be down soon, so why don't we wait a few minutes and see?" Rory answered. Alex was right behind and the girls joined their parents in the nook, sleepily yawning.

"Sam was still at the computer when we got home a little after midnight. Did he learn anything?"

"Well, we haven't spoken with him, so we'll have to wait. We don't know any more; it's upsetting and frustrating." Marc's displeasure showed on his face.

"God, you guys must feel so helpless. It's really awful, isn't it?" Alex shivered.

"Yeah," Rory answered. "It's dreadful, because we can't go through the normal channels to investigate. That is, beyond what we can find out on the internet. And Sam's pretty good at that, so…"

Just then, Sam entered the room looking disheveled and tired.

Rory got up and said, "How's it going, Sam? Breakfast is warming in the oven, so now we can eat."

"Morning everyone," Sam looked around the room. "Well, I think I went as far as I could go with the internet. I found out some interesting things. How about we talk over breakfast?"

Rory set breakfast up buffet style, on the island and invited Sam to serve himself. The girls jumped in behind him. They filled their plates and then Rory and Marc helped themselves. Amazingly, there was food left; Rory had had her doubts. She was very pleased to see that Sam had an appetite and that overall he looked better.

Sam picked at his food for a while before sharing what he'd found. Looking up, he began talking.

"Sam, we can wait until you've eaten, no need to rush," Rory said.

"The food's great, Rory, but I'm not really hungry."

"Henrique Alvarez doesn't exist, at least in the U.S., outside of law school. And I found nothing in Belize, where he claimed to be from, that would jibe with his age, or any documentation of someone with that name coming to the U.S. So, after finding nothing in a random search of other Central and South American countries, I finally discovered that Henrique came in from Mexico, obviously with forged papers. I also found that Alvarez, probably the real one, was killed in a drug war in Mexico. He'd have been about the same age as we presume the man in question is, mid to late twenties."

"Alvarez, and I still found no clue as to his real identity, came to the U.S. the summer before he and Sarah started law school. I don't know if I'm being premature, or overly dramatic, but I think it's possible that a drug cartel is involved..." Sam continued.

There was a knock at the door and Blake Ford, Rory's administrative assistant, strolled in saying, "If you'd told me there was breakfast, I'd have been here sooner. Thanks for saving some."

Before getting his food, Blake went over to Sam, "How are you doing, Sam? Sorry about Sarah."

"I'm hanging in there. Thanks for asking, Blake."

"I came over to help brainstorm. I've given it some thought and have some ideas that might be useful," Blake said, "once I get some food."

"Sam, it looks like there's some food left, if you're hungry," Blake said. "If not, I may be forced to finish it."

"I'm good," Sam said. He hadn't touched most of his food.

Sam filled Blake in on what he'd learned from the internet. Then he repeated what he'd said as Blake was arriving. "I think this may involve one of the major Mexican drug cartels. Consider the magnitude of what they've done. If only we could share this info with Sarah's dad and the people he has on the investigation. They would have the ability to dig deeper and access classified information we can't find."

Blake held up his hand to get attention until he could finish chewing. "I may be able to help out there. I have a friend who's a law clerk at the Federal Court in New Haven. He might be able to get a message to the judge, just to see if the judge is amenable to working with us. It could be risky for him, but I'm hoping he knows enough about the system by now to go to the right people. And if he nixes the idea, so be it."

"How do you know this guy?" Rory asked

"He went to Greenport HS with me, a few years ahead. Then he went to Yale Law School. And, he's engaged to my sister," Blake answered.

"That's sweet!" Marc observed. "Not bad, having a contact with the federal court. Where are you headed when you graduate?"

"I'll finish in the Spring, then have to pass the bar, and then...I'd love to be Rory's law partner," Blake said, looking at Rory.

Rory looked pleasantly surprised. "I never thought…"

"What, that I'd pass the bar?" Blake was having fun.

"Well, I assumed you'd be in law school forever," Rory gave it back. "But, seriously, I'm flattered. And I like you way more than Jeremy Katz," Rory replied, referencing a fellow attorney who had offered a partnership to her.

Sam spoke up, "Your idea about contacting your friend Nate sounds good, as long as he's comfortable with it and has access to the judge. Of course, it's tricky too because we have no idea if the judge will even concede that Sarah's been kidnapped. But, I'd sure like to share info with Sarah's father. He may have softened a bit, having to face losing her…"

Sam stopped suddenly, realizing what he'd said.

The room grew quiet as the reality sank in.

"OK," Blake said, I'll call Nate. He should still be at my sister's for the weekend. I guess I can use my cell? I shouldn't be on anyone's radar, right?"

"Far as we know," Marc answered. "Of course, I think it goes without saying that you can't call him at work."

"Don't even have a work number for him, and you're right."

Blake hit a contact number on his cell phone and within minutes was talking with Nate.

He walked outside to the porch to continue his call.

"Speaking of cell phones," Sam broke in, "I got a disposable one, left the real one at home. I'll take it only when I go to predictable places like school, or running errands. It's possible they could be tracking me."

About ten minutes later, Blake came back inside. "Nate's been away from work over the weekend, but he is friends with the judge's personal federal marshal. He's willing to talk with her and see what flies when he gets back to work."

Without warning, Sam got up abruptly, headed for the door. "I've got to get out of here, do something productive, like find fucking Alvarez!"

CHAPTER 12

Judge Carson Justice was bent over, head in hands and sobbing uncontrollably. The picture that caused him such pain had fallen to the floor.

Geneva picked it up and put it into the envelope, then went to the judge and gently placed her hand on his shoulder. Her face was grim.

Roger and George stood nearby, looking helpless. They talked quietly to each other.

Then, Roger went over to the judge and kneeled in front of him saying, "Sir, is there anyone we can call for you? How can we help?"

The judge raised his head, his face stained with tears. "You can find the bastards who did this," he said, through clenched teeth. Then, he seemed to compose himself somewhat. "You and George are off duty soon, if you don't mind, I'd like to have Carla and Andrew replace you."

"That shouldn't be a problem, Sir, I'll call the office now." Roger went off to call.

Geneva sat next to the judge and spoke softly to him. "I'm so sorry you had to see that. I see a lot of horrendous things in my line of work, but it never ceases to affect me; I mean the unspeakable deeds…" She shook her head.

"Thank you for your sensitivity. I appreciate it. Your job must be tough, indeed."

"It is," Geneva agreed, "but what I do also helps to catch the evil-doers, sometimes. I'd especially like to help shut down this operation," she said with steel in her voice.

"I'm sure you always do your best. Hopefully, we'll find more evidence that will help us apprehend these evil men."

Roger came over and said, "We've reached Carla, and she's contacting Andrew, so they should be here soon. We'll stay, of course, until they arrive."

"I can stay," Geneva offered.

"It's our watch, Gen, thanks. They probably need you back at HQ."

"True," Geneva conceded, "there's always something that needs to be done."

She patted the judge's shoulder as she said goodbye. "I hope we have some good news on this front soon. You take care."

"Thanks, Geneva, for everything," the judge replied.

Roger and George stood awkwardly. They didn't even know what had happened. And Carson couldn't bear to tell them. Instead, he said, "Why don't we order out breakfast? You guys must be hungry. There's a coffee shop down the street."

"Sounds good," George said. "I'll take orders."

"Next to the phone, you'll find a list of numbers, it's on there."

George looked, found the number and said, "Now, who wants what?"

Carson really wasn't hungry, but ordered anyway. "Scrambled eggs and toast for me."

When George had phoned in the orders for the three of them, he headed for the door. "Shouldn't be long," he said.

Roger closed the door and locked it, scanning the area in front of the house. Then he turned and went to the back of the house, checking the locks. He stopped at the French doors, which opened onto a large deck. He took in the view of the Sound.

Walking back to the living room, he said, "That's a beautiful scene out back. I didn't realize how close you were to Long Island Sound."

"It is beautiful. I really should spend more time looking at it. There are a lot of things I should pay more attention to," he said, almost to himself.

The knock at the door brought Roger to his feet and he went to check. He opened the door to Carla and ushered her in. She went to the judge.

Carson saw a frown furrowing her brow.

"You okay, Carson?" she asked.

"Won't lie to you, you'd see through it anyway; I've had better days."

Roger was still at the door, so was ready to open it when George arrived with the food.

He turned and addressed the judge, "Food's here, and so is Andrew."

George and Andrew entered one after the other.

What do I owe you, George?" the judge asked.

"Thanks Judge, but this goes on the expense account. And I guess we can leave, unless you two have any questions," George said to Carla and Andrew.

"I think we're good," Carla spoke for both of them. "We'll talk to you later."

Carson put his breakfast aside; perhaps he'd feel hungry later. Right now, he was struggling to stay upright, and to keep himself from screaming. He was accustomed to being in control; feeling anxious was a new feeling for him. It was uncharted territory.

The judge knew he needed to talk, and these two people were the colleagues he trusted most. He said, "There's some coffee left if you want it, or I can make more if we need it."

Carla got up, but Andrew waved her down; "I'm having a cup, anyone else?"

"Yes, thanks Andrew, I'll have one." Carla answered. As she spoke she rubbed Carson's arm and looked at him with concern.

"We'll talk," he assured her. "This is one I can't shove away or pretend didn't happen. I really need to talk and I appreciate the two of you coming on your day off."

"We're always on call for you, Carson. And, it's more than just a job. You've always treated us well." Carla spoke softly.

Perhaps better than I've treated my own daughter, Carson thought with regret.

Andrew came in with the two coffees and handed one to Carla. He sat in a chair adjacent to where Carla sat with the judge. He said, "I took the liberty of making another pot in case we want more."

"Thoughtful of you, Andrew," the judge said. "In case you didn't hear me tell Carla, I appreciate that both of you came in on your day off."

"Not an issue, Sir," Andrew answered. "Where your safety and welfare are concerned, that's a priority."

The judge was touched, nearly to tears, and he thought again how ironic it was that the people he worked with were the recipients of his affection, while his daughter must've felt left out in the cold. He had a lot to answer for and he prayed he would have the opportunity to show Sarah just how much he loved her.

Carson cleared his throat and began, "I was telling Carla I had to talk with you both about what just happened. I don't want you to be in the dark."

In fits and starts, the judge did his best to describe the heinous picture and the effect it had on him. Then he said, "This was the answer to my demand for proof that Sarah was alive. Unspeakable animals!" He took a deep breath, trying to move on. "That picture, I'm afraid, will stay with me for a very long time. But, I think I need to use it as an incentive to find these depraved men at all costs. I'll need you both for support; you keep me grounded. I have to find a way to let go of the hatred and use the anger instead to fight this battle." He slumped in his seat, feeling drained, but somehow relieved.

"Carson," Carla got him to lift his head. "We're in this with you, I promise. I can't even begin to imagine what it was like for you and I'm not sure I could look at the picture."

Andrew nodded as he listened to Carla, then said, "Maybe I have a typical male reaction, but I want to kill the guy; he's trash!" Andrew's eyes flashed with anger. "It's just...unforgivable!" His fists were clenched at his sides.

"Thank you both," the judge said. "I knew I could count on you to make me feel better; you've no idea what your support means."

"In the meantime, Carson," Carla said, touching his arm, "I think you need to rest. This has been a huge shock. I'll call Dr. Lin and have her come over to look at you... please don't argue," Carla said as she saw his face grow taut. "You can tell us what you were working on, whatever files you think need special attention and we will be on it."

The judge sighed, "I'm no match for you, Carla. I know I have to be at the top of my game for this, and I'm not..."

Looking surprised, as if expecting a fight, Carla said, "Thank you, Carson, for being reasonable."

"You implying that I'm usually not?" he asked, with the first hint of a smile he'd given all morning.

Carla smiled too, the tension broken. "I'll call Dr. Lin, and then you can brief us."

Andrew got up, saying, "I'm getting more coffee, do you want any, Carson?"

"Thanks, Andrew, but I think the doc might have other plans for me, and frankly, I don't mind being put under for a while."

"I hear you, Sir. I think it's for the best." And as an aside he whispered, "I try not to tangle with Carla either."

"I heard that!" Carla called from the kitchen.

"See what I mean?" Andrew shrugged.

The banter was good for Carson; he found himself smiling again. And he was grateful for the support of these two and at how comforted he was by their words and their presence. This tragedy, he realized, made him aware of just how grateful he was. Gratitude was a new concept for Carson Justice.

CHAPTER 13

Rob and Lisa had slept in late, after finding it difficult to get to sleep the night before. Lisa's mind had been particularly difficult to settle; she and Rob had stayed up late discussing the situation.

Now, it was after ten in the morning, very late for both of them to be getting up. Sun filled the room, as Lisa opened her eyes and saw Rob, propped on an elbow, watching her. Now, he leaned over to brush a soft kiss on her lips.

"Morning sweetie, how'd you sleep?" Lisa asked, smiling at him.

"Slept like a rock, after being wide awake for what seemed like hours, how about you?" Rob asked.

"Well, you were asleep by about one, and my mind was still buzzing, so I finally got up and admitted defeat. I took an over-the-counter and probably slept by two or so. I don't have that groggy feeling, so I'd recommend it if you can't sleep tonight."

"So, you want to go out for breakfast?" Rob asked.

"No, I'm feeling lazy, don't want to get dressed right now..." She gave him the look, and he knew what that meant.

"All righty then, I'm up!" He laughed at his joke.

And Lisa, glancing his way, answered, "Indeed you are!"

Lisa loved early morning sex and she needed a way to release the tension. She gave over completely to her senses, and enjoyed fully the gentle, playful lovemaking. Lisa was completely in the moment, leaving her worries behind. When finally they enjoyed a mutual release, they dozed again, entwined.

Lisa sat up suddenly, the clock read eleven-thirty. Something had awakened her, what was it? She thought for a moment. It came to her gradually; it had been a slow, hissing sound. She couldn't imagine what it was.

Looking over at Rob sleeping peacefully, she slipped out of bed quietly and went into the bathroom to dress. He was still asleep as she quietly edged down the stairs.

She went first to the front door and checked that it was locked; it was. Then, Lisa checked the back door; it too had been bolted shut. At the chief's suggestion, they'd had deadbolts installed the day before. That gave her some sense of security. But what had made that noise? She checked the gas, to make sure none was escaping; it wasn't. She just had an odd feeling about this and wanted to get Rob's take.

She heard him come down the stairs. He was dressed only in his boxers, and it looked as though he was ready for round two. Regretfully, she was now all business. "Rob, I…"

"Why'd you leave? I missed you…"

"Rob, I heard something and it scared me awake."

"What was it?" he asked, on alert.

"It was like this hissing sound, I think. I don't think I imagined it. I wasn't dreaming. I checked the doors, both are locked and I'm glad we got the deadbolts. Also checked the gas for a leak and didn't find one."

Rob had gone to the front window and was looking out. "Hmm," he said, "looks like a flat on the car. Looking more closely he said, "Fuck! Both tires on this side are flat." He ran up the stairs, saying, "Gotta get dressed and see what's up with that!"

Lisa went to look and felt as deflated as the tires were. But she'd heard a hiss; this was hardly looking like an accident. She felt fear knot her stomach. As Rob came downstairs fully dressed, she stopped him. "This was no accident; please look around before you go out."

Rob had a hard set to his jaw; Lisa knew he was pissed. So was she, but more than that, she was afraid. "Just go out and check, then come right back in. We need to call the chief and see what he thinks."

"Okay, I guess you're right." His fists were clenched; Rob hated to be a victim. He got angry.

Unbolting the front door, Rob went out, Lisa stood in the doorway, her eyes scanning the surrounding area. She saw nothing out of place.

Rob marched in and re-bolted the door. He was seething, "Four fucking tires were slashed! You're right Lise, this was no accident!" He paced the floor, venting his anger.

Trying to keep a cool head, Lisa suggested, "We need to call the chief; I think we both know what this means… do you want to call or should I?"

Rob calmed himself, "I'll call and see what he has to say."

"Where'd you put his number?"

Walking over to her purse, Lisa reached in and pulled out the card, handing it to Rob.

He dialed the chief's number. He put it on speaker, as the phone rang.

"Chief Mayer, can I help you?"

"Chief…Thom, this is Rob Higgins. We have a situation here; all four of our tires were slashed. It was done this morning before we got up. Lisa woke up about 11:30 when she heard a hissing sound. So, this was done in broad daylight!"

"Pretty brazen, I'd say," answered the chief. "Obviously it was a threat and I'd heed it were I you." There was silence on the line for a moment, then the Chief said, "Look, here's the plan, I'll get a garage we use to drive me over in a tow truck. I'll come in and talk with you while the guy's hooking up the car. Should be there in twenty-five minutes or so."

"Thanks, Thom, and we appreciate the suggestion to have dead-bolts installed; we feel a little safer. See you soon. Bye"

"Well, you heard," Rob said. "Not sure what he means by heeding the warning."

"My guess is he thinks we should leave; we're a bit exposed here. And they got a little close for comfort today." Lisa sighed. "I'd hoped we'd have a nice vacation out here. Although this morning was a treat." She smiled. "We should probably start packing up. Pretty sure that will be the verdict."

Together, they went upstairs to pack. Just as they were finishing up, they heard a vehicle crunch onto the shells in the driveway.

Looking out the window, Lisa said, Chief's here."

Rob left his open suitcase on the bed and went down the stairs. He was at the door and unbolting it when the chief stepped to the front door. "Thanks for coming, Thom. You really look the part," Rob said, as he took in the dirty coveralls and backward cap.

"Yeah, you know, I still remember my undercover days; it was always exciting. Anyway, Oh hi Lisa," Thom said as she joined Rob at the door. "The plan is to tow your car away, get new tires and bring it back tomorrow. But we want you guys outta here, like ASAP." He picked up his clipboard and pretended to write things down. "I've written out the details, so you know exactly what to do. I'll keep my phone on, so if you hit any snafus, just call. Ok, now I'll give you your 'bill' and we'll be on our way."

"You need money?" Rob went for his wallet.

"No, we'll settle up later. No charge for the tow and my pal, Gus, the owner, will give you a discount on tires. Gotta' go now." He gave the 'bill' to Rob and waved as he left.

Lisa bolted the door, and followed Rob into the kitchen. Rob was already reading the plan from Chief Mayer.

Lisa suggested, "I'm starving, why don't I make us a big brunch, while you read to me?" There was no answer, so she looked over at Rob, engrossed in his reading. She repeated, "Rob!"

He startled and looked up, "Huh?"

"I thought I'd make us brunch, while you read to me, ok?" Lisa repeated.

"Brunch sounds real good, but I want to read this over first; then I'll tell you what it says, ok?"

"OK, fine," Lisa replied, as she busied herself removing several containers of food from the fridge.

Rob surprised her by jumping up and going to the front door and unlocking it. He was back in a moment and had a key, possibly a car key, in his hand.

Lisa cocked her head and frowned, "What's that?"

"It's a car key and the car it belongs to is in the lot at the end of the beach. We're to take it, and," here Rob consulted the paper, "and drive to the train station and hustle our buns back to the city. That's basically what we have to do. OK so far?"

"Yes, and that's all we have to do? I'm feeling there's more."

"Oh, there's more, but the chief and the under-cover guys will do the rest."

"So, what's the rest?" Lisa asked, impatient to get brunch going, but curious.

"Just chill, Lise; I'm still reading."

Lisa finished the food preparation and then said, "OK, come and get it." She didn't have to say it twice. "Careful," Lisa warned, "it may be hot."

Rob ate for a bit, still reading. Then he stopped chewing and began to tell Lisa about the plan. "OK, so you know we need to leave and take that car, the beat-up Toyota, and go to the train station. Then, we'll leave the key to our house under the driver's seat, lock the car, and head back to the city. One of the plainclothes guys will get the Toyota and head back to our house, hide the car somewhere, and go into our house. That will likely happen tonight, after dark." Rob stopped to eat.

"So, will he be staying at the house?" Lisa asked.

"Yes, his job is to give the impression that someone is home. So, I guess it's fine to leave whatever food we have behind." Rob took a few more bites. "Then tomorrow, the VW will be delivered back to the house and then Thom will come to the house and pretend to talk to the guy."

"What is he going to do besides stay in the house?" Lisa asked.

"He will evidently have some surveillance equipment to scope out the area, even at night. There's supposedly a homeless guy who stays in that house down the beach; the one where we saw the two guys. The officer hopes to make contact with him and find out if he saw anything when Sarah was kidnapped, if the bad guys saw him and offered money for silence, or whatever he can find out."

"Anything else on the paper the chief gave you?" Lisa wondered.

"Ok, ok, let me think!" He paused and then said, "The chief says you should leave your cell phone here, and Sarah's, too. I guess mine's ok. Oh, yeah, and the Range Rover that followed us is a rental, leased to a guy by the name of Alvarez, ring a bell?" Rob looked up.

Lisa slowly shook her head, but something sounded familiar, "Did you get the guy's first name?" she asked.

Rob consulted his paper, then said, "Here it is, Henrique Alvarez."

The color drained from Lisa's face. "Oh my God! I have to call Sam, see what he thinks. I know Sarah told him all about this guy she dated."

Lisa reached Sam, who had texted her his new number, and he picked up immediately. "Sam, I just wanted to tell you that the chief stopped by and gave us the name of the guy who rented the Range Rover that tailed us. It was Henrique Alvarez!"

"Son of a bitch! I knew that bastard was involved; Sarah told me she thought she was being followed again…"

"Anyway, our tires were slashed this morning, all of them! So the chief ordered us to go home, like tonight." Lisa told him.

"Good luck, Lisa, and stay in touch," Sam answered.

"How are you doing, Sam?" Lisa asked.

"Not very damn good, but I'm tired of sitting here doing nothing. It's about time I got my ass in gear. Thanks for the info, Lisa, and I'll talk to you later."

Lisa looked at Rob. "I'm worried Sam is going to do something rash; he sounded at the end of his rope."

"Can't say I blame him. I'd be pretty crazy if anything happened to you!"

CHAPTER 14

Sarah awoke reluctantly, trying to forget what had happened during the night. It was difficult to ignore, since every part of her body ached and there was an especially searing pain in her groin area. She was sure he had torn the flesh of her vagina; it felt as if there was sticky blood in her pants. In fact, it felt as though she was still bleeding.

Sarah could hardly contain her physical and mental anguish, but she knew this was not the time to give in to tears or succumb to self-pity; this was a life or death fight. Sarah could not afford to appear weak, or for that matter, defiant. She had to find a place of neutrality, a place where her mind was free to work out an escape plan. She knew Henrique, though she could hardly bear to form his name. He was shrewd, but Sarah knew she was smarter. She'd seen him struggling in law school…

As Sarah thought about law school, she wondered… has this all been a set-up? They'd met when he'd approached her for help with translation, but she soon saw that he knew English well. Flattered, Sarah believed that was his way of getting her attention. But, as she looked back on the two months or so of their relationship, Sarah saw flaws that she'd been blind to at the time. He'd always been possessive and somewhat rough. But Henrique could also be unbelievably sweet. Sarah now saw this as what it most likely was, manipulation.

The door was suddenly flung open, crashing into the wall. The masked man thrust a tray of food at Sarah and said something in

Spanish. It was a reference to 'last night,' she thought and was delivered with a laugh.

Sarah listened as the man retreated. There was a discussion between him and Henrique; she could pick out his voice from the others. It seemed this thug was teasing Henrique, something Sarah had learned not to do; he hated being made the butt of jokes, even if it was mild teasing. She was right. Soon, Henrique's voice rose above the others, and then Sarah heard a loud thwack. The guy had hit the deck, she could feel the vibrations.

Then, evidently a scuffle ensued. A third voice entered the fray, as if playing referee. Henrique prevailed, bellowing at the two of them. They were all speaking so rapidly it was difficult for Sarah to grasp what they were saying with the little Spanish she knew. But the language was slowly coming back and she could catch an occasional phrase. To Sarah, it sounded as if he was reminding them they worked for him.

In the silence that followed, Sarah resumed pondering her strategy. It was to her advantage to have rebellion in the ranks. She decided to find more ways to push a wedge between Henrique and his thugs. Sarah realized she would do whatever it took to escape from this monster.

CHAPTER 15

It was Monday and Rory reluctantly returned to work. As she drove, she tried to push her concern for Sarah's safety out of her mind. Rory knew that would not help and that getting involved with her work would take her mind off her worries. And, she had a case that demanded her attention.

She'd taken on the case of a juvenile, DeSean Smith, who'd been direct-filed to Adult Court. He was fifteen and charged with a felony, Armed Robbery, so was presumably eligible to be tried as an adult. This direct-filing was a fairly recent addition to the Juvenile Act in response to a rise in violent crimes by juveniles. It was up to the discretion of the DA to approve each case.

Rory had taken this case Pro Bono, because in her mind, the direct-file was being abused. DeSean's case was just such an example. Rory had interviewed the youth at the prison; he was housed in the infirmary. DeSean was a skinny black kid from the city of Chester, one of the poorest cities in the nation. He'd told Rory he had asked an older woman if she had any change outside of a convenience store. He admitted that he'd pressured her, but denied he had a weapon of any sort. The woman claimed that he'd had a gun in his pocket pointed at her. She'd given him some change and had run off. Shortly thereafter, the police arrived, as DeSean was walking home munching on a candy bar. There was no gun found at the site of the crime, nor on his route home.

None the less, he'd been charged with armed robbery, and sent to jail.

Rory had spoken with the DA on duty when DeSean had been arrested. The DA spoke with the victim, who apparently had feared for her life because of the gun she'd assumed was in the youth's pocket. He felt the facts presented were serious enough to warrant a direct-file.

This DA, Peter Townsend, was new and Rory believed, eager to be noticed. She hadn't seen him operate in court yet, so she'd no idea what to expect. She would find out today.

As she entered her office, Blake greeted her and inquired about news of Sarah.

"Nothing yet, Blake, but I'm sure hoping you hear from Nate. I've got DeSean in court today for a decertification hearing; have you finished getting the background info I asked for?"

Blake went to his desk and retrieved a stack of papers. Handing them to Rory he said, "There you go; that's everything. It looks pretty promising."

"Thanks Blake, I'll read it over coffee." She stopped to fill her mug, then entered her office.

As she read, she nodded. It looked as though DeSean was fitting the criteria for being decertified back to Juvenile Court. Specifically, he had no prior record, not even a summary offense. He attended school regularly and was a decent student. He had parental support; both parents had visited him in prison, although they were not together. As far as Rory was concerned, this was a case that should definitely be heard in Juvenile. But, it was never a foregone conclusion it would go the way she planned. Rory had had too many cases run amok in the courtroom.

Having finished her coffee and her reading, she placed DeSean's case file in her briefcase and left for court.

Rory wished she could be somewhere else, maybe outside to enjoy this beautiful fall day, but then she thought of Sarah and realized she was lucky to be alive and doing the job she loved.

Rory walked the three flights of stairs to the courtroom. Judge Hayley Dickenson was presiding. Rory hadn't gone before Judge

Dickenson yet because the judge had been newly appointed when a senior judge retired. She was also younger than Rory, which was surprising. Dickenson had been backed by the political party in power, which was no doubt the reason for her appointment.

Rory took a seat in the back of the courtroom waiting for her case to be called.

The first several cases were requests for continuances, by either defense or prosecution, sometimes both.

The first real case involved an assault of a man by his wife. The defense attorney asked that the case be dropped since the man wished that the charges be withdrawn.

The wife, in orange jumpsuit and shackles, was quietly sobbing with her head down. Her husband looked equally miserable.

The DA asserted they would still pursue the case even though the victim wished it to be dropped. Since the perpetrator was unwilling to go for a plea bargain, he suggested that it go to trial, with the defendant remaining in prison until the hearing.

The defense attorney said he was willing to go forward with his case today.

The victim asked to address the judge, but was denied.

The woman was continued in prison for two weeks until the case could be relisted.

Oh boy, Rory thought, we've got two 'law and order' junkies in Court. And she pulled out her paperwork, making sure that she knew her stuff. The combination of these two rookies could be lethal.

Within a half-hour, her client shuffled in, flanked by two burly sheriffs. He looked even skinnier than when she'd seen him a few days before. Both parents were in the body of the courtroom and willing to take the stand on behalf of their son.

DA Townsend introduced the case, and called his first and only witness to the stand, the victim, Maddie Greyson.

At least eighty, bent over, and walking with a cane, Maddie slowly proceeded to the witness stand.

After she was sworn in, the DA addressed her: "Miss Greyson, would you please tell the Court what happened on the night of Friday, October 10th of this year that brings you to Court today."

Her voice was shaky and it was hard to hear, as she recounted her story. She basically confirmed that DeSean, identified by her in the courtroom (ludicrous, Rory thought, since he was the one in shackles) had stopped her outside a convenience store and asked if she had any change. She tried to push past him, but he took her arm and asked again. His other hand was in his pocket and it looked like he had a gun. She was "scared to death," and finally gave him some coins and ran off, calling the police as soon as she could.

Maddie clearly had the "sympathy vote;" she looked and sounded pathetic. Rory knew she would have to tread lightly to avoid making her look further victimized.

When the DA had finished, Rory addressed the victim.

"Miss Greyson, I understand you were extremely upset over what you described. I have just a few questions. I noticed you reported that you felt sure there was a gun in DeSean's pocket. Did you actually see the gun?"

"No, ma'am, he was pointin' it at me through his jacket; I knew it was a gun."

"Yet, you didn't see a gun. Did DeSean say he had a gun?"

"No, ma'am, he didn't have to, I knew he had a gun."

"Miss Greyson, are you aware that a gun was never found, either outside of the convenience store, or along the route DeSean was taking home?"

"He had a gun and it near scared me to death!" Miss Greyson was trembling.

Rory knew it was time to cut her losses. She said, "Defense has no more questions."

The DA declared the state had concluded its case and asked that the juvenile remain in jail until a hearing could be scheduled.

Rory requested permission to present her case for decertification. She walked to the bench and gave the judge copies of report cards, parental reports, and confirmation of no juvenile record or summary offenses.

Rory then addressed the Court. "This juvenile, DeSean Smith, has no record in the juvenile system and no summary offenses. He attends school regularly and is passing all of his subjects; he is a sophomore at Chester HS where he also plays football and is in Science club. Both parents are present and willing to attest to his cooperation at home. I would ask that, in light of these circumstances, the youth be decertified to Juvenile Court and released from prison immediately."

Rory sat down. The DA got up again and reminded the Court that Miss Greyson had "feared for her life," and that DeSean was a menace to the community, preying on senior citizens.

Rory rebutted his argument, stating again for the record, that no gun had been found anywhere, including in his home, which his parents voluntarily allowed police to search.

The gavel banged down and Judge Dickenson ordered that DeSean remain in prison pending a psychological evaluation to determine whether or not he was a threat to society.

Rory was speechless. She looked over at the smirking DA who apparently had no regrets about jailing a juvenile without just cause; another black on white case and the typical response. Christ, Rory thought, he wasn't even wearing a black hoodie!

Head down, Rory left the courtroom dismayed by what passed for "justice," a word so often used, yet so seldom served.

Rory saw DeSean's parents outside the courtroom and spoke with them. "I don't know what to say. I really didn't expect an outcome like this considering what he has going for him. Hopefully the psychological evaluation will be in his favor. In the meantime, visit him as often as you can and try to keep his spirits up. I'll do what I can."

Rory's words sounded lame to her own ears; she was so angry she felt she might explode. The 'rookies' had done their damage, both hoping no doubt to impress their colleagues with their hard stance on crime. It was time to start praying for another judge at the next hearing.

***

Blake was on the phone when Rory returned; she went straight to her office, too angry to even nod at Blake. She sat at her desk, feeling agitated.

Blake knocked, and then came in, the smile on his face replaced with concern.

"Bad day in court, Boss?"

Rory just nodded, not ready to talk about it.

"I've been trying to reach Sam, have you heard from him?"

"No, not since breakfast yesterday, why?"

"Well, I've tried reaching him several times and I just got his message," Blake answered.

"Let me check my cell," Rory said. "It was turned off in Court." She took her phone from her purse and looked at it. "Looks like a text from Sam," Rory said. Then, with look of disbelief on her face, she read it to Blake. "He says, 'Rory, please feed the cat, you know where the key is hidden. I had to go and find out for myself what's happened to Sarah. I just can't sit still without doing anything. I'll be in touch. XO.'"

"Holy shit Rory, he left without hearing the good news from Nate. Where do you suppose he's gone?"

"I have no idea, it's so out of character, not to mention dangerous to him and possibly, detrimental to Sarah. The kidnappers warned him…"

CHAPTER 16

Brent Hargraves, an undercover cop chosen carefully for this assignment was standing at the front door of Rob and Lisa's cottage admiring the view. He was happy to be in such beautiful surroundings, even though the job might be dicey. An African-American who normally wore his hair short, he was ordered to shave his head; they wanted him to match Rob as closely as possible. He kind of liked the look.

Also a plus, was the chief partnering him with a woman who resembled Lisa. Sharon Davies was a blond, so all she'd had to do was find a black wig. Brent had worked with Sharon before and was impressed with her intelligence and work ethic. And, he had to admit to himself, she was hot. But, work came first.

Sharon joined Brent at the door. She was scratching her head. "Fuckin' wig; I hate it!"

Brent laughed, "At least you didn't have to shave your head!"

"Yeah, but it looks good on you, while this," Sharon jerked at the wig, "looks like shit!"

"We'll keep the blinds drawn, and you can put it on only when we go out, ok?"

"Yes!" she said as she went around yanking all the blinds shut and pulling off the wig. She shook out her natural blond bob, smiling. "Much better! Did you by any chance make coffee?"

"Ummm, we could go out," Brent suggested.

"Did you actually see any little coffee shops within walking distance when we came in last night?"

"It was dark when we came in last night, so no, I didn't."

"Well, there aren't any! We're not in the village." Sharon went around flinging open cabinets until she found what she wanted. Then she made coffee.

"Want me to make some breakfast?" Brent asked, hoping she'd say "No."

Sharon smiled at him, "What a good idea! And see if there's any bread left in the breadbox over there," she pointed to the corner of the counter.

Now what have I done, he thought. "Getting a little low on provisions," Brent commented. "There is some bread, though. Maybe we'll have some toast?"

Sharon gave him a frown and then opened the door to the fridge. "Some eggs in here; can you manage that?" She sounded frosty.

Brent wasn't happy, with her request or with the implied insult.

"I don't really want any…" Brent trailed off.

"Well, there's not much food left, so I'm going to at least have a decent breakfast."

Sharon got the eggs out and began scrambling them, only two, he noticed.

Well, shit, he thought, she can have them.

"We can't get any more food until they bring the car back, and the chief called to say he wasn't sure when that would be. Why not make yourself useful and look for grocery receipts, see where they shopped."

Brent glared at her and said, "Bossy bitch," under his breath.

"I heard that!" Sharon said loudly. "And tough shit if you don't want to be working with me; it seems what I've heard about you is dead on!"

"Yeah? And what would that be?" He stood toe to toe with her, looking her in the eye.

"That you don't respect women, and you think you're 'God's gift,'" She held eye contact with him until he grew uncomfortable.

Momentarily at a loss for words, Brent left the room in a huff.

He was hurt; he'd always liked Sharon and had never 'come on' to her. Was this the way people looked at him? It took him aback, but he gave it some serious thought. He knew he flirted sometimes, but he was no lothario. And he thought he treated women respectfully, viewed them as equals. Was Sharon just angry with him or was she repeating what she'd heard?

Smelling burnt toast, Brent went back into the kitchen. Sharon was eating her eggs. He saw the burnt toast on the counter.

"Your toast was burnt," she said, stating the obvious, "so I turned the setting down and put in two more slices for you."

"Thanks," Brent said, moving over to the toaster to make sure there was no repeat. When the toast popped up, he put peanut butter on it. He turned toward the table, unsure whether or not he was welcome. "Do you mind?" Brent asked, indicating an empty chair.

Sharon shrugged in a neutral manner, so Brent took the seat.

They ate in silence, looking down at their food.

Who could hold out longer, Brent wondered. Then he almost laughed at how childish this whole thing was getting.

"Sorry…"

"Let's…"

They spoke at the same time and then laughed. Brent said, "You go first."

"Thanks," Sharon said. "I am sorry about the way I spoke to you. It's not good to feed into office gossip; I thought I was above it. I apologize."

"Apology accepted. I have to admit what you said hurt. Of course, there's a kernel of truth in it, but that hardly sums up who I am. At least, I hope not."

"Maybe we can start over; we'll be working in close quarters for a while, so let's make it as easy as possible. It's a tough enough assignment, to be sure. I've never done undercover work, have you?"

"Yes, I have and it can be very challenging, sometimes exciting. I'm not totally sure what we're supposed to be doing, but I haven't read the chief's notes yet, either." He smiled, "I agree, we should try to put our preconceptions behind us and try to get on as best we can."

"Good," Sharon said. "I'm about to read the chief's notes and then we can talk about them."

"So, what do you think of the assignment?" Brent asked when he was finished.

"It's fascinating; I've never been on anything like this. There's a lot of... intrigue. A lot of different angles. We're here, first of all to pretend that Rob and Lisa are still here. So we need to be on the lookout for any nasty business, like they did to the car, or worse." Sharon bit her lip. "And of course, we have to keep in mind that we're trying to get evidence that helps to find the victim. That really sucks, what they did to her."

"I agree, we have to keep that in mind. But also, think about the kind of criminal minds that devised a scheme to kidnap a federal judge's daughter!" Brent shook his head. "I know it's not our job to speculate, but really, what outfit could pull off this big a deal?"

"The buzz is drug cartel, either that or the mob. It's got to be something big, with a lot at stake and lots of money to back it up. And the chief got a call from Lisa; she told him that Alvarez, the guy who rented the SUV that followed them, was Sarah's boyfriend, briefly, her first year in law school. He dropped out when she broke up with him and then stalked her." Sharon said.

"Good info, but what we need to keep in mind is that they are ruthless; it seems they'll stop at nothing. So, we need to appear to go about business as usual, stroll on the beach, wait for the car to come back, then we can actually get out and do normal things."

"Like getting groceries," Sharon said. "Did you find any grocery receipts?"

"No, sorry; I'll look now."

Sharon got up a second behind Brent and together they went through the drawers.

Brent was the first to come up with a receipt. "Hey, this is from the local IGA in the village; that's where the 'underclass' shops. So, even if they are rich, they're frugal. I like them already."

"How do you know they're rich?" Sharon asked.

"Chief told me Rob's a hedge-fund manager, and they live on the upper West side in the city. And Lisa's an assistant DA. Just put two and two together." Brent shrugged.

"Makes sense to me," Sharon said, and added, "plus they have this cottage, as a second home."

"Ok," Bent said, trying to focus, "back to business. Now we know where to shop. But I think we should still keep a low profile. And I think we should stick together; we have no idea what these thugs are up to, or what they want from us, except to be sure we don't talk."

"We're supposed to make contact with the homeless guy who has been staying in that beat-up house that's for sale," Sharon reminded him. "Is it best to do that at night, or do you think we can find a way when we're walking on the beach?"

"There's a lot we'll have to finesse, and we can always call the chief. In fact, he may be coming when they drop off the car, so we should write down our questions."

A half-hour later, they were still deep in discussion and jotting questions, when the distinct crunch of a vehicle on the shell driveway jolted them back.

Brent jumped up, his hand immediately going to his weapon, and gestured for Sharon to put the wig back on. Slowly, he approached the front door.

CHAPTER 17

"I'm ready for the good news, Blake, spill it!" Rory demanded.

Blake replied, thinking for a moment. "OK, Sarah's dad, the judge, is not at work today. According to the office buzz he had Federal marshals with him on shifts all weekend. Apparently, he's upset about something, out sick, or somehow in danger."

"Blake! Pretend you are in court in front of a cranky judge. Get to the facts quick!" Rory paced like a caged tiger in front of his desk.

"Well, it confirms what we know, which may be more than the federal marshals know. Anyway, Nate's friend, the judge's personal guard, isn't in the office today; she's at the judge's house. Nate called her and asked to meet with her. He said he had information useful to the judge and the case." Blake looked pleased with himself.

"That's good," Rory responded. "Is there anything else?"

"Yes, the best part..."

"Finally!"

Blake was crestfallen at her tone, but knew enough to continue. "OK, the marshal, Carla somebody, told him to come right over to the judge's house; but said she would have to send a car for him to keep comings and goings from the house private." Blake finished in a rush.

"Wow!" Rory was momentarily speechless. "That's very good news. I'm sorry I was so bitchy, I just get impatient. And I'm sorry

Sam didn't stick around to hear it; he might've stayed if he'd known."

"Maybe, but I do understand how upset he is, and any action must seem better than none. Anyway, Nate will probably get back to me after his meeting. Maybe then we can shoot off a text to Sam."

"We should send him to meet with the judge; that might be incentive enough to get him to come back."

The conversation was interrupted by the ringing of Blake's phone.

***

Nathan Burns, Blake's soon-to-be brother-in-law, sat in the back of a black, government-issue SUV. Following the phone call to Carla Nelson, it seemed that everything moved double-time. Nate was whisked into the car and off they went. He was nervous; as a law clerk, he'd never actually spoken with the judge, but had often seen his performance in court. Carson Justice was smart as a whip, quick to decide, and overall intimidating. Nate wasn't sure he'd actually talk with the judge today, but he thought he might, since he was going to the judge's home.

Before he was quite ready for it, they'd arrived. Nate was ushered out of the car and into the house quickly. A marshal he didn't know, Andrew Milano, he soon learned, answered the door, but Carla was right behind him and greeted Nate warmly.

Carla escorted Nate into the living room, and gestured toward a chair. She took a seat opposite him and spoke, "Thanks for coming, Nate. Obviously, your call intrigued me and I thought we'd best talk in person. You know this is a very sensitive subject…"

"Of course," Nate agreed.

Carla continued, "I need to know what you know, the reason you called me. Let's start there."

Nate's mouth was dry and he swallowed a few times before speaking.

Carla asked Andrew to bring some water.

Nate took a big gulp and then spoke. "Yesterday, I got a phone call from my fiancée's brother, Blake. He works at the law office where the judge's daughter, Sarah interned over the summer. Blake had gotten a call from Rory Chandler, his boss, who told him that Sarah had been kidnapped off the beach in East Hampton while staying with friends there."

Carla's face betrayed her; Nate knew instantly that she already knew this. She nodded for him to continue.

Nate related everything Blake had told him. Then he said, "I wasn't told what they'd found while researching on the internet, because we didn't want to say too much on the phone. Blake thinks, and I agree, that someone, maybe Sam, should talk with the judge in person and that it would be best if you continue to collaborate with him."

"Collaborate with whom?" the judge demanded as he entered the room in his bath robe.

Nate stood immediately and introduced himself to the judge.

Carla took over, asking the judge to sit while she explained what she and Nate had discussed.

Nate was thankful when Carla repeated what he'd told her almost verbatim. After finishing, she turned toward Nate and asked, "How'd I do? Did I forget anything?"

Nate shook his head as he tried to gauge how the judge was taking it. The judge looked, interested, Nate decided.

The judge trained his gaze on Nate, who felt a bit uncomfortable under scrutiny. Then he spoke, "Young man, Nate is it?" Nate nodded. "It's a bit unsettling that so many people know about this; what are your thoughts about that?"

"Well, my soon-to-be brother in law, Blake, is trustworthy. I've known him since high school; we're friends and I respect him. And from the way I've heard him talk about his boss, who runs a law firm; I can only conclude that she's top-drawer, too. Then, there's Sarah's boyfriend who interned with Sarah last summer at the firm, who's in his last year at the University of Pennsylvania Law School, and he's in love with Sarah. Oh, also, Rory's husband, Marc, is a forensic psychologist. All of these people love Sarah and are willing to do anything to find her. Sam would probably be the person to come here and speak with you in person, because he's the most involved." Nate was pleased that he'd hit all the important points.

Carson Justice nodded at Nate, then asked Carla, "What's your take on this?"

"I've known Nate since he's been here, as a law clerk, almost two years, and I know his uncle, Judge Harley Burns, and respect them both as competent professionals. And Carson, I believe these people Nate's mentioned have Sarah's best interest at heart. At the very least, I think you should meet with Sam Logan and decide for yourself. It looks like a good opportunity to find out more about Sarah's captors. We haven't had too much to go on."

The judge sighed, "That's true enough, Carla." Then he turned his attention to Nate. "Thank you, Nate, for coming forward. As I said, I'm sure you had some misgivings coming here, but the information from your friend will hopefully help us find Sarah."

The judge stood and shook Nate's hand. As he left the room, he turned to Carla, "I'm going up to rest, please get all the information from Nate so we can reach Sam Logan."

Nate breathed a sigh of relief as the judge left the room. It did not go unnoticed by Carla, who said, "I know, he has that effect on people. He can be intimidating, but he's quite a nice person and treats his staff well. Thank you so much for coming to us. Before you leave I need to get information."

***

Blake answered his phone on the second ring. When he heard Nate's news, he said, "Great! We just have a minor snag at the moment. Sam has now gone missing, no doubt to do his own investigating. We don't know where he is, but hope to track him down before the meeting with the judge. But if not Sam, someone will come. Thanks for doing this, man."

CHAPTER *18*

Chief Mayer, dressed in his "garage chic" attire, stood at the front door of the cottage. Brent heaved a sigh of relief. "Hey Chief, wasn't sure who might be paying us a visit; I was feeling a little edgy."

"With good reason," the chief answered. "Well, here's your car, where'd you leave the Toyota?"

Brent told him and asked him the few questions they'd written down.

The chief answered, "I'd like to talk with you a bit, so why don't you come out to the car and let me pretend to show you some things."

"OK, I'll follow your lead," Brent answered.

They walked out to the car, while Sharon remained in the house.

The chief pointed to the tires, kicking them, and bending down to point something out. Brent watched, as if interested.

The chief said quietly, "I don't want you two going out at night; you can do surveillance with the infrared goggles from inside. For now, you can go out during the day and try to make contact with the homeless guy, Joe, staying in that abandoned house. If anything at all comes up, call me at once. My secure contact number is on this sheet." He stood up and handed Brent the 'bill.' Just as he was turning to leave, his cell went off. He answered immediately, "Mayer here…what? Which marina? Ok, I'll be right there."

The chief waved to Brent as he left.

Brent took the paper and headed for the house. As he opened the door, he almost knocked Sharon over.

"Jeez, I guess you want to know what the chief had to say," Brent said, smiling.

"Well, yeah, so out with it!" Sharon demanded.

"He doesn't want us to go out at night; says we can do surveillance from inside with the goggles. We can go out during the day, acting as the other couple, umm…"

"Lisa and Rob," Sharon supplied.

"Yes, we should do what they would've done. And he wants us to try and make contact with that guy Joe, in the abandoned house. Oh, and he gave us a secure number to use any time we need to call him." Brent handed Sharon the paper with the number on it.

"That's it?" Sharon inquired.

"That's it for now." Brent answered.

"Ok, then I guess we can go shopping now, as soon as I get this god awful rag on my head," Sharon said, tugging the wig into place.

"It's part of being undercover, Sharon; suck it up!" Brent was getting tired of her complaints.

"Easy for you to say…" Sharon muttered.

"You can call the chief and ask for reassignment, if you can't handle it," Brent said.

Sharon walked to the car in a huff.

"Do you have a list?" Brent asked.

"I know what we need, no worries; I'm not a moron!"

As they got to the car, Brent looked into the car window. "Uh-oh, do you drive stick?"

"You mean you don't? How have you gotten by?" Sharon laughed, "Give me the keys."

They got into the car and Sharon adjusted the seat. "In case we're being watched, how do we account for the change in drivers?" Sharon asked, as she pulled the seat forward.

"Shit, who gives a fuck? Do you really think they'd notice?" Brent was frowning.

"Well, I'm only suggesting we follow the chief's orders." Sharon answered.

"Then, come up with an idea," Brent countered.

Sharon chose to ignore his remark, but considered checking with the chief.

The village was not far, only about ten minutes away. "Boy, it really is different once the crowds leave," Sharon noticed.

As they neared the grocery store, Sharon made a quick turn to the left, instead of turning into the lot.

Brent looked at her quizzically, and she said, "Don't look back, but there's a black SUV behind us; I'm going to try and lose it, just in case."

"I'm not going to look in the rear-view, but you can glance at the side mirror and let me know when we lose the guy."

Brent stole a glance at the mirror and told Sharon, "The car is one back, there's a little Kia behind us now. But the black car is close to the Kia."

Sharon drove a bit above the speed limit, and when they approached an intersection, she gunned it through a yellow-to-red light. She made the first right, taking her out of the village and towards the open road where she had many options to divert.

"Looking good," Brent said, turning around to look for the car. "No cars behind us now. You think it's safe to head back to the IGA now?"

"I think we need to go back to the cottage first, to make sure that no one tried to get in while we were gone. And why don't you call the chief on his secure number and let him know."

Brent called the chief. "Mayer here, what's up Brent?"

Brent told the chief what had happened and he replied, "Why'd you do that? You guys were on a completely legit shopping errand. Do me a favor and use the diversionary tactics only when necessary, Ok? I've gotta go now; someone suspicious has been hanging around one of the marinas. Bye."

"So what'd he say? You look upset," Sharon said.

"Chief said the diversionary action wasn't necessary, since we were on a legit errand. I guess he thinks we're real rookies," Brent added, frowning.

"Shit, he's right. My bad. I guess I got too caught up in the moment. Don't worry, I'll take the blame," Sharon added.

"Hey, I didn't stop you, so I'm in it equally. Remember, we're a team."

"Thanks," Sharon said smiling. "Guess we should go back to IGA."

The shopping went quickly and Sharon was ready to check out. Brent disappeared saying he wanted to get a few more things.

He soon came back with ice cream and a six-pack of beer.

Sharon eyed the beer suspiciously and said, "I'd run it by the chief, if I were you. We are on duty 24-7. That's part of being undercover." She threw his phrase back at him.

Brent said nothing but didn't remove the beer from the cart.

They drove home in silence. Brent was fuming.

It was lunch-time when they got back. They took the groceries inside and put them away, saying not a word to each other.

An unfamiliar ring tone sounded.

Sharon grabbed what turned out to be Lisa's phone. An "unknown" number came up. She glanced at Brent with a furrowed brow. "Hello," she said, trying to sound confident as her knees were knocking.

"Hello, Lisa," a strange, echoing sort of voice said. "You're still there, didn't heed the warning. I wonder what it will take to get rid of you!" An eerie laugh, devoid of mirth lingered in Sharon's ear as the line went dead.

CHAPTER 19

Sarah awoke suddenly; the boat had slowed to a stop. It had been making frequent stops Sarah presumed, to keep out of sight as much as possible. It was difficult for her to keep track of the days, mainly because she'd felt drugged so much of the time. She wasn't sure if it was Monday or Tuesday; it seemed like an eternity that she'd been gone. Sarah was hungry; she couldn't remember when she'd last eaten. She struggled to keep her mind alert and to stave off the anxiety she knew would cripple her.

What kept her going the most was her love of Sam, and, of course, her 'second family,' Rory, Marc, the twins, and Blake. She knew they loved her and were probably going crazy trying to find her. She had faith in them and believed they were smart enough to find her.

In contrast, her anger and hatred towards Henrique engaged her mind in strategies of escape. She'd been working at the duct tape, biting it, in hopes of freeing her hands. Sarah was attuned to the schedule of her abductors, when they were likely to feed her, or come in for other reasons. Henrique hadn't been back; Sarah was grateful for every day she didn't have to deal with him. The guy who'd always been the one to interact with Sarah had been replaced since the argument when Henrique had hit him. This new guard was not aggressive, and in fact appeared almost friendly in contrast to his predecessor. Sarah hoped to be able to manipulate him. Beyond that, she hadn't formulated a plan, other than to be alert for opportunities.

The boat had definitely stopped. She wondered how long they would stay, if they had finally reached their destination. Sarah could only guess at where they could be. With any luck, they could be somewhere on Long Island Sound near Connecticut, her home. A few tears slipped out as she thought of home, and she began to think about her father. He must know by now.

Something clicked in her brain as she thought of her father. The last time she'd seen him, he'd spoken to her about one of the cases that was on his mind. It was atypical that he discussed any cases with Sarah, but perhaps because she was almost a full-fledged lawyer, he was more comfortable.

It was the case of a minor drug runner from Mexico. He'd been given a sentence of 8-10 years, yet his attorney was requesting a hearing for parole after only two years. And it wasn't because he'd been an exemplary prisoner; he'd had two failed escape attempts. So Sarah's father was concerned that somehow he was a bigger player and the drug cartel might be involved. This concerned the judge, and as a result, Sarah worried. She hadn't been able to talk with anyone about that. But she had told Sam she thought she was being followed again. It turned out her instincts were right on that one, unfortunately.

The two had to be connected somehow, Sarah thought. She wished her mind wasn't so muddled, a result of the drugs and her heightened anxiety. She would find a way out of this, no matter what.

CHAPTER 20

After resting, Carson Justice was looking at the files Carla had brought over; he was feeling better since his conversation with Nathan.

He sat at his desk, trying to capture a thought that kept flitting away from him. Thinking of Sarah was distracting him. He was trying to remember a case that had troubled him. What was the guy's name?

To jog his memory, he looked through the cases on his desk. Carla had put "Gonzales" on top. He opened the file and began to peruse it. This was definitely the case, he realized as he read through it; now it was all coming back to him. Gonzales had been convicted of transporting heroin from Mexico to the U.S. It was a large quantity, thus the stiff sentence of 8-10 years.

He'd been imprisoned in the San Diego Federal Prison after his conviction. An unsuccessful attempt at escape had taken place soon after his incarceration. The decision to transfer him to a Federal prison in Berlin, New Hampshire, was based on its distance from the Mexican border. And Carson Justice had received the case because the prisoner was on the list to be transferred to the Federal Prison in Danbury, CT., as soon as it was transformed from a women's to a men's prison, which was in the works.

Gonzales had been in the Berlin facility for under a year when another, nearly successful, escape attempt had been made. Yet, his attorney was requesting a parole hearing after only two years of confinement.

The judge was almost certain there was help from inside or outside; probably both. In any case, there was money changing hands, he was sure. Prison guards were not well compensated for their dangerous job. Not that it made it ok, just understandable. It was difficult to find good guards.

For this reason, Carson suspected a Mexican cartel, perhaps the most powerful one. Gonzales's lawyer had scheduled this hearing, despite an unfavorable report from the prison. It was, however, unusual for them to risk so much for a "drug mule."

A light went on in the judge's head. Could it be that the cartel had kidnapped Sarah in an effort to force him to grant parole? Horrific, but effective, he had to admit. The meaning of this was either that Gonzales was a major player in the cartel or he knew too much, maybe both. Perhaps the plan was to kill Gonzales upon his release. Either way, the judge needed to talk with Gonzales.

"Carla, can you come here, please?"

Carla appeared quickly. "What do you need, Carson?"

"I think I may have hit on something. Can you arrange to have Juan Gonzales brought from the Berlin prison to the holding cell at the courthouse tomorrow? It has to be done on the QT. I'll speak to the warden and tell him it's of utmost importance that he alone knows about this. Two of our best marshals will transport him. They should leave at once; it's a five-hour drive each way. I'll go back to work tomorrow and I need to speak with Gonzales."

"So, this is case you've been trying to remember." Carson nodded. "I thought so, that's why I put it on top," Carla said.

"Yes, I'm glad you did; the name resonated immediately. There's definitely something wrong here; no way is he eligible for parole. Makes me think this is the reason for Sarah's abduction. The bastards haven't told me yet what it is they want, so if I can figure it out first, at least I'm a step ahead of them."

"Oh, and before I forget to tell you, I've reached Blake Ford, the guy who knows Nate and booked a room into a local B&B for Wednesday. Set the appointment for 2 p.m.; does that work for you?" Carla asked. "Nate isn't sure who will be coming, because several of Sarah's co-workers worked together getting information."

"Yes, I'll put it in my book. I may actually have some information to share, after I speak with Gonzales."

"Do you think you should be the first person to talk with Gonzales?" Carla's brow was furrowed. "We do have marshals quite adept at these kinds of negotiations…"

"Well… Carla, I think you're right. I'm too emotionally involved to do it. Also, since I'm hearing the case, it's improper. Who did you have in mind?" the judge inquired.

"Well, Andrew's quite good and that makes one fewer person we need to involve. I'll ask him; he should be here in a few minutes."

"Andrew would be perfect, if he agrees. And I think maybe, along those same lines, Roger and George would be good transport officers." He paused, "and now, I'm going back to Gonzales's file to see if I can find anything else."

CHAPTER 21

Chief Mayer answered on the second ring; he knew the call was from Brent.

"Thom, we have a situation here, thought you should know. Sharon just answered Lisa's phone and well, basically, we got another threat. The guy said something like, 'you're still here, you didn't heed the warning,' we don't know what to make of it but it looks like they're going to up the ante."

"I think you read it right, Brent. So, it looks like we'll have to do the same. I don't like it at all. You and Sharon need to stay in, at least for now, until we get a few more undercover guys on board."

"You don't think we're safe being out during the day? I mean, we'll be careful. I think we'll go nuts just sitting inside, plus, it will change our normal routine." Brent answered.

"Well, I think that was the intent of the call, don't you? It would be reasonable for you to stay in," the chief countered. "They've followed you and threatened you in the same day. So they're still here and still watching."

"But I think staying out of sight would make this just drag on longer, you know? Why not stick it in their faces and be ready for a response?" Brent asked.

"I'm of two minds. Actually, I do like the idea of drawing them out. On the other hand, I hate putting you two in jeopardy. I need time to think on this and get some more officers involved. In the meantime, until you hear from me, please don't go outside, promise?"

"Ok, promise," Brent said. But he wasn't happy.

"Ok, for now, I've got to interview a guy they found hanging around asking questions at a marina. Just what we need, more complications. Stay alert! Bye." The chief rang off.

Brent looked at Sharon, "You heard? He wants us to stay in until he can get more officers on the scene. I did push back, but he needs time to come up with a plan. He encouraged us to do that as well."

***

Chief Mayer arrived at the marina on Gardiners Bay. He spoke with the owner, who said, "This guy, he's waiting in the office, I didn't tell him you were coming. Anyway, I noticed him looking around and then he asked if any of the boats were for hire and if any had been taken out in the past few days. I remembered your phone call about the same thing, and thought you might want to talk to him."

"Quick thinking, Harv, thanks. I'll just go in and see what I can find out."

The chief opened the door to the office and startled the young man sitting there. He didn't look suspicious, but he appeared nervous.

"I'm Chief Mayer," he said, holding out his hand. The young man shook it, and said, "Sam Logan."

***

"The chief said we should do surveillance, so we might as well get started.

"You're right, Sharon," Brent conceded. "I'll take the upstairs; use the binoculars and be sure to stay out of sight."

97

They went to their separate locations. Soon Sharon called up to Brent, "There's not much I can see from down here, what with all the beach grass and scrub pines. Should I come up?"

"Not so fast, if someone is coming toward the house we want to know," Brent called down.

He smiled as he heard her reply. "Okaaay..." He knew she liked to be in on the action, an adrenaline junkie like himself.

Not that he was getting any action, Brent thought as he scanned with the binoculars; he had a view of the parking lot at the end of the beach, and he could see much of the beach itself.

Just as he'd decided to go to the other side of the house, he noticed movement in the parking lot; an old truck, it looked like a Chevy, had pulled in and parked. The driver took his time getting out of the truck, and when he did, his movements were furtive. He looked around several times, then ducked into the bushes leading to the beach. The guy was also partially hidden by a cap and sunglasses, hardly unusual for the beach. His clothes were unremarkable; he wore jeans and a long sleeved shirt.

Brent was losing him and quickly went to another window. It looked like he was headed in the direction of the dilapidated house, the one where the homeless guy reportedly stayed. "Sharon, c'mon up, quick!"

He didn't have to call twice, Sharon was there in a flash, "What's up, Brent?" she asked, breathless.

"Shit! I just lost him; see that patch of brush over there?" He pointed. "Well, this guy just got out of that truck in the lot and ran toward the house that's deserted. Can we see it any better from downstairs?" Brent asked.

"Don't know, I'll check," Sharon called as she ran down the stairs.

In a moment, Sharon had focused her high-power binoculars in the general direction of the house. It was several houses down the beach, but the houses were staggered, so she had a small view space from the corner of the living room. "I can see a very small part of the house," she called up to Brent, "but there aren't any windows. If I could go out on the deck…"

Brent took the stairs two at a time, "You heard the orders. But, I might just try to sneak out while you keep watch…"

"Okaaay," came Sharon's response, which Brent had come to recognize as displeasure.

"Look, I'll take the heat if the chief finds out…" Brent rationalized.

Sliding the deck door open from a crouching position, Brent carefully and slowly made his way to the deck, almost at a crawl. There was a largish scrub pine below which would shelter him as he tried to see the house.

He found a window on the entry floor, essentially a basement, and focused on it, adjusting the glasses for maximum magnification. He settled in to patiently watch. Were his eyes fooling him or did he see shadows of movement? He looked intently. He was right; there was movement, and it appeared to be quick, almost violent. He continued to watch. When he saw no further movement, he scuttled back inside.

"Upstairs, quick!" he motioned to Sharon as he bolted up the stairs. Brent knew just where to look, and he focused the glasses on the parking lot. Sharon followed his lead.

Soon, they both saw a man, running in a crouched position toward the truck. As they watched, he jumped in and took off. Brent tried to focus on the license plate, but he could see only that it was a New York plate.

"What do you suppose that was?" asked Sharon.

"I'm not sure, but my gut says it wasn't good," Brent replied.

***

It was full dark, as Sharon and Brent finished a hastily prepared dinner of hot dogs and beans. They were still waiting for a response from the chief, since their phone call to him reporting what they'd seen. The chief had continued the ban on going outdoors, but they could watch with their night goggles. He said he'd find a way to get back with them.

Sharon was growing restive. "Why don't you go upstairs with the goggles, while I clean up the kitchen?" she suggested to Brent.

"OK, can't hurt to stay busy until we hear from the chief." Brent grabbed the goggles and went upstairs.

Sharon gathered the dishes and put them in the sink. The pile was growing, so she sighed and put herself to the task of washing them. She hadn't signed on for KP duty, she thought glumly.

Gathering up the trash they'd accumulated in the last couple of days, she frowned at the bulging garbage bag, which was beginning to smell. This was unacceptable; it needed to be emptied. The trash can was outside the basement door. They should've just hauled it inside. Too late for regrets, Sharon thought, as she carried the bag down the steps to the basement. She didn't turn the light on, as there was enough light from the street lamps. She walked quietly to the door; seeing nothing, she unlocked the door and quickly stepped out.

Just as quickly, a large hand went over her mouth before she could utter a word.

CHAPTER 22

Berlin Federal Prison was quiet at this hour, well past midnight. Roger Land and George Anderson, the two federal marshals, accompanied by the warden, John Harding, were striding quickly down the darkened hallway. At the end was Gonzales's solitary confinement cell where he'd been housed since his last escape attempt.

The warden unlocked the cell and the three went inside. Gonzales was apparently sleeping; he made no movement when they entered. Harding went to the side of the cot as the marshals flanked him. He said to the prisoner, "Gonzales, get up, you have an appointment."

Juan Gonzales sat up, looking around in confusion, which quickly morphed into anger. "What's happening?" he demanded. "Where's my lawyer? He's the only one I talk with!"

Uh-oh, thought George, he's already surly. He was hoping this wouldn't be a wasted effort.

"On your feet!" ordered the warden. The marshals stepped in to offer assistance, each grabbing one of Juan's arms and hoisting him to a standing position. The prisoner made himself a dead weight, making it necessary to drag him. Gonzales continued to struggle, and though the marshals were stronger, the smaller man put up a fight.

As Gonzales's energy began to flag, the warden managed to cuff first one wrist and then the other. Soon the shackles were in place and Gonzales was quickly ushered out of his cell and out the adjacent door, which led to the basement. The prisoner was not cooperating, so he was nearly carried downstairs to the transport vehicle. He was shouting obscenities the entire time, some in English, some in Spanish.

George, playing 'good cop' said, "Look, man, you're making it tougher than it needs to be."

Sputtering with rage, Gonzales blurted, "You come in and drag me from bed, don't tell me nuffin'; how you 'spect me to act?"

"Ok, fair enough," George replied, "we're taking you to a holding cell at the courthouse in New Haven."

"My hearing ain't today, and it sure's hell's not in the middle of the night! You think I'm stupid? I want my lawyer; you can't do this!"

George rolled his eyes, though he wasn't surprised at the prisoner's response. There was no point in continuing the discussion, now that the 'L-word' had been introduced for the second time.

Gonzales was placed in the back of the vehicle, where George had the privilege of joining him.

George settled in, putting earbuds in to make the next five hours bearable. It helped, but he could still hear the ranting, although it was somewhat muted.

CHAPTER 23

The trash bag fell from Sharon's grasp. She had no time to react as she was forced into the basement and the door was slammed shut.

Hearing the loud noise, Brent appeared at the top of the steps, turned on the light and took in the scene.

"What the fuck is going on?" He ran down the steps, grabbing the young man standing next to Sharon.

"Hey, please, let me explain," the stranger said, as Brent held him. "I'm Sam Logan, Sarah's boyfriend. I'm just trying to find out what happened to her. When I saw lights on in the house, I was suspicious; I knew Rob and Lisa had left; she called me. You aren't Rob and Lisa, I've seen pictures!"

"I really can't comment on our investigation here, but if you want to help Sarah, you need to stay out of this. In any case, I'll have to call the chief," Brent answered.

"Oh shit!" Sam said, frowning.

Just then the basement door opened, and the chief came in. Looking at Sam, he said, "Not you again, I told you to go home! You're not helping us find Sarah."

"Well, you haven't found her yet!" Sam accused.

"You have no idea what we've been doing, but again, your presence here is compounding our efforts. This time, I'm taking you in and charging you with 'obstruction of justice', and I need to give your Miranda warnings."

"I know my rights, I'm in law school…" Sam responded.

"Oh God, save us from the lawyers! In any case, Mr. Logan, for the record, I must give you your rights."

Mayer then cuffed Sam and took him upstairs, depositing him in the living room.

He closed the door and took Sharon and Brent into the kitchen. "What were you thinking, Sharon? I distinctly told you to stay in at night. The intruder could've been one of the thugs we've been tracking, instead of just a pain-in-the-ass lovesick boyfriend!"

Brent was listening, but not saying anything. Then he said, "Chief, of course Sharon didn't do the right thing, but sometimes...."

The chief was quick on the uptake, "What, you were in on this, Hargraves?"

"No, Sir, I think it was simple force of habit; Sharon's a bit OCD, can't stand a mess."

Sharon glared at him, although she knew he was trying for levity.

Brent started again, "The intel we gave you earlier, about the activity in the house down the beach would not have been possible without going out onto the deck. I made that call, and it paid off."

"Yeah, I noticed on the way here that it would've been mighty difficult to see that from inside the house. Then, when Sharon stepped outside, I began thinking that both of you were playing by your own rules." He wasn't smiling.

The chief relented a bit, "When I give orders, I expect them to be followed. Bottom line, I can't afford to lose either of you! I trust I've made my point."

Sharon and Brent both nodded.

Chief Mayer responded. Looking toward Brent, he said, "No question that your information saved Joe's life. If you hadn't seen what looked like violence and reported it, he might have died. By the time we got to him, he barely had a pulse. He's in South Hampton hospital, and it looks like he'll pull through. So, you took a calculated risk, Brent and saved his life."

"So, what if the perp comes back to finish the job?" Sharon asked, her brow furrowed.

"We have an undercover guy there, dressed in grungy clothes, and looking bruised. Actually, we hope he does come back; he'll get a surprise." The chief smiled. "In the meantime, we hope Joe recovers enough to talk; he should have plenty to say."

"And, where does that leave us; what do you expect us to do?" Sharon asked.

"Okay, you can carry on as you would normally, as Rob and Lisa. Obviously, the goons think that's who they're dealing with, and we have two extra guys patrolling the area." The chief produced a two-way radio, handing it to Sharon.

"That's how they'll contact us?" Brent asked.

"Yes, and vice versa. The contacts are Stan and Viv; that's all you need to know, and here's the code," Mayer said, handing slips of paper to Brent and Sharon.

"So, any questions?"

"Not really," Brent said. "I gather from what you've said, we should carry on like before."

"Yes, that's right. If you need immediate help, use the two-way. If we need to discuss something, you can also relay that by radio and I'll get back to you."

Sharon asked the chief, "Will I get written up for this?"

"No, consider this a verbal warning."

"Thank you, Chief, I appreciate it," Sharon said.

"One other caution, if you judge it necessary to go out at night for any reason, call Stan or Viv and they'll have your back."

"Are they on duty 24-7?" Sharon asked, eyebrows raised.

"Good question. Stan and Viv will always be on duty; those are the code names, but they may be different people. Now, I need to get Sam Logan to the station; maybe an overnight in the cell will give him some clarity."

Opening the door and finding an empty living room and an open window, the chief exploded, "Jesus Christ, what the fuck?"

CHAPTER 24

Rory was at work early, as much to hear about Nate's discussion with the marshal as she was to deal with her own work.

Blake was at his desk when she arrived; she knew from his expression that he had some news.

She held up her hand as she entered, "Let me get some coffee first, I'm dying to hear what you have to say." She quickly poured coffee and took a seat opposite Blake.

"Good news from Nate!" Blake began dramatically. "Not only did he speak with the marshal, he also talked with the judge, who he said was rather intimidating. Also he's obviously very bright."

"OK, good start, what else?" As usual, Rory was impatient to get the news.

"Well, the judge listened to him, and then told his marshal, Carla, to get my information, so she can contact me…"

"Wow! So have you heard from them yet?"

"Well, no, but," Blake glanced at the clock, "it's not eight a.m. yet, so…"

"Yes, I guess we have to wait, but that's good news," Rory said. "At least it's a glimmer of hope; I guess that's the best we can get for now."

"It is, but I'm a bit apprehensive, you know…"

"Sure, that's understandable, but we'll collect all the information we can and sit down and discuss it. I haven't heard from Lisa since they got back from East Hampton. I don't know if she knows what's going on out there. She did leave me a new cell number to call her, so I think I will."

"Why don't you wait until I hear from the marshal, let's not get ahead of ourselves," Blake said.

"You're right, it's just that I feel like I have to do something…and I'm worried for Sam; he hasn't gotten back to me."

"I hate to state the obvious, but…" Blake started.

"Don't say it. I know I have a lot to do, but I'm worried about Sam and Sarah; it's making me crazy!" Rory's lip trembled.

"And you already know that worry accomplishes nothing," Blake answered, parroting back the advice she'd often given him. "We're doing all we can for now. And until Sam wants to reach us, I guess we have to trust his judgement, dubious as it might appear."

"You're right," Rory mumbled, "I do have lots to keep me busy. That reminds me, I have to see if I can expedite the psychological for DeSean."

With that on her mind, Rory went straight to her office. She knew the psychologist who would be administering the exam, and called her.

"Dr. Simon's office, how can I help you?"

Rory recognized the cheerful voice, "Good morning, Samantha, this is Rory Chandler, is the doctor in?"

"The doctor is at the prison, and I believe she's seeing your client, DeSean, this morning," Samantha replied.

"Would you please ask her to call me when she gets back?"

"I'm sure that will be her first priority, Rory. Bye now."

Rory hung up and allowed herself a fist-pump, "Yes!" All too often her clients languished in jail, waiting for the wheels of justice to move. She was pleased that Carole Simon was not only a good psychologist, but also sensitive to the clients she served.

She checked that off her list and went on to other items.

Rory was intently studying another brief and didn't hear the knock on her office door.

Blake came in, smiling.

107

Rory immediately shoved her work aside and asked, "What's up?"

"Sam is booked into a B&B in Branford, near New Haven on Tuesday and will meet with the judge on Wednesday. If we don't find Sam by then, one of us will have to go; we have to meet with the judge!" Blake said.

"Well, that's a start," Rory said, beginning to feel some hope. "I need to call Lisa, I'm wondering if she's spoken with the chief in East Hampton. And I guess she needs to know about Sam, even though she won't be happy."

Rory called Lisa's new cell number and left a message. "She didn't answer," Rory told Blake, "but then she's a DA, so she may be in court."

"I want to talk to Roland. He may have some thoughts as to where Sam might be."

She dialed Roland's cell. He answered immediately. "Hey girl, it's been awhile, what's up with you?" She heard the smile in his voice, and hated to deliver bad news.

"Well, you knew about Sarah's kidnapping when Marc called you. But there's more, so if we could meet for lunch today at the Towne House, I'll tell you all about it, and I have some questions."

"Of course, I'll meet you, noon ok? Sorry about Sarah, I'll help any way I can." Roland's voice held a somber note now.

"Thanks, Roland, I can always count on you. Noon's good. I'll make reservations to be on the safe side. Bye."

"He's the best," Rory said, aloud. Roland was a state trooper, and good friend.

He was the only gay trooper she knew of, but he kept it buttoned up at work. She figured it might be because being black and gay might be too much for the establishment. He'd told her only because she'd agreed to represent his partner in a sex-discrimination suit, a case she'd won.

CHAPTER 25

The judge was in his office at the courthouse feeling better than he had in several days since the awful business with Sarah had begun. He was glad things were moving now and he reminded himself to stay in the moment and focused on his work.

Carla and Andrew were in the office briefing him on the transport of the prisoner during the night. Andrew had spoken with George and Roger and was reporting back to the judge.

"Well, Sir, I guess it was to be expected, Gonzales has never been particularly cooperative. He's always had this air of entitlement, as if he didn't really belong in prison."

"Most probably fed by the belief that he'd be sprung by his cronies," the judge noted dryly.

"Quite possibly," Andrew continued, "and he nearly was, on two occasions, as we know. Fortunately, during both attempts there were a few guards not 'on the take' and sharp enough to stop it."

"The warden has an ongoing investigation into those attempts, which may itself prove a deterrent. He also has a few officers under special surveillance and will fire them in an instant if there's any hint of involvement. He runs a pretty tight ship."

"You're right, Judge, but he also treats his staff well and thus has a good deal of loyalty," Andrew added.

"So, who's going to interview Gonzales? Anyone besides you, Andrew?" Carla asked."

"The DA on the case, Dan Sommers, will be there and I'm wondering if we should offer Gonzales a public defender?" Andrew looked at the judge.

"Well, of course, he needs representation, but I doubt if the presence of a PD will persuade him to talk. We need to at least make the attempt." The judge stopped for a moment to think.

"I just hope it's not an exercise in futility," Carla interjected.

"It has to be brought home to him," the judge said, looking at Andrew, "that his associates might not have his welfare in mind. In fact, I'm not at all certain they don't plan to kill him upon his release."

"That's what I plan to use as a lever, see if we can get him to 'sing.' I'll have to discuss it with Sommers, see if he'd be willing to strike a deal with Gonzales. Does he know what's going on?" Andrew asked the judge.

"We need to make sure he does. Carla, can you call his office and ask him to come over?" Carson asked.

"Will do," Carla answered as she picked up the phone and spoke with the receptionist. "He'll be right over," Carla told the judge.

"Thanks, Carla." He turned to Andrew, "Do you have any particular style, any questions you usually lead in with?"

Andrew thought for a moment, then said, "It all depends on what I'm picking up from the person I'm questioning. I know he's played the 'tough guy' so far, but often that's a flimsy façade. I'll be looking for any vulnerabilities…"

Just then, Dan Sommers entered the office. "Judge, you wanted to see me?" He nodded to Andrew and Carla.

"Yes, Sommers, please have a seat. We have a rather delicate situation here."

CHAPTER 26

Chief Mayer had been sleep-deprived in the last few days and he was feeling it; he was out of fuel, but had to keep going. Sam Logan sat in the cell, and Mayer wasn't ready to release him. Sam hadn't asked for his call either. What was up with that, the chief wondered. He wanted it resolved soon so he could get on with more pressing matters. But he was damned if he would let him go unescorted.

***

As he drove to the hospital, the chief's main concern was whether or not Joe Hayes, the homeless man, would pull through. He had come to learn in the past few days that Joe was a veteran of the Vietnam War and was estranged from his family. Joe never got the psychological treatment he needed after the war and had just drifted downward. The family had been contacted and his sister, Charlene, was now en route to the hospital from Connecticut. One of the chief's officers would meet her at the Orient Point ferry and bring her to the hospital.

After spending several minutes with the unconscious man, the chief was about to leave the hospital room when the patient coughed. Hayes's eyes began blinking rapidly and he seemed to be trying to speak. Mayer rang for the nurse, who came into the room immediately.

"He seems to be waking up," the chief told the nurse.

The nurse, Emily Dayton, went over to Hayes and propped him up on his pillow. "Do you want some water, Mr. Hayes?" she inquired gently.

He nodded as he looked around the room, appearing anxious.

Nurse Dayton brought water to the patient and held the cup while offering him the straw.

He quickly drained the cup and held it out for more. She refilled the cup and he drank more slowly this time.

The effort seemed to sap his energy and he let his head drop back to the pillow.

The nurse asked, "Mr. Hayes, are you feeling better? Can you talk?"

He nodded, then looked toward the chief.

"I'm Chief Mayer, East Hampton Police. We found you beaten in one of the houses out on Gardiner's Bay. We want to find out who did this to you."

The nurse discreetly left the room, saying, "Just hit the call button if you need me."

Hayes's voice was hoarse, but he tried to speak, "Am I under arrest, Officer?'

"No, you're not, but we are interested in finding who did this to you and we will offer you protection from them. They might've killed you…"

Hayes looked frightened and didn't speak.

"Believe me, Mr. Hayes, these men are ruthless and will stop at nothing. Please tell us what you know so we can find them."

"But, when they don't find me in the house, they'll come looking for me," he reasoned.

"We hope they do come back to the house, Mr. Hayes, because we have a surprise waiting for them. You see, we're trying to stay ahead of them. So, whatever you can tell us will help. By the way, we've contacted your sister, Charlene, and she's taking a ferry from Connecticut. She should be here soon."

Hayes was visibly moved by this news, a tear trickled down his cheek. He wiped it away saying, "Thank you." After a moment, he seemed to reach a decision. "I'll tell you everything," he said.

The chief said, "I have a recorder here, do you mind speaking into it?"

"No sir, I don't."

Chief Mayer first spoke into the recorder giving the date, time, location and name of the informant. Then he said, "Go ahead Mr. Hayes, tell me in your own words what happened."

Before he spoke, Hayes asked for more water and the chief filled his cup. Then, he began to talk. "I guess it was Friday last week. It was near dark and I was going to go out on the beach. I like to get some fresh air…but I heard a commotion, a struggle going on, so I held back and stayed in the shadows. I saw two men grab a girl off the beach and carry her away. I'd seen her walk on the beach before and knew where she was staying; she just liked to pick up shells and watch the water. Anyways, I got real scared and went back in the house so they wouldn't see me."

"Can you describe the men, Mr. Hayes?" Chief Mayer asked.

"No, it was too dark, but I could hear them talking, not in English, something foreign like. And they were rough with the poor girl. I wished I could've done something…"

"Did anything else happen?" the chief inquired.

"Well, I went back in, like I said, and I finally went to sleep. It seemed like I'd just got to sleep when I was waked up, rough. And there was this man; he was big, dark and scary. He shook me and said, 'What did you see?' He spoke English, but not real good. I told him I didn't see nothin' and he shook me some more. I got real scared and told him what I saw. He told me he'd give me money if I watched the house where the girl stayed, and he'd be back to find out. If I told anyone, he drew his finger across his throat and I got the picture." Hayes dropped back on his pillow, his eyes fluttering.

"Mr. Hayes, if you want to rest now…" the chief began.

"No, there's more...I don't want to forget. Same guy came back, couple nights later, maybe Sunday, asked me what I saw. And I told him I saw the couple, the black guy and the white woman leave in a different car; their car had been towed away. And they didn't come back. He gave me a hundred and left."

"Was it the same guy that came the next night?" the chief asked.

"Think so, but couldn't say for sure; he just banged his way in, woke me up and started smacking me around, saying, 'You lied, you lied!' Then I passed out, don't remember nothin' 'til I woke up here."

CHAPTER 27

After an early supper, Rory, with the twins' help, cleared the dishes away and tidied the kitchen. She prepared for the meeting to discuss finding Sam and she pulled together information they had for the meeting with the judge.

"Anything new since we spoke?" Roland asked with a smile as he entered the house without knocking.

Rory shook her head and Marc got up to shake Roland's hand, "Hey, good to see you, man. Coffee?"

"Not for me, thanks," Roland answered.

Rory got up and gave Roland a hug, "You'll have some tea, if I make it, won't you?"

"Sure, if it's no trouble…"

"For you? Never a problem." Rory went about making the tea while Marc and Roland seated themselves in the breakfast nook.

Before the tea was ready, Blake came in. Helping himself to coffee, he went to join Marc and Roland.

Rory came over with the tea and handed it to Roland. "Everyone have what he needs?" They nodded. She brought a bottle of water for herself and took a seat.

Taking a deep breath to settle herself, Rory said, "This meeting is to discuss what we know so far and see if we can come up with any ideas for finding Sam. I'm sure he wants to talk with the judge, so that should be a huge incentive if only he would contact us."

Blake asked, "Did Lisa ever get back to you?"

"No, now that you mention it, she hasn't. I forgot I'd called her..." Rory answered.

As if conjured, Rory's cell trilled and she answered, mouthing 'Lisa.'

***

After an animated conversation with Lisa, Rory ended the call and turned to the others.

Taking a deep breath, Rory addressed them, "Well, that was Lisa. She called because Chief Mayer of East Hampton just called her. Sam is sitting in a jail cell in East Hampton, and has numerous charges against him. He's apparently been hampering the chief's efforts to investigate Sarah's kidnapping."

"What did he do exactly?" Roland asked.

"He was first questioned because he was hanging around a marina, asking questions about boat rentals. I guess the chief alerted marinas in the area to be on the look-out. The chief talked to Sam, didn't charge him, but told him to go home and leave the investigating to them."

"So, I'm guessing he didn't heed their advice," Marc said.

"You might say that," Rory answered. "His next move was to try to break in to Rob and Lisa's house. Then, after he'd been cuffed by the chief and left alone in a room, he escaped and had to be hunted down. So, yeah, he's accumulated several charges."

"So, now what?" Blake asked.

"The chief wants him out, but he won't let him out on his own. He'll probably drop the charges if Sam leaves and doesn't come back. I got the chief's number from Lisa; I'll give him a call and probably head up to East Hampton after my court case tomorrow. Let him sit a bit more."

"I wish I could go with you, Rory," Marc said. "But I have to testify in the city tomorrow..."

"I'll go with you," Blake offered.

"I really need you in the office, Blake, and I don't mind traveling alone."

"You sure you don't want to spring him tonight?" Roland asked.

"Well," Blake said, "he's been real fucked up since Sarah was taken. God knows what he's thinking. Plus he needs to be in Branford by tomorrow night for his meeting with the judge the next day."

Looking at her watch, Rory spoke, "Okay, you've convinced me that we should get Sam tonight. It's just seven, and it will be a long night, but worth getting him back as soon as possible."

"That sounds good, Rory; I'll go with you. It's a lot of driving and I'll feel better knowing you have my assistance." Roland offered.

"And I'd like to go too." Marc put in.

"But you have an early case in the city."

"Fuck it, I'll go anyway, I really want to," Marc said.

"Ok, we'd best get on the road; I'll call Mayer and get the address to put in the GPS."

"Well, I guess I'll see you tomorrow," Blake said.

"Yep, and now you have some time to see your girlfriend tonight," Rory smiled.

Rory went upstairs to tell the twins, while Marc got the Prius out and punched in the address in East Hampton.

***

They'd made good time to East Hampton, Rory thought. True, they'd hauled ass, but there wasn't much traffic. It was just before eleven p.m. when they'd arrived.

Mayer was there and was happy to release Sam. He agreed to hold the charges open until Sarah's case was resolved, and would consider dropping them if there was no more interference from Sam.

Roland agreed to drive home, while Marc sat in the back with Sam.

Sam looked as bad as Rory had ever seen him; he was unshaven, dirty and looked generally unhappy. He sat with his head in his hands.

Rory had no need to question Sam on his judgement, she figured when he was ready to talk, he would. But she did think it was important for him to know about the breakthrough with the judge.

So, she finally broke the silence. "Sam, the reason we came for you this late is because you have to go to Branford tomorrow and meet with the judge the next day."

Sam's head came up and he registered a weak smile. "Really? He's really going to see me? How did you guys hook that up?"

"You may recall that Blake called his friend Nate, who's a law clerk at the federal court in New Haven," Rory said.

"I sort of remember that, but it seemed like a long shot. Look, I know you must all think I'm an asshole; I have no excuse. I've just been so devastated over Sarah's disappearance that I can hardly function. I felt like I had to do something to find her. As it turns out, I've been a dismal failure!" Sam sighed.

"We weren't judging you, man, we were concerned for your safety. The guys in East Hampton have many armed undercover officers out there. We're just glad you didn't get yourself shot," Marc said.

"And now, you have a great opportunity to talk with the judge," Rory said.

"I won't fuck it up, I promise!" Sam said. "I'm sorry for the added stress I put on you guys, I know you've been upset about Sarah, too. I can't explain it. I had to get moving and at least try to find out where she was."

"That's what 'second chances' are all about, Sam," Roland weighed in.

"And what better chance than to meet Sarah's father," Marc put in.

"From what she's told me, he's rather intimidating and aloof; at least that's how she's described him," Sam said.

"He may have changed since Sarah's abduction," Rory said. "You never know."

CHAPTER 28

Andrew Milano, the federal marshal, along with Dan Sommers, an assistant DA, had spent most of the day questioning the prisoner. They'd brought in a Public Defender to represent Gonzales's interests.

Despite generous offers, thinly veiled threats, and a variety of 'good cop/bad cop' exchanges, Gonzales had remained defiantly silent. Refusing to talk with the PD, he demanded to see his lawyer. This option was not offered.

Andrew and Dan left the room, leaving the PD and the two marshals, Roger and George, who would eventually take him back to prison.

They walked to the judge's chambers without talking. Andrew was dreading the conversation with the judge. He was frustrated, exhausted and feeling defeated. He hated to have to pass on such a dismal report to Carson Justice. Apart from disappointing the judge, he was disappointed in himself.

They reached the judge's chambers; Carla greeted them in the outer office and buzzed the judge to let him know they'd arrived. He sounded enthusiastic as he told her to send them back, and asked her to join them.

Andrew's mouth was dry, and he was feeling dejected. He and Sommers entered the judge's chambers and took seats silently.

Carson's cheerful greeting and smiling face slowly faded as he noticed the expressions on both men's faces. He tried for humor, "Well, don't all talk at once!"

Andrew started to speak, but found he couldn't. He got up and poured water for Dan and himself. He took a sip and then asked if anyone else wanted water. Getting no takers, he gave Dan his water and took his seat.

He tried again to speak, but was interrupted by the judge.

Carson held up his hand, and said, "Ok, I think I get the picture. You guys look like you've been through the wringer. Look, we knew it was a long shot from the beginning, but we had to give it a try. And I doubt any other team could've pulled it off better than you two, so stop beating yourselves up."

Andrew now spoke, "Carson, we did give it hell trying. Gonzales is a punk, but he's not stupid. He knows who's signing his paycheck and it's not us! He has no reason to believe us and every reason to believe his thugs will get him out and send him right back to work in Mexico. We tried every angle and he's not budging."

Sommers joined in, "I went to the top and got permission to offer him the best possible deal if he talked -- immunity and the witness protection program. He laughed in our faces."

"Oh, and we're pretty sure he understands English well enough, but we had a translator to make sure he understood everything. He displayed not an iota of fear at the possibility of his men turning on him, which, incidentally, I think is a real possibility..." Andrew's voice trailed off.

The judge picked up the conversation. "Look, Andrew and Dan, I don't doubt that you've left no stone unturned. As I said, it was a long shot from the beginning. So, what now?"

Sommers spoke, "We're leaving him for a spell, to catch our breath, get some dinner, let him stew..."

"Then, we'll go back and give it another try, see if we can wear him down," Andrew added.

"Make sure he's fed," the judge interjected, "we don't want him to have any opportunity to accuse us of cruelty."

"When he gets to his lawyer, he'll try to throw the book at us anyway," Andrew commented. "But, sure, we'll feed him."

"First, have yourselves a nice, long dinner, you deserve it." Judge Carson Justice said, dismissing them.

***

The walls were thin and Sarah could often hear her captors, dominated by Henrique, talking among themselves. Some of her Spanish was coming back to her as she listened intently to their conversations. She hadn't been able to get the gist of what they were saying, but she could pick out some words.

Sarah heard a cell phone buzz and Henrique answered. He began speaking rapidly and seemed to grow more agitated as the conversation went on.

He shouted, "estupido!" and evidently hung up his cell. Henrique seemed to be filling in his lieutenants about the call. Sarah understood, 'fracaso,' or failure, and then 'mision,' or mission. Then he said, 'no tuva alternative,' which Sarah thought meant he had no choice. Henrique commanded 'venga!' which Sarah interpreted as 'come' and then, 'quedarce.' Sarah thought he'd ordered one of his men to go with him and one to stay. She prayed it would be her most recent guard who'd remain, as she heard the loud stomping fading away. Then the distinct sound of a motorboat starting up filled the air. The noise gradually grew fainter until she no longer heard it.

Sarah held her breath, afraid to move. She wondered where they were going; they must be close to land since it sounded as though they'd taken a small boat.

She'd managed to free her hands of the duct tape, keeping one long strip to put in place when her guard showed up. There had been no more 'visits' from Henrique. Sarah figured he'd made his statement, which was always about power, not lust. He also seemed to make it clear to his underlings that she was his, alone, to use as he saw fit. And he seemed to have lost some trust in her first guard, as he'd not been back.

The boat was silent, but for the quiet lapping of the water. Sarah wondered how long she'd have to wait to find out who her guard was. She figured if it had been the first one, he'd have come in already to taunt her, or worse, to abuse her. She wanted to look around her tiny cabin, now that her hands were free, but she dared not make a sound.

What had happened to make Henrique leave in such a hurry? It seemed clear to her that one or more of his henchmen had failed to do something on their mission. And evidently, Henrique alone could save it. The mission was, of course, the reason for her kidnapping, for which she was beginning to formulate a possible scenario.

Sarah thought back again to her last conversation with her father, when he'd revealed his concern about the parole hearing of a convicted drug runner. Her three captors were Spanish speaking, and Henrique, who had contrived to meet her and develop a relationship with her, was in charge of this operation. It seemed plausible she was being used to gain the freedom of the guy—she forgot his name—who was up for, but not deserving of, parole.

But, she was still captive, so what had gone wrong with the 'mission?'

Sarah heard footsteps coming in her direction and quickly replaced the tape. She breathed a sigh of relief when her guard entered the room. He brought a tray with breakfast on it and said, uncertainly, "OK?"

"Si," Sarah answered, then asked, "café, por favor?" He nodded and left the room.

Chapter 29

After spending a few more unproductive hours with Gonzales, Andrew had reported back to the judge they'd made no more progress. In fact, the prisoner seemed more determined than ever to thwart them.

The judge had instructed Andrew to tell the marshals to take him back to the prison after sunset, well after the courthouse closed.

"Andrew," he'd said, "this in no way reflects on your abilities, so go easy on yourself."

While Andrew had appreciated the judge's words, he was more than disappointed in himself and wondered what he might've done differently. He finally reached the conclusion there was little more he could have done, because Gonzales seemed sure he'd get out of prison soon and apparently had faith in his co-conspirators.

***

A few hours later, Milano returned to the cell, telling George and Roger it was time to go.

Gonzales resisted and had to be physically pulled to a standing position. Roger went to the door, stepped out into the hallway and checked to make sure there was no one about. He signaled to George and the two marched Gonzales out the door, while Andrew brought up the rear.

The three were scarcely over the threshold, when a masked figure sprang into view, his gun aimed at Gonzales. George shoved the prisoner back into the room and fell on him, taking a bullet to the arm. Roger opened fire on the retreating attacker. He saw the masked figure grab the back of his leg and he thought he hit him. Then the shooter ducked into a stairwell and vanished.

Andrew was the first to recover from the shock and called security, ordering a lockdown of the courthouse. Then he called 911 and asked for an ambulance to be sent.

Gonzales appeared dazed and frightened. George was checking the blood flow from his wound, which was substantial.

Roger came back into the room, out of breath. "Looks like I hit him. I started to follow him down the steps, but lost him, then realized it might be more important to help you. Is George okay?'

"I've ordered a lockdown and called an ambulance for George; he's been wounded," said Andrew.

Roger looked at George for the first time, concern etched in his face. "Jeez, man, we need to stop the bleeding!" He pulled off his belt and made a primitive tourniquet.

Andrew was in communication with security, "Yeah, Glen, when the ambulance arrives send the EMT's up to the cell block ASAP! Have you seen any evidence of the shooter? Oh, well, how long 'til you can get back-up? Ok, we need another marshal to replace George, too. I understand…"

Addressing George, with his gun pointed at Gonzales, Andrew said, "Shouldn't be too long, in fact…" as he spoke they could hear the approaching sirens, "sounds like they're almost here. Hang in there man."

George was pale and shaken, but said, "I don't think this is too bad, I've been wounded before."

Within minutes, two EMS techs arrived at the door with a gurney. They quickly spotted the wounded man and carefully lifted and secured George.

Roger spoke, "I'll escort them down to be on the safe side; in the meantime, until I come back, lock yourself in."

"Good idea," Andrew answered. "Take care, George, I'll see you later."

Andrew closed and locked the door, feeling somewhat uneasy after the violent scene that had just taken place. He wondered if Gonzales grasped the fact that the bullet had been meant for him. Having spent the day talking to the prisoner, he could barely stand to look at him. But he wondered if this turn of events would change Gonzales's frame of mind.

"Are you all right?" Milano asked the prisoner, as he cautiously watched him struggle to get up off the floor.

Gonzales looked dazed, then said, "No, man, my shoulder hurt, and my leg. Get me some pain pills."

"Sure, we'll have a doctor look at you," Andrew answered, taken aback by his continued attitude of entitlement and wondering what it would take to break this guy.

CHAPTER 30

As darkness settled, Brent looked out over the peaceful waters of Gardiner's Bay. He thought about the events that had happened since his arrival on Sunday night, and realized with satisfaction that they were making progress.

Sharon came from the kitchen and stood behind him, "Beautiful, isn't it? We haven't had much time to appreciate it. By the way, I washed, you dry."

Brent turned to her with a smile, "You don't need to remind me, I've been trained. Yes, this place is gorgeous and I was just thinking of all that's happened in a few short days." He walked to the kitchen to tackle his chores, which in fact, he rather enjoyed.

Sharon followed him and continued the conversation. "It's amazing that Joe lived and will recover; your eagle eyes saved him, I think."

Brent brushed the compliment aside, saying, "Speaking of which, since it's dark, we need to get those goggles on and watch the parking lot and the house."

"I'm on it," Sharon replied as she took the steps at a run.

Putting away the last dish, Brent called out, "I'll be right up."

By the time he got upstairs, he found Sharon focusing on the parking lot. "I'll have a look at the house," he said. "Presumably, Viv and Stan will be hiding out somewhere. It would be great if we nailed this guy tonight."

"If whoever beat the homeless guy comes back to check on him…"

"Or comes prepared to bury him," Brent supplied.

"It seems they left him for dead, but for your quick response." Sharon complimented him again.

This time, he responded, "Look, Sharon, I'm no hero. I just happened to be at the right place at the right time."

"And you did the right thing immediately. Give yourself more credit, you're a good cop. That's just between us, I won't go bragging on you!" Sharon smiled.

"Ok, ok! Thanks, I guess." It was tough for Brent to accept praise, but deep down, he did appreciate it.

"Looks like a quiet night," Sharon commented.

"That's just when you have to stay alert; it's easy to get lulled into complacency."

"You're right, should I make some coffee?" Sharon asked.

"Not a bad idea; I can keep an eye on both spots," Brent replied.

"Got it." She pulled the goggles off her face and left them dangling around her neck as she went downstairs.

Sharon looked out over the bay from the kitchen window as she prepared coffee. Seeing movement on the water, she stepped closer to the window and put on her goggles. She called to Brent, "Get to the deck side; I think I see a small craft landing!"

Brent moved swiftly to the other side of the house. "Alert Stan and Viv!" he yelled. "This could be our guy!"

Sharon got on the two-way radio and immediately reached Viv. She said, "xm930 reporting; small craft landing on beach near our cottage."

"Copy that; we're on it!"

"It's been reported," Sharon said breathlessly, as she joined Brent upstairs.

Brent, deep in concentration, said, "Why don't you go watch the house and I'll join you if he moves in that direction; just don't want to lose him."

Sharon moved into position, intently watching the house and keeping one hand on her two-way. Seeing movement near the house, she called to Brent. "Is he still in your sights? 'Cause I'm seeing movement near the house."

"I've still got him; he's walking toward our house now. Maybe you're seeing Viv or Stan." Brent replied.

"Could be," Sharon sounded uncertain. "What do you think, Brent?"

"For now," Brent said, "just keep watching. My guy is zig-zagging between houses; I'm coming over!"

"Ok, now it seems the person I'm watching may be aware of your guy, but not moving; it probably is Viv or Stan," Sharon whispered.

"I haven't lost sight of my guy; he's looking around. Don't think he's spotted the undercover and it looks like he's about to go in the back…"

Just then, the suspect turned and opened fire on the undercover cop.

"Holy shit, Sharon, did you see that? Did our guy go down?"

They watched as the gunfire was returned. The perp quickly ducked into the house, with the undercover cop in pursuit. Then silence.

Sharon and Brent waited anxiously. "Should we go help?" Sharon asked.

"They'd radio if they needed us; just wait," was Brent's answer.

Before long, someone emerged from the house and Sharon's two-way began to buzz. She hit the talk button and heard, "ID." Sharon replied, "xm930, over…"

"Suspect captured," said Stan. "Chief is sending someone to take the suspect to headquarters. Todd, the officer inside, will accompany them. No injuries, good work! Over and out."

Their relief was palpable, when Brent said, "You know, I hate to bring this up, but there may be two guys on this detail. It wouldn't hurt for us to keep watching, in case another guy shows up."

"You've got a point, but I'm wondering about the boat; what do you think we should do about that?" Sharon asked.

"I don't think we should do anything; remember, we have strict orders to stay inside. But maybe you could radio your question and also ask if we should be on the alert for another thug."

"Good idea." Sharon got on her radio again and asked her questions. The reply came. "We're taking the boat, need it for forensics, and good idea to keep watching for an accomplice. Chief will probably call you later. Keep up your vigil. Over and out."

"I bet there's another guy out here," she said, "I doubt they'd send the one guy without backup..."

"I think we have to assume that. Even if they planned to remove a body that would take two." Brent weighed in. "Maybe the first one was going to report back to someone."

"So, if one came by boat, the other may drive, but why?" Sharon asked.

"Let's think about that from their point of view," Brent conjectured. "First of all, they hadn't approached by water before, and we wouldn't have seen them if you hadn't been in the kitchen...by the way, what happened to the coffee?" Brent teased.

"Aw, shucks, I just got too busy...do you think I could chance it now?"

"Well, I could sure use it now, since it looks like we'll be up for a while."

CHAPTER 31

Pedro Lopez, currently known as Henrique Alvarez, a lieutenant in a prominent Mexican drug cartel, was wounded. He'd been hit twice, in the knee and the thigh. Both wounds hurt like hell, but the thigh was bleeding the most profusely.

He'd wedged himself into the far corner of a janitor's closet and was trying to use the rags he'd found there to staunch the blood flow. Fortunately, the closet was jam-packed with equipment— a janitor had already been in to remove some cleaning supplies— but had not seen Pedro.

Pedro had no idea how long he'd be safe here; he'd heard the alarm to lock down the courthouse. He cursed himself for not being more careful. Carlos, who'd accompanied him from the boat, didn't do well without direction; God only knew what he'd do. Just so he didn't call the boss. His bungling of this hit now put him in fear for his own life. That's how it worked. You fuck up, you get fucked. Everyone was expendable, he knew that, and he'd been lucky so far.

He'd tried to call Carlos, but no there was no cell service inside the courthouse. He wondered how long Carlos would hang around and risk getting caught with the car they'd stolen down by the beach. Of course, he had given Carlos strict instructions to stay near the car and out of sight until he heard from him. He'd also instructed him to find a suitable doctor, in case he needed one. He needed one now.

But, Carlos was not the sharpest and he might also be nursing a grudge against Pedro because he'd smacked him around. Then again, the smack-down might've put Carlos in fear of more pain. Pedro had found fear to be a powerful motivator.

Squashed in the back of a janitor's closet and in total darkness, Pedro was afraid. Fear was an emotion he rarely felt; he was not usually on the receiving end. He didn't like it and he resolved never to let it happen again. He would get out of this, and when the judge capitulated to his demands, he'd move up in the cartel.

But, he worried that perhaps he hadn't killed Gonzales. That fucking marshal had pushed Juan back into the room. What if Gonzales had just been wounded? Would he sing? Pedro didn't think so. Juan had a mother in Mexico and he knew what would happen to her if he talked to the feds.

As he was thinking about the situation, Pedro thought again about how foolish numero uno had been to allow one of his top men to go on a routine drug run. Gonzales was no drug mule. But now, it appeared he was expendable because he knew too much.

It also occurred to Pedro that this mission was failing; he just hoped he could right it before the big boss found out. Pedro had to keep a lid on this; he couldn't afford to be caught in the courthouse.

Pedro's ears perked up as he heard talking in the hall outside of the closet. It sounded like a couple of janitors talking about the lockdown. They'd been summoned to speak with the marshals. That could mean only one thing; they would be ordered to thoroughly check their closets. Or worse, a marshal would accompany them in that process. Hearing the footsteps die away, Pedro carefully moved from his place in the corner. He gathered up the bloody rags and stuffed them in his pocket. Inching his way to the door, he was quiet and careful not to knock anything over. His hand hovered near the firearm in his belt.

When he reached the closet door, Pedro took a deep breath and slowly opened it. He looked both ways, then hurried to the stairwell closest to him, bolted through the door and closed it quietly.

CHAPTER 32

It was late, Sarah thought, as she pondered what the absence of Henrique and his lieutenant meant. She knew it was dark because her new guard hadn't bothered to blindfold her when she went to the bathroom. He'd also given her privacy and allowed her the luxury of a shower. That was a huge boost to her morale. Sarah believed he was basically a decent person caught up in a dangerous game.

She was thankful for every minute the other two were gone, but she worried what might have happened. If they never came back, she was sure she could escape. The guard in charge had become increasingly indulgent with her.

She'd been using Spanish words whenever they came to her and had begun to teach Jesus—he told her his name was Jesus— a few English words, through pantomime. What a relief it was for Sarah to have a respite, however brief it might be, from the ominous presence of Henrique and his first mate. As she thought about the names she'd heard when her captors talked, besides Jesus, Sarah deduced that Henrique's real name was probably Pedro and his sidekick was Carlos.

While Pedro and Carlos were gone, Sarah managed to move about her cabin and use her hands. She found there was a large drawer under her bunk. Inside, Sarah found a treasure-trove. There was bottled water, packaged peanut butter crackers, protein bars, as well as crossword puzzle books (with a worn-down pencil) and some children's story books. All of which led her to believe that this boat had been stolen from a family and she fervently hoped that they'd reported it.

Sarah enjoyed the snacks, which were far more nutritious than what she'd been fed. And the bottled water was a Godsend.

After her explorations around the room, she was careful to put the tape back in place on her wrists. The last thing she wanted was for Jesus, truly her savior, to be on the receiving end of Pedro's horrific temper. For Pedro, Sarah realized, it was all about control. It had been his need to control her that had ended the relationship. She was glad she could think of him as 'Pedro' now, because it further distanced her from their relationship.

Sarah was feeling sleepy now; the shower had been relaxing. She hoped she could sleep; she hadn't been drugged since the duo had left the boat. Thinking happy thoughts of being home with Sam and all of her other friends and—she thought, with a pang— her father, she drifted off to sleep.

CHAPTER 33

Carson Justice was in his office having been debriefed about the situation by Andrew Milano. Quite a turn of events! He sat thinking before he spoke.

"So, a thorough search turned up nothing. Do you suppose the assassin got out before the lockdown was in effect?"

"That seems to be the consensus. There was only Glen Messick on duty when I called for the lockdown; one marshal was on dinner break and the other had not reported for his shift. So, there were a few crucial minutes when he could've escaped. They've done a clean sweep; gone through all the closets, emptied everything out. There's not a sign of him. Of course, a small crew will remain vigilant through the night." Andrew exhaled with resignation.

"And the prisoner? Where is he?" Carson asked.

"He's still here; we took him to the basement lockup. He has two guards. There's less access down there and most of the staff don't know about it."

"Including yours truly. I've had no knowledge of it," Carson admitted. "I'm thinking perhaps Gonzales needs some time alone to ponder his situation. In the meantime, we need to find out if he has any relatives in Mexico and take them into protective custody. That way we'll have a bargaining chip if Juan decides to cooperate."

"We were thinking along the same lines, Judge, and we're already looking into his background. As we suspected he's not your typical drug mule; he's near the top. Why he was sent on a routine drug exchange is a mystery. But, it's clear the cartel wants him out, dead or alive." Andrew spoke decisively.

"Well, that's good news." Carson looked at his watch. "I'd best get home; I've got that meeting with Sam tomorrow…"

"Sir, I'd advise you not to go home alone. In fact, if you can wait a few more minutes, I'll take you home and stay with you." Andrew offered.

"Thank you, Andrew, I appreciate that." Carson knew he looked haggard and needed sleep. He had a last thought, "The courthouse will open as usual tomorrow, right? I don't want any undue speculation. It'll be a miracle if we can keep this under wraps!"

"We'll do our best, Carson. Let me call a few key people and we'll be on our way."

Andrew reached for the phone.

***

The fugitive, Pedro Lopez, was indeed running scared, but he was still in the courthouse. Through stealth and cunning he'd managed to stay ahead of the posse of marshals.

It had quieted down; they seemed to have given up. It might be a trap, he knew, but he couldn't stay in one place for too long. He'd spent some time in the women's bathroom. That had enabled him to clean his wounds. He'd also stuffed clean paper towels around the thigh wound; it looked awful and he knew he would need treatment. He hoped Carlos would redeem himself and try to find a doctor who would see him as soon as he was free. Truth was he didn't have much confidence in Carlos.

In the meantime, where to hide? Where would they be least likely to look? It came to him in a flash; the judge's chambers. Assuming the judge had left, that was the perfect place. And, as a bonus, when the judge arrived tomorrow he'd be there to greet him. Pedro smiled for the first time since the mission had started to go south.

He left the shelter of the bathroom and headed out to look for the judge's office. Stopping by the elevator, he read the names of judges on this floor. It was the second floor and Carson Justice was not on the list. Pedro cursed inwardly, not wanting to take the stairs to another floor. He knew that only administrative offices were on the first floor, he'd hidden in one just before the courthouse had closed. So, that left the third and fourth floors.

Pedro slid along the wall to the stairwell, opened the door soundlessly and closed it behind him. His hearing was acute and he stood silently, listening for any activity. He heard muffled conversation, but couldn't tell if it came from above or below him. So he stayed where he was, motionless.

The noise came closer and he heard the door above him open; before it had closed, he'd already ducked back into the second floor. Fuck! This is where they're coming next! Now what?

Pedro made for the nearest janitor's closet, figuring they wouldn't look there again. It was conveniently close to the stairwell and he'd soon hidden behind some large equipment. Now he held his breath and waited.

He heard footsteps coming perilously close to where he was hidden. They stopped near the closet and he could hear them talking. It sounded like there were two marshals.

"Should we check the closets again, Chuck? What do you think?"

"I don't think we need to, we just did, what, twenty minutes ago? They all seem to think he's gotten out somehow. Why don't we finish checking this floor and then go for coffee? Sound good to you, Marv?"

"You're the boss! Sounds good to me. We can meet up with the other teams and see what they've got." Marvin answered.

Is this a trap? Pedro wondered from his hiding spot, not moving an inch. He heard the footsteps recede, but he remained unmoving. Finally, he heard the door to another stairwell close and all was quiet.

Still, he waited. When he felt confident that no one was left on this floor, he opened the closet door slowly and quietly. Peering into the hallway, he poked his head out and looked both ways. It looked safe, so he went for it.

Again, he slowly proceeded to the stairwell, staying close to the wall. Entering the stairwell, he stood silently until he was sure he heard nothing.

Pedro started up the steps to the third floor. From far below, he heard a door close, but no footsteps came in his direction. He continued moving slowly and quietly up the stairs. Reaching the third floor, he looked through the window. Seeing nothing, he opened the door to the third floor. Again, Pedro walked to the elevator and looked at the names of the judges. And there it was: The Honorable Carson Justice, office # 5. Bingo! Pedro congratulated himself, but was careful to continue moving stealthily.

He soon found the judge's chambers, and though the office was locked, he found it pathetically easy to open. It was a spacious office, as befitted a Federal judge; he looked around the room, dimly illuminated by the street lights.

Seeing the huge desk, Pedro soon sprawled out underneath it, finally feeling he could let down his guard and perhaps rest until morning. He'd already formulated a plan.

CHAPTER 35

Chief Mayer had slept in after a few late and very exhausting days. He was late getting to the office, but was pleased with what he and his officers had accomplished. It had actually been quite exhilarating, nothing like the usual "off-season slump." But it was nice to take a moment to contemplate the events of the past several days.

He phoned Brent and Sharon at the cottage; Sharon picked up, "Hi, Chief. What's up?"

"Lots," he answered enigmatically. "Why don't you come to my office, as soon as you've had breakfast?"

"Oh, we've eaten; we'll be right over!"

The chief smiled; he loved the enthusiasm of youth. And he had to admit to himself that this case had ratcheted things up quite a bit; he hadn't seen this kind of action in years.

Talking with Rory, her husband and the trooper had given him new information and a different perspective. It was also good to hear his intelligence would be shared with the judge and that the Federal marshals would be involved. He sat drinking his coffee slowly and enjoying some relaxation; he hadn't had much for the past few days.

So, all things considered, it wasn't a bad thing that Sam Logan had showed up, although at the time it was a distraction. He was sure Sam would be otherwise occupied in the next few days and hopefully the case would be resolved.

A knock on the door interrupted his thoughts and Sharon poked her head in. Brent was right behind her. They looked like two eager puppies. He smiled and welcomed them.

"That was quick; hope you didn't break the sound barrier! OK," the chief said, "last night, we brought the probable attacker of Joe Hayes into custody. We were fairly certain he hadn't acted alone and his partner would expect to hear from him. We got a translator in so there would be no mistaking what was said." He stopped for breath.

"So, this suspect wouldn't talk, but we have prints and should be able to find out something about him. Anyway, we went pretty hard on him, letting him assume he'd killed Joe. He stayed tough, sort of cocky; I guess the cartel trains them for that. We've offered him immunity if he cooperates, so that gives him something to think about. And, he matches the artist's rendering of one of the suspects given by Rob and Lisa."

"But, how can you do that, I mean give immunity?" Sharon asked.

"Well, we can't, but the Feds can..."

"I thought we were alone in this operation," Brent said.

"We were until yesterday. I know I'm getting ahead of the story, but I met the victim's, that is Sarah's, colleagues from Pennsylvania, when they came to pick up Sam last night. It was Sarah's boss, Rory, her husband and a PA State trooper. They've been mounting their own investigation. They've been in touch with the judge, Sarah's father, and are sending Sam to talk with him. Obviously, they needed all the information so they can join forces with the judge. Carson Justice obviously has the best resources at hand, so the more he knows the closer we can get to finding Sarah. Chief Mayer stopped to catch his breath.

"Wow, that's incredible! What a day you had," Sharon remarked.

"Yeah," the chief agreed, "and I slept like a baby last night. Not that it's over, but we know a lot more than we knew a few days ago."

"So what's next?" Brent asked.

"Well, if the partner comes back to the house looking for our suspect, he'll have a surprise waiting for him, you know, our undercover guy," the chief answered.

"And then?" Sharon asked.

"We're trying to work that out now. Of course, after the meeting with the judge and Sam, we'll have a more complete picture and a better idea of what we can do."

"So, what do you want us to do?" Sharon was nothing if not direct.

"Well, I think you can go to the cottage and pack up. Then bring the car back here and we'll notify Rob and Lisa to come get it. Of course, until this is all over, they won't be going back to the cottage." The chief nodded to Sharon and Brent, saying, "You two have done a great job! We'll keep you on the team until it's all over."

"You mean I can take this friggin' wig off?" Sharon asked.

"Once you return the car you'll be off undercover duty," the chief answered.

Just then, the chief's phone rang; he held up a finger, and they waited while he answered it. "Yes, yes, this is Chief Mayer." He nodded his head a few times, as a smile spread across his face. "I'll be damned! Out of South Hampton, close enough. What took so long? Ok, got it. Yeah, sure, but the original name was 'Early Riser,' a 36-foot cabin cruiser, blue and white. Of course there will be some other identifying marks they can't get rid of. Got it; thank you so much! Right, bye now."

The chief was excited as he relayed the information to his officers. He told them that a cabin cruiser had been stolen from a marina in South Hampton. "The family had been away, and just returned home and reported the theft. Gotta make some calls…"

"OK, we'll be back later this afternoon," Brent said.

Sharon and Brent left, fist-bumping as they went out the door.

***

It was late when Carson Justice woke up. He'd had awful dreams, nightmares really, and had awoken with a leaden feeling in his stomach. He took a shower, hoping to revive himself.

Feeling marginally better when he'd finished, he dressed and went downstairs.

He was grateful to see Andrew as he came downstairs.

"Good morning, Carson, how'd you sleep?" Andrew asked.

"I tossed and turned all night, had nightmares…"

"No wonder, what with all the stress you've had! Maybe you want to stay home today?" Andrew sounded concerned.

Carson sighed, relieved. "You think I should?" he asked.

"I think you should." Andrew said bluntly.

The judge felt as if a huge weight had been lifted from him. He realized he'd been dreading going back to the courthouse.

"I've spoken with security today. The courthouse is open, as you wished, but they are 'quietly observant.' Why should you go back until we're absolutely certain it's safe? It's a huge building and difficult to secure." Andrew answered.

"You know, I had a bad feeling about going there; I guess that's what my nightmares were about. Thank you, Andrew, for making the decision easy for me." Carson was not accustomed to trusting his gut feelings, or allowing others to make decisions for him. A sense of gratitude engulfed him.

CHAPTER 36

To the casual observer, it appeared to be business as usual at the New Haven Federal Courthouse. Regulars, however, would notice there were more marshals about. And they were stationed at every exit. News of the events of the day before were restricted to the few people directly involved; it had been kept confidential and out of the press.

Pedro Lopez remained under the judge's desk. He'd slept fitfully and ached all over from his wounds and his cramped muscles. But it would all be worth it, he'd convinced himself, when the judge came in and found him. That one thought had kept him going through the long and uncomfortable night.

He looked at his watch again. It was after ten-thirty! How did judges get off coming in so late, he thought, his anger rising.

Underneath the anger, a small finger of dread began to creep up his spine. The question, 'what if he isn't coming in?' whispered in his ear. This was a thought he could not tolerate; his plan was perfect. He'd imagined it over and over in his head; even now as he thought about it, excitement raced through him. The judge would come and he'd have his revenge. He would show Numero Uno how important he was to the organization.

As the minutes ticked away, he began to notice his throbbing wounds, his aching muscles and the sweat trickling down his face. Each moment took away some of his resolve.

At eleven-thirty he'd all but given up his grand plan. It was imperative that he come up with an alternative, one that involved a clean getaway. His mind fought against it, but the physical reminders were becoming too insistent to ignore.

Normally, Pedro was sharp and disciplined, but the pain was getting to him. He realized with a jolt that his body could soon betray him if he did not act.

He didn't abandon his original plan; he just revised it to allow himself to consider the possibility of an escape scenario. He'd noticed traffic and conversations outside the door of the judge's chambers. It seemed to be a normal day. He hadn't heard any whispered discussions about the events of the previous day. There was no indication anything was different. But of course, it would be to his enemy's advantage to keep it quiet. That didn't mean they weren't more than usually suspicious of anyone leaving the courthouse.

How could he leave without being noticed? He thought about this for several minutes, finding it hard to focus. But he was determined to find a way out; there was always a way out.

It dawned on him; the people who weren't noticed were the most commonly seen ones, the lawyers with their briefcases, the cleaning people, and, he thought suddenly, the judges! The place was filthy with judges. A plan began to emerge.

Pedro eased out of his hiding place slowly and quietly. His muscles screamed as he tried to stretch, but he ignored the pain. He crept to the judge's wardrobe, slowly opening the doors and looking inside. No fewer than four robes were hanging there. Several pairs of shiny black shoes were on the floor. There were even clean white shirts and black ties. He was looking at a virtual goldmine!

The plan took shape in his mind; the robe would hide his tattered and bloodstained clothes, the weapon would be hidden and there were no metal detectors at the exits. He looked in the mirror; his four-day stubble didn't look 'judicial.' He went into the judge's private bathroom and soon found shaving supplies.

144

Once finished shaving, he looked around in the cabinets, searching for something...there it was, talc. He liberally sprinkled it in his hair, smiling at the result. Pedro had made himself look perfectly respectable.

As he was coming out of the bathroom, he heard a click, like the door was being unlocked, and he slid into the wardrobe, closing the door behind him. Sweat trickled down his back and face as he stood, immobile, listening.

"Don't look like the judge's comin' in today, Leo. Not much to do in here."

"We can empty the trash, that's about it, Nora, you think?"

Pedro heard the clanking of trash cans, then, an exclamation.

"Oh, look here, Leo, looks like the judge cut hisself!"

"Yeah, maybe shavin', you think?"

"Well, whatever, it's none of our business, Leo."

The door soon clicked shut and Pedro, drenched in sweat, remained still for a moment, collecting himself.

Emerging from the closet, Pedro re-entered the bathroom, to clean himself. How thoughtful, the judge even had deodorant. Looking in the mirror at his clean shaven face and gray hair, he was satisfied that he would not be noticed.

Finding that the judge's clothes fit, although the shoes were a bit too large, Pedro dressed as carefully as if he were facing a jury. The irony of this thought did not escape him. With a final look around the office, he seized upon a manila folder and picked it up.

His disguise in place, Pedro strode confidently out of the office, leaving the door unlocked.

***

Inside the basement lockup at the courthouse, Juan Gonzales was hungry. He hadn't spoken to his guards, which had changed at least once. He knew they would feed him, but he wouldn't ask for food. So far, his determination had carried him through. He would not talk.

But he couldn't control the thoughts that popped into his mind, outside of his control. He'd held out in prison for two years and during two failed escapes. His attorney had seen him frequently and had kept up his hopes for release.

Now, he was left to his own devices; there was no lawyer to turn to. Worse yet, his mind continually played back the scene from last night. Try as he might, he could not change the fact that the bullets, taken by the marshal, were meant for him. And the horror on the face of the man who saved him was not pretend; Juan knew terror when he saw it. He'd seen it many times on the faces of his victims.

His thoughts were interrupted as he smelled the fragrant aroma of roast beef and soon the guards were passing his lunch to him. They respected his silence and said nothing, merely delivered his food. He couldn't complain about his treatment; it had been humane. And the food, well, that was far better than what he'd had in prison. This roast beef sandwich was no exception.

But, Juan wondered, why has no one tried to talk to me? He should be happy after yesterday's inquisition, but he couldn't understand it. Why weren't they talking to him now? Were they leaving him to rot down here, in the bowels of the courthouse?

Hating to admit it, Juan had to face the obvious; he would have to take care of himself. Regardless of the fact he'd been high up in the organization, that he'd commanded respect and fear from his lieutenants; he might now be a liability. He would have to see how he might manipulate his guards.

Juan thought back to his glory days, when anything was possible, and anything could be bought, if you were willing to pay the price. He'd begun to think of himself as invincible. He'd longed for the days when he'd been a drug-runner, a very good drug-runner, outsmarting border patrols and law enforcement. And Juan had loved the adrenaline rush.

That was why, Juan thought with a flash of regret, he'd done the unthinkable. Just for the hell of it, he'd crossed the border with a huge load of heroin. Juan had not taken into consideration that law enforcement had become more sophisticated since his last run.

Juan was a forgotten man. Or was he?

By the time he'd finished his lunch, Juan had made a decision. It was unthinkable, but he had no choice. For now he had to at least pretend to cooperate with his enemy and see where that would lead. He needed a way to get out.

Juan rose from his cot and walked to the barred door. "Guard!" he called, "I would like to see the men I spoke to yesterday."

CHAPTER 37

Sharon and Brent returned to the cottage to have lunch and pack up their things. Even though they'd been there only a few days, Sharon knew she would miss this place.

Getting out of the car, Sharon said to Brent, "We can leave the car open since we'll be packing up. It will probably take more than one trip out, at least for my stuff. The trunk of these Beatles isn't exactly roomy."

"We can also stow stuff on the back seat if we need to," Brent added. "Let's get the packing done before we eat lunch and then divvy up the food."

"Sounds fine," Sharon said listlessly, dragging her feet towards the house.

"I get it Sharon, I don't want to leave, either."

She shrugged in response, "Might as well get it over with."

They entered the house and went straight up to their rooms. Brent finished first, and stopped to look in Sharon's room. She was moving slowly and deliberately. "I'll take my stuff to the car," he said.

Sharon looked at his gear. "Is that all you've got?"

"Yep," he said, hefting his duffle bag, and tossing some blankets over his shoulder.

Sharon continued to pack, watching him out the window. He threw the blankets into the back seat and then put his duffle into the trunk. Looking up, he saw Sharon at the open window and yelled, "Don't worry, there's room for your stuff in the trunk. Is there anything you want me to come get now?"

"Sure, thanks; my large bag is packed, and I can bring down the tote bags."

Meeting Brent at the door to her room, she handed him the large suitcase.

"Holy shit! Did you steal the silver?" Brent grimaced as if he could hardly carry it."

Sharon stuck her tongue out in response, knowing it wasn't the most mature of responses.

He shook his head, laughing, as he lugged the bag down the steps. Sharon wasn't far behind with the rest of her bags. Once everything was stowed in the car, they went back in to make lunch.

Sitting outside on the deck, enjoying their lunches, little was said between them.

Sharon broke the silence. "It would be fun to come back here; it's a great place."

"Yeah, too bad you have to be a millionaire to have a place out here."

"You can always rent, off-season. Maybe we'll get to meet Rob and Lisa, see if they ever rent it out. It could happen…"

"Anyway, we'd best take a last look around, pack up the food, and go back to the station. We're done here." Brent said.

"Might as well," Sharon sighed.

Brent checked the house while Sharon loaded up the food.

The two walked out into the bright sunshine and stashed their remaining goods in the trunk.

Sharon got into the driver's side and started the car. "Ok, off we go. Bye bye, beach house!"

Brent slid down and relaxed in his seat, looking out the window at the panorama of beach, sea and sky.

They didn't talk and Sharon drove slowly, trying to savor the beautiful scene.

Without warning, the quiet was shattered. A deep voice with a distinct Spanish accent ordered, "You drive where I say!"

Brent's head snapped back to see a masked man, emerging from under the blankets, put a gun to Sharon's head. He addressed Brent. "You do anything, and your wife gets it."

Sharon gasped. Then, realizing he thought they were Rob and Lisa, she played along.

"You have to listen to him, Rob!" she pleaded, noticing the look of recognition on Brent's face.

"Sure, Hon," he told her. And to the man, he said, "Please don't hurt my wife, we'll do whatever you say. Do you want money? What do you want?"

Sharon noted with satisfaction that Brent was playing the role seamlessly. Her mind was in survival-mode and she began to hatch a plan to outwit the thug.

"I want you gone," the man answered with a sneer. "Do as I tell you…turn here!" he demanded.

Sharon turned the car onto an unfamiliar and little-traveled road. She knew if she didn't do something quickly, they'd both be goners.

She accelerated, hoping that the bumpy terrain might knock their captor off balance. It did, momentarily. When he recovered, he hissed in Sharon's ear, "Slow down or …" To demonstrate, he grabbed a handful of Sharon's hair, and pulled.

That was the diversion Sharon was looking for and she had to smile as the man looked with shock at the wig in his hand. She accelerated again, turning the car left, then right.

Brent wasted no time lunging toward the back seat and struggled to get the gun. Waving the gun wildly, their hijacker got off a few shots, took out the passenger side window, and a bullet whizzed by Sharon's head as she ducked. Then she increased the speed, until she was sure Brent was in charge.

Sharon slammed on the brakes and leapt from the car. Then she helped Brent as they dragged the large, swarthy man from the car. This time, she put the gun to his head, as Brent cuffed him.

CHAPTER 38

Sam awoke when the sun, glistening off Long Island Sound, poured into the east-facing window of his room at The Kelsey House. He'd arrived late the night before and, after accepting a glass of port wine from the inn-keepers, had gone straight to bed.

Upon awakening, he could see the water all around. It felt as if he were on an island. Curiosity drove him from the bed as he went to stand by an open window.

The view was breathtaking; he could see that the house rested firmly on top of a huge outcrop of rock. Looking east, he saw the sound following the coastline in a northeasterly direction. The place was enchanting.

Lost in the view, he was startled when he heard a small tap on the door.

"Breakfast in twenty minutes, if that suits you," called a female voice.

Quickly donning a robe, Sam strode to the door and opened it. "Good Morning, and yes, I'll be ready in twenty minutes. What a beautiful place you have!"

"Thank you, we like it too. See you at breakfast! By the way, I'm Sue." And she was off to prepare breakfast.

Sam was happy that Sue introduced herself; he couldn't remember if the inn-keepers had given their names in the flurry of arriving and getting to his room last night. They were very nice and welcoming, he remembered, providing all the comforts of home. Sam dressed in casual clothes, since his meeting with the judge was in the afternoon, and he wanted to take a look around before then.

When he went down for breakfast, the table in the dining room was set. A young couple, probably honeymooners from the look of them, sat at the table. He introduced himself and they did the same. Jane and Henry were indeed, on their honeymoon, and began to gush with praise about the inn and the area. They told him of local places of interest and how long it would take to get to them.

"Thanks for the information. I'm here on business, so won't be staying very long, but maybe I can get to see something before my meeting this afternoon." Sam smiled at their enthusiasm.

Before he could say more, Sue brought in the first course, a bowl of fresh fruit. Sam was ravenous and began to eat immediately.

He slowed down, realizing he might appear crude. Just then, his cell buzzed. Sam excused himself and walked outside to the wrap-around porch to answer it.

"Hello, Sam? It's Carla, Judge Justice's marshal. I hope your lodgings are to your liking."

"Hi, Carla, are you kidding? This place is gorgeous! And I'm about to have what looks like a gourmet breakfast."

"Oh, it will be, if I know Sue. So, I won't keep you, I just wanted you to know that you won't be meeting the judge at the courthouse. I'll send a car for you at about 2:30? A marshal will be picking you up and you'll be taken to the judge's house. You have my number if you need to call. I'll see you later. Bye."

Sam lingered outside for a moment after the call ended, taking in the fresh air with the unmistakable smell of the sea. He filled his lungs and began to feel some of the anxiety drain away. It had been a stressful several days.

Back inside, the second course, an egg mixture inside of a puff pastry was being served. Sam forced himself to eat more slowly and began to converse with the young couple.

Realizing that his time was limited, they recommended that he do the Thimble Island boat tour. The tour left a few miles up the coast and it sounded very interesting.

The third course was announced by its fragrant aroma before it arrived. It had to be blueberry muffins, Sam thought. And he was right.

Returning to his room after breakfast Sam gathered his things and prepared to go on the Thimble Island tour. He thought wistfully about the young newlyweds. How happy they seemed. And he thought about Sarah, hoping he would have a chance to marry her. They loved each other. Why should they wait? So what if they were still in law school? Seeing the newly-weds had given Sam a new perspective, and losing Sarah had added an urgency to the idea.

He took the stairs two at a time. Meeting Sue on the landing he asked for directions to the Thimble Island tour. She looked through her file of brochures, and handed him one. "You're in luck, there's one in about a half hour. They close at the end of the month; I think you'll enjoy it."

"Thanks so much, I really appreciate your hospitality." He left smiling as he walked to his car.

Sam drove along the coast with the windows open so he could take in the air; it really lifted his mood. So this was where Sarah had grown up, in a beautiful, serene environment. He began to feel more confident about the meeting.

He drove through a quaint area near the wharf with restaurants and shops, soon finding the pier from which the tour boats left.

Within minutes, Sam was seated on the top deck of the Sea Mist; it was half-full and Sam noticed that he was probably the youngest person aboard, excluding a young couple with a baby.

It was interesting as the guide, Captain Mike, talked about the history of these once uninhabited islands, most of which were now owned privately. There were several mansions, partially hidden from view. Some islands had small communities of more modest homes. All seemed to be closed for the season.

The largest island, Horse Island, was owned by Yale University, in nearby New Haven. There was just one building to be seen, an old house, the cupola rising above the dense trees and shrubs. Whereas the other islands had no boats moored nearby, this island, Sam noticed, had a small cabin cruiser partially hidden in a sheltered cove tied up at a dock. He narrowed his eyes and looked closely. Had he seen movement on the boat, or was he imagining?

Curious by nature, Sam asked Captain Mike, "Are there usually boats at Horse Island?"

"No, not usually, but then, it's Yale, so they pretty much do what they want. Yale is big business around here!"

Thanking the captain, Sam went back to his seat to enjoy the rest of the cruise. It was relaxing and enlightening. He was glad that the couple had recommended it. But he continued to look at the lone boat docked at Horse Island.

CHAPTER 39

Brent and Sharon were leaning against the VW, with the prisoner sitting on the ground next the car, spewing obscenities (Brent assumed, but they were in Spanish) when Chief Mayer arrived with two other officers.

The chief got out of the cruiser with a big smile on his face and greeted the two.

Taking stock of the scene, the chief said, "Well, well, looks like you caught up with the second accomplice!"

The prisoner glared at Mayer and said, "Fuck you police. I don't tell you nothing!"

"Hey, bud, you don't have to, I think we learned all we need from your pal," the chief lied.

That shut him up, but his face registered hatred, with just a hint of fear, Brent thought.

The chief turned his attention to Brent and Sharon. "Nice job, you two! Can't wait to hear about how you lost your wig, Sharon…"

"Oh yeah," Sharon laughed. "I never thought I'd be happy to have that monstrosity on my head, but I think it saved our bacon!"

The chief shook his head. "Well, my friend," he said, addressing the prisoner, "it's time we got you to the station." He nodded to his officers and they stepped in to escort the angry suspect to the squad car.

"You can take him in and book him; I'll ride back with these guys."

The judge was sitting in his home office, studying the notes he'd taken on all the elements of Sarah's case so far. He was getting ready for his meeting with Sam, set for the afternoon. He was looking forward to meeting Sam, and at the same time, was apprehensive. He hoped Sam deserved Sarah. He quickly chided himself for the thought, because couldn't the same be asked about him?

A knock on his door interrupted his thought processes; he put down his notes and said,

"Come in."

Both Andrew and Carla greeted him and quickly entered. They seemed to be bursting with news, and he wasn't sure it was good.

"Sit down, tell me…" he encouraged.

"Well," Carla began, looking at Andrew, "there's news from the courthouse, and it's really good that you stayed home today…"

The judge, curious, said, "Continue…"

Andrew continued, "It's a long story, but the essence is this: the shooter did not leave the building last night as we'd all assumed. He somehow eluded all of the marshals."

"So, around lunch time today, one of the security guards at the exit took notice of a 'judge,' in robes, leaving the court house with a brief, headed for the Federal Building. He thought it unusual for the judge to leave the building in his robe. When he called him back, the guy took off. He ran out through the courtyard and took the underpass to Court Street, with several security guards after him, and somehow, he disappeared again. They later found the robe and other of the judge's clothes, stashed in a dumpster, but no trace of the guy."

"So, of course, another search of the courthouse was ordered," Carla continued, "and the door to your chambers was found unlocked. There was evidence of someone having been there; your wardrobe was open, and we assume it was your robe he took."

The judge, taking it all in, sighed. "It looks like he was waiting for me, and, with your excellent advice, Andrew, I stayed home. Thank God!"

"We're all plenty relieved, I can tell you that," Andrew answered.

"It may be awhile before you can get back into your chambers, so if there's anything you need, we can get it. The perp had apparently spent time under your desk; they found blood stains on the carpet. He also used your bathroom to shave, pretty brazen I'd say. Anyway, he left behind a treasure trove of DNA, fingerprints, and who knows what. It appears he planned to make a clean getaway."

"And from what you've told me, he did!"

"At least for now," Andrew was quick to point out. "He made his escape so quickly, no one really got a good look at him. But, with all of the evidence he left behind, we'll find out. He's got to be running scared and he's injured. He'll make a mistake."

Andrew's cell buzzed and he answered immediately. His face broke into a smile as he listened. Then he turned to the judge, "That was from Corey, in lock-up… guess who wants to talk?"

CHAPTER 40

Sarah woke up feeling refreshed for the first time since her captivity had begun. This past night she slept soundly without the gnawing anxiety that had been ever- present. Not that she was out of the woods, far from it. But she was now able to think clearly without the interference of whatever drug they'd been giving her.

She paid close attention to the noises she heard, alert to the potential arrival of her dreaded captors, Pedro and Carlos. Right now, she heard only the gentle lapping of water and bird song. These sounds would normally lift her spirits, but with each minute, she felt her fate closing in on her. Interrupting her thoughts, Jesus knocked and then entered with her breakfast tray.

"Buenos Dias," Sarah said, smiling. "Gracias maravilloso!" Sarah knew Jesus had gone to great lengths to please her. He'd made scrambled eggs, bacon and toast. She could also tell he was happy with her praise and probably pleased with himself.

Jesus put the tray down, then holding up his finger said, "Y café!" Then he left the room, leaving the door ajar, presumably to get her coffee.

She had started eating when he returned with the coffee. "Muchas gracias!" Sarah said, with feeling. Jesus smiled and left.

With her stomach full, more replete than she'd felt since her abduction, Sarah engaged her mind in planning an escape. As much as she'd appreciated Jesus's kindnesses, it complicated things. She couldn't now think of escaping and leaving him to face the wrath of Pedro. Jesus had treated her with dignity, had never waved a gun at her, nor did he carry one. Any escape attempt she made would have to include ensuring Jesus's safety. Anything less would lower her to Pedro's level.

Jesus came in for the tray and Sarah smiled again, rubbing her stomach. Impulsively, she gestured to Jesus, pointed to herself, then pointed up. She said "cubierta?" hoping she got the right word for 'deck.'

A look of fear slipped across his face, then he held up his finger and said, "Espera!" and left with the tray. The door was again left ajar, leaving Sarah to wonder if he wanted her to make a run for it.

He came down quickly and motioned her upward, saying "Date prisa!"

Sarah left the room in her shuffling gait and laboriously climbed the ladder to the deck.

Jesus was behind her, guiding her up.

The sea air hit Sarah's face like a winged angel, the familiar smell bringing tears to her eyes. "Muchas gracias!" She looked at Jesus, letting him see the tears as they fell.

She took in her surroundings, noticing they were anchored at a dock off what appeared to be an island, a heavily forested island.

***

Rory was at work early; she missed Sam already and prayed that things would go well for him today.

When the front door opened, she smiled. "Hi Blake! Good to see you."

"Thanks, Rory. I couldn't sleep, kept going over all the details of our discussion. I hope we hear from Sam soon and hope it goes well with the judge. I know he was a little anxious about the meeting. On the other hand, he's much happier than he was, since he's right at the center of the action."

"I agree, but while I'm waiting to hear, I have plenty of work to do…"

"Right, how's DeSean's case going?" Blake asked.

"It's looking up. The psychologist saw him yesterday and I know she's written a favorable report. She's going to email it to me. I'll try to set up a hearing for later in the day. And if I don't get the same two morons who ran the last hearing, he may have a shot at release."

"Katrina's been encouraging me to get involved in the Big Brothers program, which helps kids like DeSean to have a better future. I think I might consider it."

"I think you'd be good at it. Why don't you sit in on the case?"

"I'd love to," Blake replied.

When they were seated, Rory said, "I have a gut feeling this will be over soon. I think the meeting between Sam and the judge should give us some forward momentum."

Blake was smiling. "Wouldn't it be nice if this whole nightmare was behind us?" He sighed.

"I know it's hard for all of us, playing the waiting game, but we've accomplished a lot in the past few days, and I do feel it's going to pay off soon."

Her email notification came up at that moment. Rory retrieved it and printed the five page report, nodding her head. "Yes, yes, that's good. It's the report I'd hoped for," she told Blake. And she proceeded to read it more carefully. Then she looked up, "Here, Blake, have a look, see what you think."

Rory dialed the DA's office to schedule a special hearing, and she decided to enlist the help of the head DA, Connor McClain, with whom she'd worked closely on a recent case. "Leigh, hi, it's Rory. Is Connor in? Thanks, I'll hold."

After a brief conversation, Rory hung up the phone and turned to Blake. "McClain has assigned Stan Como to the case and they'll get a senior judge, Thank God!"

Blake looked up from the report. "This looks good, he should be released. I'd like to meet him after the hearing, assuming it goes as expected."

"Of course, and I'm going to need some help preparing a memo. You up to that?"

"Sure thing," Blake answered.

CHAPTER 41

Carson's head was almost bursting from the information he'd been taking in from several sources. He felt a small seed of hope bloom in his heart. Everything they'd found out was leading to the final goal of freeing Sarah.

The kidnappers were making mistakes, big ones. He just hoped they didn't harm Sarah as a result; he couldn't bear that thought. His meeting with Sam was in fifteen minutes. Another marshal, Roger, had been sent to get Sam when Andrew had to leave in a rush to talk with Gonzales. The outcome of that was, as yet, unknown.

His phone rang and startled him, then he picked up. "Carson Justice, can I help you?"

There was a pause before he heard the metallic twang of an engineered voice. "You need to give up Gonzales if you want your daughter back!"

"He's in Intensive Care, they're not sure he'll live!" The judge lied without remorse.

"You find a way to get him, if you want Sarah! I give you twenty-four hours from now! And this stays out of the news, understand? Not a word!" The line went dead.

Carla was standing in the doorway, an inquiring look on her face.

Carson put his head in his hands. "That was the kidnapper, just when I thought we were seeing the light at the end of the tunnel! He's given us 24-hours to hand over Gonzales. I told him Juan was in intensive care, but that didn't matter to him. Christ, he'd just as soon have the body! He also insisted nothing gets in the news. I agree with him there. But how do we control the news?" Carson asked.

"They're getting desperate, Carson. They no longer have the advantage…"

"Ah, but they do; they still have Sarah!" The judge went silent.

"We have twenty-four hours, and a lot more information than they know. We'll find her, Carson, we have the time and the resources. And we've already put a lid on the news." Carla spoke with assurance.

The pep talk helped. Carson lifted his head and began leafing through his notes. "Sam should be here any minute. We'll have more Intel then and maybe get this thing over with."

The phone rang again and the judge cringed. Carla answered it. She listened, then hung up. "It's ok, it was Roger. He's on his way with Sam."

The judge relaxed a bit, whispering, "Thank God, I wasn't ready to speak to that animal on the phone again."

"I've made coffee, would you like some?"

"What I really need is a double-scotch, but sure, I'll have some coffee. Let's wait for Sam and see if he wants some, coffee, that is. Not scotch." Carson tried for a smile.

There was a knock at the front door. Carla said, "It must be them," and went to let them in.

Carla met Sam at the door, introducing herself. She led him to the judge's office.

Sam strode into the room, displaying more confidence than he felt, as the judge stood to shake his hand.

"Thank you so much for coming, young man. I look forward to a discussion with you."

"It's an honor to meet you, Judge." Sam said. "Your tenure on the bench has been exemplary."

"Thank you, Sam. And please call me Carson. Truthfully, I'd give all this up," he waved his arm around the room, which displayed diplomas, honorary awards and other testaments to his stature in the legal community, "to have Sarah safe. This whole ordeal puts everything in a new perspective."

Momentarily at a loss for words, Sam said, "Sarah's a wonderful person; I can't imagine how difficult this is for you. I know it's knocked me to my knees."

"Thank you for saying that, I appreciate it. Sarah had a wonderful mother; it hit us both when she died so young. Sarah's a lot like her mother, actually," the judge said, as if realizing it for the first time. "It's so good to meet you. I think we understand each other's pain, loving Sarah as we both do."

"Thanks for saying that, Carson, I...I wasn't sure how you'd accept me."

"Understandably, especially if you knew that I wasn't much of a father to Sarah. As I said, things are much different now, or at least they will be when I get, when we," he amended, "get Sarah back."

Sam nodded, and the judge said, "We should get to work." He began to list his information in bullet form. When he noticed Sam taking notes, he said, "No need for that, let me make a copy for you..."

Carla, entering with the coffees, said, "I'll do that Carson. Sam, is there anything you want copied?"

He pulled several pages from his briefcase and handed them to Carla. "Thanks, that would be helpful; we can each read and compare what we have."

Sam and Carson were drinking their coffees when Carla handed each a copy of the other's notes. Carla turned to leave. "Just give me a shout if you need anything else." The judge nodded.

"Why don't we just read, and see where the information fits, then we'll discuss it, Ok with you?" the judge asked.

"Fine," Sam answered, already starting to scan the pages.

***

After a half-hour of studying the material, they heard a knock on the door, and Andrew stepped in. "Sorry for the disturbance, judge, but I think this is important…" He looked at Sam and introduced himself.

Carson said, "Sit, Andrew, let us know what you've learned." The judge leaned forward with interest.

"Juan talked, sir. He gave us a fair amount of info. Of course, we have to verify everything. The deal is we have to secure his mother's safety before he gives it all up. We can do that, right?" Andrew asked.

"We will have to bring the Bureau into this. We can take his mother into protective custody, but when it gets to the Witness Protection Program, the FBI will have to take over."

"Ok, well we can at least offer that, right?" The judge nodded. "Any idea of the time frame on that?" Andrew asked.

"I can tell you this, we'll make it a priority; let me make a few calls." Carson got on the phone while Andrew and Sam quietly discussed the new development.

Hanging up the phone, the judge turned to Andrew, "You got the information from Juan about his mother's name and whereabouts?"

"Yes, I finally did; he really didn't want to give it up. Bottom line, he had to trust us. I guess he decided we were the only hope."

Andrew riffled through his sheaf of papers, pulled out one from the pile and handed it to the judge.

Carson took the paper and read it. "Once we run this, we should have Gonzales's mother by tomorrow, with any luck. We still have two guys in East Hampton, one's been caught and is in police custody; the other is likely to be snared as well. So far, the guy they've got is stone-walling. They're a tough bunch." Carson's energy was beginning to flag, thinking of all that had to take place.

"So, it sounds like we may learn the names of the major players in the kidnapping from Juan. Sarah said two guys grabbed her, but that doesn't mean there weren't more," Sam said.

"Sure, there probably are more, and it's possible that Juan didn't know who was involved, but I'm thinking he can help us."

"Henrique Alvarez, which is probably an alias, was involved with Sarah for a short time in law school; did you get to that in my notes, yet, Carson?" Sam asked.

Carson leafed through his notes until he found it. "Yes, that was her boyfriend in her first year of law school." He couldn't hide the look of distaste on his face.

"Sarah dated him for only a short time, but it was hard for her to shake him loose; he started stalking her. He stopped only when she threatened to take him to court and have a restraining order imposed. But he left her with a verbal threat, something like, 'you'll be sorry.' She took him seriously, got a roommate, never went out alone. She was afraid of possible repercussion for quite a while. He's a strong suspect, I think," Sam said. "Plus, it was his name on a rental car that tailed Rob and Lisa in East Hampton."

"What was the make of the car, if you know?" Carson asked.

"It was a black Range Rover," Sam answered.

"Interesting," Carson said. "There was a black Range Rover involved in hand delivering a message to me from the kidnappers…"

"Yes, well, quite possibly this man targeted her from the beginning; perhaps the plan was brewing then. After all, he left law school as soon as she broke it off," Sam added.

Andrew Milano stood up and said, "I need to get back to Juan, let him know that you're on it and we may have a reply as soon as tomorrow. Can I tell him that, Carson?"

"You can, and thanks, Andrew, for all of your hard work; it can't be fun."

"For sure it's not fun," Andrew answered, "but every once in a while, you catch a break."

He smiled and waved as he left.

"So Sam, have you had a chance to look over my material?" Carson asked.

"Most of it, Sir," Sam answered, scanning the notes quickly. "I think I have the gist of it, and it's reassuring that so much of it dovetails with what I found on the internet and from what Sarah's friend Lisa has reported."

"That's true," Carson said. "The final resolution will be the toughest part, I think, and I pray it comes soon. That bastard Alvarez, it must've been him on the phone, gave me twenty-four hours and by God if I have to stay up for the next 24, I'll get this done. I'll get my Sarah back!" Carson was both shaken and empowered by his own words.

"I'm with you, Judge. I think we can do it."

Just then, Sam's cell vibrated in his pocket. He looked at it and said, "I think I need to take this. It's Trooper Johnson."

"Hey, Roland, what's up?" Sam spoke into the phone.

The judge watched as Sam's face creased into a smile.

"Holy sh…Wow! Man, when it rains, it pours! I'm with the judge now. I'll pass it right along, yep, I'll let him know how to reach you, and thanks, buddy! See you soon. Bye."

Sam composed himself as he put away his cell and looked at the judge, who was smiling.

"Well, get on with it; don't leave me hanging!" Carson said.

"That was Trooper Johnson, relaying information he'd received from East Hampton's Chief Mayer. Anyway, they caught the second guy. Right now they're trying to play them against each other, feeding them false info. Neither has bought in yet, but depending on what Gonzales has to say, we might not need them. "

"Yes, everything except where Sarah is. We'll have to find a way to push one of these guys to find that out."

"Right," Sam agreed. "Oh, more big news; East Hampton just got a report that a 36-foot cabin cruiser was stolen from South Hampton. The owners were away and just got back."

Sam stopped talking. The judge looked up to see an unreadable expression cross Sam's face.

CHAPTER 42

Pedro had narrowly escaped the security guards as he attempted to exit the courthouse. He'd moved quickly and hoped that no one had gotten a look at him. That would not be good; news traveled fast to Mexico. What could he do? He knew his choices were diminishing and events were spinning out of his control.

He was sitting in the park across from the courthouse, hiding in plain sight, as it were.

He'd gone into a gas station bathroom and had removed the talc from his hair. Underneath the judge's robe, he still wore his ripped and blood-stained clothes. He knew he looked disheveled, so he played that up. Pedro found a discarded shopping cart and filled it with trash. It was next to him, as he sat, head down, feigning sleep. People didn't really look at the homeless.

Pedro had put in a call to the judge, trying to convey more confidence than he felt. He wanted this to wrap up soon, before it got to the press, before his boss found out. He had given the judge twenty-four hours to hand over Gonzales and ordered him to put a lid on the press. He had no idea whether Juan was dead or alive, and no way to find out.

Pedro hadn't heard from Diego and Ricardo in East Hampton, so had no idea what was going on there. And the third guy, Hernando, who was in charge of making sure the homeless guy didn't talk, hadn't yet been successful in finding out if the guy was dead or alive. Pedro was seething with rage; how could everything have gone so wrong? It wasn't supposed to go like this.

And that fucking moron, Carlos Diaz; where was he? Pedro had given explicit directions as to where he should meet him. And he'd been waiting twenty-minutes! Carlos had said he was 'down by the river,' wherever that was. But he should be here by now. Carlos had dumped the first stolen vehicle and was now driving a blue Honda civic. Pedro lifted his head a bit to look toward Church St. He saw no blue cars of any description, and was growing more agitated by the moment. He pushed back the scenarios of betrayal that began to spin through his mind.

Pedro startled when he felt a small tap on his shoulder. It was Carlos and he was gesturing toward a car, a blue Honda, parked a few yards behind where he sat. Flooded with relief, Pedro shuffled along behind him without raising his head.

Once inside the car, Pedro exploded on Carlos, grabbing him by the throat and asking where he'd been and what had taken him so long. Carlos was not as deferential as Pedro expected and thought he might need another physical reminder of who was in charge. But the pain in his leg was becoming unbearable, so he questioned Carlos as to where he could get medical attention.

"Found a medico," Carlos replied.

"Well, at least you're good for something," Pedro admitted. "Where?"

Carlos handed him a map and pointed.

"You're sure about this?" Pedro asked, not ready to give up his anger.

Carlos shrugged his shoulders and drove, but apparently wasn't very impressed with Pedro's anger. Something had happened to change his attitude. Pedro would have to reassert himself in a more aggressive way. But that would have to wait; the throbbing pain was unbearable.

Following the map, Pedro said, "Turn here," as they approached Columbia Avenue off Church Street. Pedro noticed this was also Route 1, so would be heavily traveled. He kept his focus on the road, and when Washington Street came up, he indicated that Carlos should turn.

This neighborhood was what Pedro had been hoping for. It appeared to be largely Hispanic and gang signs were evident. He scanned both sides of the street for the doctor's office as Carlos drove. Young men hung out on street corners, looking menacing. It made Pedro smile; they had no idea what 'tough' was. They should come to Tijuana.

Carlos slowed the car, and pointed, "Medico." True, there was a small sign indicating a doctor's office and it appeared to be open. Carlos parked the car and the two got out.

Pedro knew they did not look out of place in this neighborhood and felt confident that the doctor would see him.

Pedro told Carlos to stay with the car. Carlos leaned up against the car and gave off attitude.

Entering a small waiting room, Pedro saw it was empty save for an older, rough-looking woman, possibly Hispanic, but more likely 'mixed,' she looked him in the eye and said, "Yes?"

"I'd like to see the doctor," Pedro said, as he displayed a roll of cash.

Apparently unimpressed, she picked up the phone, and said, "Patient coming back." She gestured for him to go through another door.

Pedro, who'd grown accustomed to better medical treatment since he'd been living in the states, found the place shabby and assumed he'd get inferior treatment here. But he had no choice.

Dr. Velasquez was Hispanic and did have a medical degree on the wall. The printing was too small for him to make out the school, but Pedro was pretty sure it wasn't Yale.

He told the doctor he had two gunshot wounds and pointed to them. Dr. Velasquez instructed him to drop his pants and lie down on the table.

Pedro gasped as the doctor put pressure on the wounds. The doctor pursed his lips, and said, "Not good. We'll have to take the bullet in your thigh out. The other one is less serious."

"I have money," Pedro showed him his bank roll. "I'll pay whatever…"

Dr. Valasquez went to his office door and opened it, calling out, "Gina, I need you back here. Put the 'closed' sign on the door." And to Pedro he said, "Someone with you?"

"Yes, my friend is outside with the car," Pedro replied. "Why?"

"This will take some time and you won't be in any shape to drive."

CHAPTER 43

Rory and Blake were waiting in the back of the courtroom for her case to be called. Rory felt confident that DeSean would be decertified back to Juvenile Court, but there was always that kernel of doubt; she'd learned to be wary of court outcomes.

She was glad that Stan Como, once her nemesis, now her trusted colleague, would be the DA on the case. They had successfully worked a case recently and she'd found it was helpful to be on good terms with district attorneys. In the end, both sides wanted to come to the truth. Ideally, that's how a good system should work. She knew it often didn't.

When DeSean's case was called, finally, Rory joined her client at the defense table. She nodded across the aisle to Como.

Judge Jenkins, a veteran on the bench with a reputation for fairness, directed the DA to introduce the case.

"Your Honor, this is the case of DeSean Smith, a juvenile who was direct-filed to adult court, sent to the county prison and charged with Armed Robbery. At the last hearing, the decertification was denied and the juvenile was held over for a psychological evaluation to determine his potential risk to community safety. I believe Your Honor has the completed report."

The judge nodded and said, "I have read the report. Ms. Chandler, do you have anything to add on behalf of your client?"

"Yes, Your Honor, as you have already read the report, I will call the Court's attention to the last paragraph, which states unequivocally, that 'Despite some lapses in judgement, this youth does not appear to have sociopathic tendencies, nor does he appear likely to act out in a violent manner in the community.' The psychologist is not at liberty to make specific recommendations to the court, but it appears that it would serve no purpose to continue to pursue this case in adult court." Rory looked to the judge.

"Thank you Ms. Chandler. Is there any other information you wish to give the Court?"

"Yes, Your Honor, I would only repeat what I said at the previous hearing. There was no gun found in DeSean's possession, nor along the route he travelled home. His home was immediately searched, with permission of his parents, and again, no weapon was found. DeSean is a tenth grade student at Chester High School, is passing all subjects, and plays on the football team. His parents are both here and are more than willing to take him home today."

"Thank you, Ms. Chandler. Mr. Como, is there anything the State wishes to say?"

"Yes, Your Honor. The District Attorney's office, while not in any way condoning DeSean's actions, concurs with defense, especially since this youth has no prior record with Juvenile Court, nor any citations. We believe he can be held accountable in their jurisdiction."

"Very well, then, the Court will order DeSean Smith's immediate decertification to Juvenile Court. He is to be released from prison, and escorted to Juvenile, for their determination." She banged the gavel.

Rory smiled her thanks to Stan Como and he smiled back and winked.

CHAPTER 44

Sam's thoughts were interrupted as the phone rang and the Judge took the call.

"Carson Justice here." Sam watched as the judge listened intently, and a slow smile spread across his face. "Kudos to your department, Frank. I can't believe you were able to take care of this so quickly." He paused to listen. "Yes, yes, I think we have to do that if we want Gonzales to talk…OK, good we'll talk soon."

Carson was beaming when he looked up at Sam, "They have Gonzales's mother in custody. She's a bit distrustful, understandably, but once she talks to her son on the phone, it should move the process on. Can you believe it?"

"That's incredible," Sam agreed, "how were they able to manage it so quickly?"

"She's been under surveillance for some time, because Gonzales is close to the top of the chain of command in the Corizon Cartel—that's news to us, by the way. They were aware of the attempt on his life, so were especially attentive."

Just then, Andrew Milano came in. Before he could speak, the judge informed him, "They have Gonzales's mother in custody; we need to arrange a phone call between the two so that Juan will have reason to talk to us."

"Jeez, that was fast!" Andrew marveled. "By the way, Juan gave us two names; the two guys the East Hampton police have in custody: Diego Cortez and Ricardo Aguilera. It killed him to give up anything; he's so dead set against diming out the cartel. That's the number one sin, and it's been drummed into all of them. By the way, do you know if his mother's out of Mexico yet?"

The judge was writing down the names, then looked up and said, "I'm not sure, I didn't ask, but it seemed they had just picked her up. But for sure I'll find out when they call back. Why don't you go down and tell him. Once we get his mother on the phone, we'll call you downstairs."

Andrew thanked the judge and rushed from the room.

Sam said, "I'll call Trooper Johnson and give him this info; should help their investigation. Do you want me to get Chief Mayer's phone number?"

"Good idea, then I can call him personally. The phones in the courthouse are secure."

Sam made the call and Roland gave him the Chief's phone number, but said he would call Mayer with this new information. Sam relayed his conversation to the judge.

"Thanks, Sam," Carson said as he wrote down the number. The judge was more animated than Sam had seen him since he arrived. He said, "Things should start moving pretty quickly once we get the phone call behind us; can't happen too soon for me. I've still got that 24-hour ultimatum in my mind." He grimaced.

"This is a big break, it should move the whole process along; once Gonzales feels safe enough to talk…"

"Yes, that's the big if, when he'll talk and how much he knows, not to mention how much he'll be willing to give up." Carson was still frowning. "We're up against the clock here."

"But, we're giving his mother and him asylum in the witness protection program, right?" Sam asked.

"Yes, the Bureau is involved officially now; they picked up Juan's mother. And they will offer the WPP to them. I can't imagine he would reject that offer; the Corizon Cartel has its tentacles everywhere, as he well knows. He's wily, though. I wish I felt I could really trust him."

"And Gonzales probably doesn't trust us either. Maybe he wonders if the Feds can keep his mother and him safe, but he can't risk going it alone with his aging mother," Sam added.

"You're right," Carson said, "but the Bureau has a very good record of keeping their witnesses safe. They have safe houses everywhere, and they often move the people in their custody if there's the slightest risk of a breach."

"Honestly, Judge, it seems like Juan's only course of action. It might not be a perfect life, but he has to consider his mother," Sam said.

The phone rang and the judge sprang to life. "Carson Justice here," he said. "Yes, yes, we're ready as soon as you are; I'll put you on hold and call our marshal. Yes, we have a translator. By the way, where are you? Excellent. Ok, hold on..."

The judge called Andrew, "We've got Mrs. Gonzales on the line; by the way, they are at the airfield, ready to fly out of Mexico. How are things at your end? Ok, excellent! Frank, from the bureau, is on line one and when I hang up you can talk to him and get this moving."

***

Sarah stood on the deck of the boat, tears streaming, and pointed towards the mainland, saying "Mi ciudad," letting Jesus know she was looking at her hometown, across the water. Then she said, "Mi padre..." She began trembling; she was overwhelmed with emotion. Seeing the coast of Connecticut on the sound was a balm to her. How to get there was another matter. But now that she knew where she was, she knew she could find her way home.

Sarah sat, head in her hands, sobbing with both relief and frustration. She was so near...

Jesus tapped her on the arm and gestured to himself, said, "help," and pointed to Sarah.

Not sure that he understood what he was saying, she asked, "You help me?"

"Si," he repeated, "I help you!"

"Por que?" Sarah asked, not quite sure she could believe him.

Sarah looked up at Jesus as he said, with anger in his voice, "Mi hermano, Henrique, muerto!" He shook his head sadly, but had fire in his eyes.

It suddenly dawned on Sarah, and she asked, "Henrique Alvarez, your brother?"

"Si," Jesus replied, fists at his side.

"Quien?" asked Sarah, although she was certain who had killed the real Henrique.

"Pedro Lopez; asesino!"

Sarah shrugged her shoulders with her palms up, trying to convey the question "Does Pedro know who you are?"

"No!" Jesus answered emphatically. "Mi madre protectora. Ella es muerte; cancer. Mi solo."

Sarah nodded and said, "Lo siento." And she was sorry for this kind man who had lost his brother to murder and his mother to cancer.

"Gracias," Jesus replied. "I join cartel, mi nombre es 'Jesus Sanchez.'"

Then Jesus said, "you go now!" He pointed towards the wooded island, gesturing with his hand, "Go!"

"No," Sarah said stubbornly, "you come; I help you!"

Jesus was kneeling, cutting off what remained of the duct tape. He looked at her with a mixture of hope, disbelief, and not a little fear.

They both heard the sound of a boat motor in the distance, glanced at each other in terror, and scrambled off the boat, and onto shore.

CHAPTER 45

Back in East Hampton, Chief Mayer and his officers were taking turns questioning the two suspects. They'd been peppering them with questions, alternating between 'good cop,' and 'bad cop,' with no obvious results. The two had been kept apart, but neither was about to break his silence.

Sharon and Brent were sitting in the office with the chief. They'd both had the opportunity to interview the subjects. And both concluded it was a good 'learning experience,' but Sharon wondered aloud now to the chief, "How do you guys do this on a daily basis? It's frustrating and exhausting!"

"True enough, it is frustrating. But I have to say, that since I don't deal with gang members on a daily basis, I've never encountered any suspects this brazen and utterly uncooperative." Chief Mayer sighed. "Fortunately, we don't do this every day, and definitely we don't have this much action in the off season. So, chalk one up to experience and hope this is the worst of the suspects you will ever have to interview."

"I guess you're right," Sharon said. "By the way, how's Joe Hayes doing?"

"I saw him yesterday, and his daughter was with him. She plans to take him home with her when he's discharged, which should be soon; he's much better. I think seeing his daughter and actually having a home and a future to look forward to has boosted his morale and helped his recovery."

"That's good news," Brent said. "By the way, I saw the VW sitting outside; when can Rob and Lisa come to get it?"

"They can get it whenever they want; it's been dusted for prints and repaired so it's ready to go. But they won't come back out until it's safe to stay in their cottage. They don't really need the car in the city. Also, they would like to meet you two when they come; I think they're curious." The phone rang and the chief answered. "Hey, Roland, you got something for me? Yeah? No shit! Let me write this down." He couldn't keep himself from grinning. "Maybe this will do the trick; who knows?" He listened, then said, "Ok, good, I'll be happy to talk to him, and you can call any time! Thanks, Roland, I'll get right on it."

"Ok, team, the two 'gentlemen' staying with us now have names, courtesy of Juan Gonzales. They are Diego Cortez, and Ricardo Aguilera. This could put a hitch in their giddy-up; shall we post bets on who cracks first?"

***

Joe Hayes was, indeed, feeling better. He was filled with gratitude. First, that he'd survived the vicious beating, and second that he'd been reunited with his daughter, whom he'd longed to see. His mind was foggy on the details of how they'd drawn apart, but he knew he'd been lost for a very long time. Joe realized now, from talking with the hospital social worker, he'd been suffering from PTSD since he'd come back from Viet Nam. The hospital social worker had told him of a very effective treatment and had made sure that Joe's sister, Charlene, knew how to access it.

Bart Graham, the officer posted outside Joe's door, poked his head in to see how Joe was doing. They chatted for a bit; Joe told him he might be leaving soon.

Bart said, "Glad to hear that you've made such a good recovery; I'll miss talking to you. I'm gonna' pop down to the cafe for a couple minutes; you be ok while I'm gone?"

"I'll be fine, my sister should be here soon," Joe answered.

"Ok, I'll let the nurse know," Bart said as he left.

Joe picked up the book Charlene had brought for him; it was Nelson DeMille's "Plum Island," one of DeMille's earlier novels, and maybe one of his best; Joe couldn't put it down. He had forgotten how much he loved to read, but his sister had not forgotten, God bless her!

Glancing at the clock, Joe noticed it was time for the nurses' shift change; it was always quiet around this time, as the nurses gathered in the office to share information. Charlene usually came at about the same time, too and the doctor would be in soon to talk with them both. He hoped it was good news; that he could go home with Charlene today.

Joe went back to his reading and became engrossed again in the story. A quiet footfall registered, but he paid no real attention. When he heard his door close, he looked up quizzically.

A man dressed in scrubs and a surgical mask with a black beard poking out from beneath, appeared at the bottom of Joe's bed. He did not know this man; a prick of fear tingled on the back of his neck. The buzzer to the nurses' station was under the covers, near his hand and he urgently pushed the button now. The light above his bed went on, alerting the intruder that the nurse's station had been called.

The man moved quickly towards Joe, brandishing a scalpel. Joe picked up the pillow, trying to protect himself from the knife. As the man came within striking range, Joe chucked his water pitcher straight at him.

Joe's door flew open as the head nurse came in. She took in the situation immediately and pressed the emergency alarm.

The intruder quickly headed out the door. Joe could hear heavy footsteps coming toward his room. He heard Bart yelling, "Stop, or I'll shoot!"

The attacker turned back into the room, grabbing the nurse and holding the scalpel to her throat. He said not a word as he dragged her out the door.

Joe heard a door open and then slam closed; soon he heard running feet charging down the stairs at the end of the hall, apparently in hot pursuit.

His day nurse, Emily, came into Joe's room and went straight to his side. "Are you ok, Mr. Hayes? Let me have a look," she said in a soothing voice.

"Is Kristin ok? She came in and scared the guy off, but he grabbed her," Joe was very upset.

"Yes, Mr. Hayes, I saw that. He ducked into the stairwell and the cops and security guys followed. I don't honestly know how she is, but if I know Kristin, she'll get out ok." A tear slipped down Emily's cheek, and Joe guessed she was trying to be brave for him.

Then she frowned and said, "This shouldn't have happened! Did your guard leave you?"

"He did, just for a moment to go to the cafe; he said he would notify you."

"I was in the office with the other nurses, so I guess he missed me. But still, this should not have happened; not a breach of security like this."

"I'm just thankful to be here; that's twice in a week I've cheated death. I'm worried about Kristin; she came to my rescue, and look what happened." Joe said.

"She was just doing her job; we all know that emergency situations come up and we try to be prepared…"

There was noise in the hall again; Emily and Joe looked up to see Bart rushing through the door and with him a bedraggled Kristin.

Emily ran to Kristin and hugged her, asking, "Did he hurt you?"

"Not as much as I hurt him," Kristin grinned. "I kicked him in the balls; he was getting on my nerves. Anyway, he let go and Bart grabbed me and brought me in. A little excitement, huh?"

Bart came straight to the bed, "Joe, are you ok? I'm sorry, this was my fault entirely. I can't tell you how awful I feel; I should know better not to let my guard down, ever."

"Mr. Hayes is fine, thanks to his quick thinking," Emily said to Bart. "And it's good of you to accept responsibility, but really, there's enough blame to go around. The nurses' station wasn't covered, for one. By the way, where is the attacker?" Emily asked.

"I got off a few shots, aimed at his legs, but it was tough since he had Kristin in front of him. Once Kristin freed herself—by the way, good for you, Kristin—I'm pretty sure I hit him. There were some security guards pursuing him across the parking lot when we came in. He'd flung off his hospital garb, but kept the mask on; still we have a general description of his height, weight, complexion." Bart informed them. Then he asked Joe, "Did you recognize this guy from before?"

"No, but I never really saw the other guys that good, I mean well enough to describe them. I can tell you he's dark, swarthy, I guess I'd say, with a black beard. A big guy, probably bigger than the one who beat me. The chief is trying to leave the impression that they killed me—well they damn-near did—but, there's at least one who knows different now. Hope they catch him," Joe said.

"Don't we all!" Bart said. "Speaking of which, I need to call the chief," Bart added.

"Guess I can't put it off any longer. I apologize in advance for any undue noise." Bart gave a wan smile and left the room.

CHAPTER 46

They jumped onto the dock and scrambled up the rocky coast. Sarah had put the second-hand sneakers on to give her better traction. She took off into the woods with Jesus close behind. It was nearly impossible to run through this dense forest.

She remembered from her many tours through the Thimble Islands, that this particular island was filled with poison ivy, but that was the least of her worries now.

Sarah gestured for Jesus to join her behind a tree. They stood and listened. The sound of a boat motor was coming closer; Sarah put her finger to her lips. They stood stock still, listening.

After a few tense moments, the sound faded. Sarah concluded it must be a tour boat, but she wasn't sure they still ran in October. No matter, Sarah thought, it wasn't Pedro and Carlos.

They pushed on through the trees and tangled vines. This island belonged to Yale, Sarah knew, but wondered why it seemed unused. Right about now, she would welcome an invasion of Yale students.

Trudging along in silence, Sarah kept alert for any unusual sound, but heard only bird song. There were many different kinds of birds on the island; it had become a refuge for them. The sound of lapping water had receded. She knew there was a house here, but wasn't sure where. It was most likely locked, but they might be able to find a way in. She hadn't been on this island since a middle-school field trip.

Motioning for Jesus to stop, Sarah pulled out two bottles of water she'd brought from the boat. They both drank as if they'd been in the desert, soon finishing their water. She hoped there would be water in the house. They should probably walk more slowly, to preserve their energy for when they really needed it. Sarah managed to convey this to Jesus and they slowed down, carefully heeding the huge roots that crossed their path.

After several more minutes of walking, the house, a big old house, came into view. Sarah pointed towards it, motioning Jesus to follow her. As they approached the house, Sarah noticed evidence of what had most likely been a tennis court. This had obviously been a private home, what she would call a mansion.

The house had been beautiful in its prime, and was still in decent shape. There must be a way in, Sarah was sure, and soon they found a window around the back of the house, that was easily broken to allow them entry. Looking up, Sarah noticed the house had a cupola on top, piercing through the pines. It would be a great place to look out over the water. The house would be a good place to lay low for a while, she decided, and climbed in the window, with Jesus right behind.

***

Dr. Velasquez had finished the surgery on his patient. He injected morphine, enough to keep him under for a while. The doctor needed time to think. He practiced in this neighborhood because he knew that poor Latinos often were denied good medical care. He was not in it for the money; he was actually still idealistic. He'd studied medicine at Yale, and had decided to stay in the area.

Of course he'd patched up many a bullet wound, and when he had these young men and women in his office he tried to talk some sense into them. He wanted to help them envision another future for themselves.

But this man, coming in with wads of cash, trying to buy silence, this man was an affront to the doctor's sensibilities. He was not from the neighborhood, that was obvious, and he'd just assumed that because this was a poor Hispanic area, his money would buy him anything.

Dr. Velasquez closed the door to his office, and went to talk with Gina, his wife and receptionist. "Gina, I need to talk to you." She turned and smiled at him.

"This man, I don't have a good feeling about him. What do you think?" The doctor always discussed difficult issues with his wife, having great confidence in her wisdom.

Gina got straight to the point, as usual, "He gave me the creeps, the way he came in flashing his money, like he could buy us. He assumed that because you have an office in this neighborhood, you have no scruples. I resent that."

The doctor smiled affectionately at his wife. "You never pull any punches, Gina, one of the things I love about you. The big question is what should I do? This might be a dangerous man, one who the authorities should know about. For sure, he's not local, but his English is good. I just have a bad feeling about him..."

"Well, we're on the same page there," Gina smiled. "Go with your gut, George. By the way, how long will he be out?"

"Long enough, and I can give him another injection, if need be. Now, will you go in and watch the patient, while I use the phone?"

Gina left the room. The doctor went to the front window and looked out. He saw a man leaning against a blue Honda. He decided to talk to him first, to see if he got a different feeling from this man.

He opened the front door and motioned for him to come in. The man, well-built, almost stocky, with dark hair and eyes, walked with a swagger.

The doctor addressed him in Spanish, first making sure he was his patient's friend. Then he told him that the operation was complete, but that it would be at least an hour before the patient could travel.

The man shrugged, looking at his watch, and asked if there was any way he could leave sooner. He seemed annoyed at the wait, the doctor thought.

"Not without compromising his recovery," the doctor answered abruptly.

Again, he shrugged, showing no compassion or concern and went back to lean against the car.

Dr. Velasquez was glad he'd spoken with the other man. He could tell from his accent that he was from Mexico, and his attitude bespoke a callous nature. That had cinched it for the doctor. He would notify the authorities in New Haven.

CHAPTER 47

Bart Graham stood before Chief Mayer, with more than a bit of trepidation. He was aware of the chief's legendary tirades. And he could feel one coming.

The chief took his time, sipping his coffee, apparently mulling things over. He looked up and said, "Now Lieutenant, tell me again just what happened."

He didn't sound angry, Bart thought, but there was the sense of tension in the air, like a tightly wound spring. He cleared his throat and went through the entire story again. He tried to emphasize the part where he freed the nurse, and shot at the suspect's legs. He also made much of the fact that these shots had enabled the security guards to subdue the man and get him into the hospital, where he was currently under guard.

"Well, let's hope the hospital security is better than ours was," Chief Mayer said tightly. Then he sat back in his chair, pursing his lips and apparently thinking.

Bart continued standing at attention, waiting for the proverbial other shoe to drop.

Finally, the chief said, wearily, "Sit down, Bart, and please tell me what you were thinking, and what, if anything, you learned from this fiasco."

Bart sat, his knees almost buckling under him. "I got careless. It had been quiet the entire time I was guarding the door; I knew that two suspects had been taken into custody, and I assumed that he'd be fine while I went for coffee. I know that assuming is a thinking error, and complacency cannot be allowed in police work.

These are things that I already knew. What I learned was never to forget those two important tenets. It was unforgivable on my part, and I will be plagued by the possibilities of what could have happened for the rest of my career, which," he grimaced, "may be cut short."

The chief sighed; leaning forward, he steepled his fingers before he spoke. "Bart, you're a good man, and have always been a good officer. The situation demands that I take some disciplinary action, though it doesn't please me. I'm going to direct that you take two weeks paid vacation, which you have coming to you, and then two weeks unpaid. You can give the impression that it's a month without pay. I think you have learned a priceless lesson, the hard way, and your analysis of it is flawless. I appreciate that you take full responsibility. Please leave your badge and gun with the receptionist and I will see you in a month."

"Thank you Chief Mayer, I really appreciate your understanding." Bart got up to leave, but first walked over to shake the chief's hand.

"Would you please send in Sharon and Brent on your way out?" the chief asked. Bart nodded as he left.

The duo appeared almost before the door had closed. "What's up?" Brent asked.

"Why don't you two sit first; there's another twist to our already tangled case."

He explained that a third suspect had turned up at the hospital to dispatch Hayes, and that he'd almost been successful, but was now in the hospital with gunshot wounds.

"Jeez, we were so sure we'd gotten both of the perps out here; I'm guessing we don't know his name."

"No, Sharon, not yet, but they are still questioning the only suspect offering information, in New Haven." The chief frowned. "I suppose it's not imperative that we push these guys, unless they actually know where Sarah is being held. You see, that's information that Juan Gonzales might not have. At least he hasn't given it up yet."

"Ok, so I'm guessing we're keeping the heat on, what with the new suspect," Brent said.

"Has anyone questioned the guy in the hospital?"

"No, last I heard, he was in the OR. When he's up to it, we'll start interrogating him. Just found out from the judge the kidnapper gave him 24 hours to produce Gonzales. So, you guys ready to go back? You want to switch guys or stay with the one you have?"

Sharon replied first, "I'm more than a little tired of Diego; you want to try your skills on him?" She looked at Brent.

"Sure," Brent replied. "I'm not crazy about Ricardo either. You know these guys are so brain-washed into not diming out; it's probably one of the few things they value."

"That's true," Chief Mayer agreed. "But at some point they've got to think about cutting their losses. I think it's important that they know we have the third, and, hopefully, the last of their group in custody, at least the East Hampton branch. I'm thinking this last guy may have been the conduit between East Hampton and New Haven. See what you two can dig up and then I'll have another go at it," the chief said, dismissing them.

CHAPTER 48

Dr. Velasquez had just finished dialing 911, when the front door crashed open and he was faced with the man he'd just spoken to. The man was waving a gun, and commanded, "Hang up!"

The doctor realized, with a sinking feeling, that he'd been right to distrust him. He prayed that the 911 call had gone through. The phone began to ring again.

"Don't pick up! You do as I say now! I am taking my friend and you will help." He came close and prodded the doctor with his gun, pushing him ahead toward the office door.

The doctor had no choice but to do as he was told. He opened the office door to see a horrified look on Gina's face, and the unconscious patient on the gurney. Gina composed herself and said nothing.

"You two take Pedro to the car, now!"

The patient's name had unconsciously slipped out, the doctor surmised. He said to Gina, "Would you please get the wheelchair?"

The intruder followed Gina to the closet, which was padlocked. She took out a small key to open the lock. The wheelchair, as well as prescription medications, were kept here. She wheeled the chair out and brought it over to the gurney.

The doctor and his wife struggled to get this large, unconscious man into the wheelchair. He kept slipping down; he was a dead weight. The doctor spoke to the other man, "Look, we're going to need your help. He can't sit upright, so you need to hold his legs."

Thinking it over briefly, the gunman shoved his weapon in his waistband, and moved into position to help, saying, "One wrong move and she gets it!"

The doctor nodded and the patient's accomplice grabbed Pedro's legs and held them in place. The trio awkwardly moved toward the front door; their progress was slow, but that might give the police time to arrive, the doctor thought.

At the front door, the gunman stopped, took his pistol out of his belt, and opened the door, looking carefully in all directions. Then he motioned them forward.

They almost lost the patient as they maneuvered down the steps and onto the uneven pavement, but he was caught in time, no thanks to his 'friend.'

When finally they had deposited Pedro onto the back seat, in a prone position, he began to stir. He looked up as his eyes rolled around without focus, and said, "Carlos, que?" His eyes closed immediately and he apparently slipped back into unconsciousness.

Satisfied, the accomplice closed and locked the car door. He motioned for the doctor and his wife to go back inside. As Dr. Velasquez glanced up he made eye contact with some young men he knew on the corner. They looked on with interest, but said nothing. He prayed they would help, and wondered what was in store for Gina and him once inside.

He soon found out, as the intruder, probably Carlos, if Pedro was at all coherent, ordered them into the closet that Gina had recently opened. The key was still in the padlock. The door was slammed behind them, and they heard the padlock click shut.

***

At the judge's home in Branford, the information was flowing and the phones were buzzing. The judge was pleased the pieces of the puzzle were coming together, slowly. But the most important piece, Sarah's whereabouts, had not been revealed. The lump in his stomach was still there and would be until he had Sarah in his arms. He couldn't allow himself to indulge in negative thoughts, as there was still much to be done.

Gonzales's mother would be landing soon, and then, perhaps, Juan would 'remember' where Sarah was being held. Looking at his watch, the judge saw that it was nearly 5p.m., and he mentally calculated the hours until the ultimatum, at 1p.m. tomorrow. There was no time to lose, but he knew events would progress at their own pace.

The phone rang, and Carson immediately picked up for Andrew. "Yes, Andrew?" The judge was sure his impatience showed. "He gave up the name of the third man in East Hampton? Wait, can you spell it?" He grabbed a pen and scribbled the name. "Geraldo Banda? Got it. Is Juan still claiming to know nothing about where Sarah's being held?" Carson felt the panic rising again. "Do you believe him?" He asked. "OK, I know you're doing your best, and I appreciate any information you get. I'll call the chief with the latest. Bye."

Carson looked up at Sam and Carla, "I guess you heard, we're still getting information, but no word about Sarah." He sighed. "I need to call the chief, maybe this new name will help to crack one of their suspects. It's amazing how many thugs are involved in this."

The judge picked up the phone to call Chief Mayer, sharing the new information with him. "So, Geraldo is still unconscious? Yeah, sure, we're up against the clock here...Chief, I just had a thought, what are the chances the medical staff could administer Sodium Pentothal to Geraldo when he regains consciousness; I can deal with the legal part. Ok, appreciate it. Talk to you later."

"That's a brilliant idea, Carson," said Sam. "You know, since 911, there's been a resurgence of the drug for interrogating suspected terrorists. Sometimes you hit the jackpot with it. Let's hope..."

CHAPTER 49

Carlos took off with a squeal of tires. He was in a panic; he had no one to tell him what to do, and his unconscious partner was in the back seat.

His impulse was to speed, but he knew that would only attract undue attention to him and his car. Ordinarily, he would dump the car and steal another one. He couldn't do that now; he'd never get Pedro out by himself. In fact, once he got to the harbor, he wasn't sure how he would manage. Jesus couldn't help him; there was only one skiff and he'd stashed that in the reeds when he and Pedro had come ashore.

After driving nearly fifteen minutes, he pulled over on a side street. He had to think, and he knew that really wasn't his strong suit. He'd always taken orders, not without resentment, but he usually did as he was told. Carlos felt a lump of fear in his stomach, as he imagined telling Numero Uno that he had fucked it up, that he couldn't get Pedro back to the boat. Or worse yet, that he'd gotten caught.

It occurred to him then, the most important thing was to keep them from getting arrested.

So, he had to lay low until Pedro was awake and could move by himself. Carlos looked at his watch; the doctor had said it would be an hour before he could be moved, so he had another forty-five minutes to kill. It was driving him nuts, but what could he do? For all he knew, the police had a description of the car and maybe even the license plate, though he doubted that.

But still, Carlos knew the best thing for them was to get as far from the scene as fast as possible. He looked in his side mirror, preparing to pull out, and saw a police cruiser pull into the street and drive toward him.

***

Juan Gonzales's mother, Maria, had just landed in New Haven, escorted by two FBI agents. She was frightened by the whole experience; she'd never been out of Mexico. The FBI men had been kind to her, which surprised her. She'd always thought of them as the enemy. She understood English better than she'd let on, so was able to listen to their conversations, but Maria hadn't heard anything to alarm her.

She longed to see Juan, her only son—her only living relative— who'd been away from her for so long. It was hard to believe she would actually be with him, soon. She hoped that he'd learned something from prison; that he was now willing to get out of the cartel. He'd always been so hard-headed, had never really listened to her. But she'd continued to pray for him.

As they deplaned, the agents carried her two bags, all she'd been allotted. It didn't matter that she'd left much behind, everything she knew was about to change completely, for the better she hoped.

Maria was escorted to a black SUV parked on the tarmac, far from the commercial planes. She settled herself in the back seat, ready to see her son and begin her new life. She just hoped that her son was ready to do the same.

***

Andrew Milano was waiting at the back entrance of the courthouse. The SUV arrived, and the agents got out first to converse with Milano. Their mission would be complete when Maria Gonzales was delivered to the holding cell.

Maria was helped from the car. Andrew introduced himself and said as simply as he could that he would take her to her son. She obviously understood, as tears began to course down her face. Andrew put his arm around her shoulder to steady her. They walked into the courthouse, the agents trailing behind.

Maria was taken to a small conference room in the basement, near the holding cell. The FBI agents took their leave, and Andrew called Juan's guards, instructing them to bring Juan.

The guards, as a show of faith, had removed the cuffs from his wrists, but left the leg shackles. Juan was brought to the conference room.

As soon as his mother saw him, she ran to him, embracing him and saying, "Mi hijo, mi hijo!" Juan held his mother in front of him so he could see her. He said simply, "Madre."

Andrew wished he could disappear, but knew that was out of the question. He took a seat in the corner, while Juan and his mother were allowed to converse.

After a while Juan asked Andrew, "Where will my mother be staying tonight?"

"That depends how quickly we can wrap this up. I don't mean to be callous, but until the judge's daughter is recovered, you will have to remain here. We will take your mother to a safe house, after the two of you have had dinner together here. We'll stay in touch with you by phone, and you can speak with your mother whenever you wish."

"How will I know she's safe?" Juan wanted to know.

"It stands to reason that since we've gone to the trouble of finding your mother and bringing her here, we're unlikely to go back on our word now. Besides, we're sure you have more information, and thus more incentive to talk. We have every reason to want to keep you safe, and your mother as well."

Juan listened, but appeared skeptical.

Andrew said, "Look, I know you're not accustomed to people being truthful; you think we're out to get you. But we're not. We're out to get your bosses, the kingpins of the cartel. By the way, it seems obvious they are out to get you. It's in our best interest to make sure they don't kill you, so you can testify against them."

Juan flinched as he pondered this, then asked his mother, "Madre, what do you think?"

"I think," Maria spoke English, "that these men are good. The men who brought me here showed me every kindness. I cannot say the same for the men who rule you in Mexico." She paused, looking at Juan, "We have a chance for a new life, and better, I hope."

Andrew was stunned, by her command of English and by her wisdom. But, wasn't that always the way of mothers, he thought. It seemed she'd turned the tide for Juan; his face had softened, and Andrew prayed that this would make the difference.

***

Outside of Dr. Velasquez's office, Paco and Luis, who'd just observed the doctor and his wife taking an unconscious man to a car, were debating whether or not they should do something. On the one hand, the doc had always been good to them, taking care of them when they were sick or injured. He also tried to steer them in the right direction, away from gang violence. On the other hand, they didn't dime people out.

Luis said, "I didn't like the look of that guy; looks like he was forcing the doc and his wife, like he maybe had a gun on them. The doc looked me in the eye; I think he wanted help. It don't hurt to just take a look and see he's ok; what do you think?"

"I don't know, I like the doc and all, but I ain't no snitch," Paco answered.

"You don't know the guy, how you bein' a snitch? That's bullshit, man, I'm goin' in, you do what you want."

Paco hesitated, "Ok, I'll go." He looked around to see if anyone was watching.

The two walked to the front door, which had a 'closed' sign on it. They knocked, but there was no answer. Luis gestured with his head to go around the back, saying, "We didn't see 'em leave, so they must be in here." He knocked on the back door, then listened. He thought he heard movement, like banging.

Luis said, "They're in there, I hear, like, banging; we need to go in." He found a good-size rock, smashed in one of the windows in the door, then reached in and unlocked the door. The two youths entered.

Now they could hear the banging more clearly, "Who's there?" the doc asked, his voice muffled.

"It's us, Luis and Paco; we thought you might need help."

"Thank God you're here; we're in the closet, see the padlock? Is the key in it?"

Luis looked, "No, it ain't; where is it?"

"I have one in my pocket," the doctor answered, "I'll see if there's room to slide it under the door."

The boys looked at the bottom of the closet door. "It don't look like there's room," Paco said. "You have another one somewhere?"

"We should have another." They could hear the doc asking his wife. "Do you know where the extra key is?" They couldn't hear her reply.

The doctor answered, "It's locked in the desk, but since we can't pass any keys out to you, that doesn't help."

Luis thought, then said, "You got a screwdriver and hammer in here? I think we can pop the pins out of the hinges…"

"Good thinking," Dr. Velasquez answered. "Can one of you run home and get the tools? I don't have any in the office."

Paco answered, "I'll go get 'em; we got tools at home."

"I'll stay here, Doc," Luis said, "make sure the bad dude doesn't come back."

"I think we've seen the last of him, at least I hope so…I really appreciate you guys coming in here to check on us. We won't forget that."

"You've always been good to us, Doc. Me, my family, all of us…"

A few minutes later Paco rushed back into the office, out of breath, but with the tools.

"We got the tools now, Doc; we'll give it a shot," Luis said.

The two worked together to pry the pin out of the lowest hinge. It was rusty, and tough to budge.

Hearing the struggle, the doctor intervened. "I do have some WD-40 in the bottom drawer of my cabinet across the way; that might help."

Paco went over to check and came back with the can. Pushing Luis out of the way, he sprayed generously, while Luis held his nose.

"That shit smell bad," Luis said, waving his hand in front of his nose. "Let's try it now."

The two set to work again on the hinge. Slowly, the pin gave, and the bottom hinge was undone. Paco sprayed the middle and upper hinges, while Luis kept his distance.

From inside the closet, the doctor said, "Sounds like you got one of them; good work."

"Yep, and we'll get the other two; have you out in no time," Paco said.

The second one came free, and Luis told the doctor, "One to go…"

They needed a chair to reach to top hinge, so it was a bit trickier to pry free, but finally, it dropped and they pulled the door open.

Dr. Velasquez and his wife emerged, looking frazzled, but happy.

Gina hugged them both, and said, "Your mothers will be very proud of you; I'll make sure to tell them."

"Just glad you're ok," Luis said, embarrassed.

"If it wasn't for you two, God knows how we'd have gotten out. We did call 911 before being locked in, before the gunman made us take the patient out to the car, but apparently they thought it was a prank call. We'll call again; you guys can go, but we'll have to tell the cops how we got out. They may question you," the doctor said.

"That's ok," Luis said. "This time we ain't done nothin."

***

Chief Mayer was able to get in contact with Dr. Thatcher, the medical director of South Hampton Hospital; they had been friends for years through their Lion's Club association.

"Hi Matt, it's Thom Mayer; thanks for taking the call. I know you're always busy."

"Oh, you could say that, especially when we have intruders trying to kill our patients," he chuckled. "It'll be awhile before you live that one down, Thom."

"Don't I know, but seriously, it's good that your security is on the ball. Ours is, usually. I hope to look at this as an anomaly; the officer's on furlough."

"Thom, I trust you and your guys, and I agree it's not likely to happen again. Can you clue me in on what's happening?" The doctor was curious.

"You have no idea what it's been like for the past several days, not the usual off-season stuff, for sure! I can't tell you everything, but suffice it to say we're dealing with some dangerous dudes from South of the border. There are lives at stake and we need information from your would-be assassin, whose name is Geraldo Banda." The chief paused, "He's not likely to give up the info voluntarily, so..."

"What are you suggesting?" Dr. Thatcher suddenly was on guard.

"Nothing draconian, I assure you," the chief was quick to say. "What we need is for your staff to administer Sodium Pentothal to Geraldo, while he's asked a series of questions."

"What? Can we legally do that?" The doctor asked in disbelief.

"Trust me, this comes from New Haven, as in Federal Court? I've been assured that the legal aspects will be taken care of."

There was silence on the line, then, "I'd need to hear it from the source, Thom, you understand my predicament; I have to answer to the board."

"I totally understand, Matt, and believe me, this is no ordinary situation. I will have the judge call you and explain. But there is a time constraint here, so it has to be done as soon as the patient has regained consciousness and is deemed ready for this procedure," the chief explained.

"That's a tall order…"

"I know that, and if it weren't a matter of life and death we wouldn't be having this conversation. The information is crucial and this may be our only hope," the chief said, "really, we're desperate."

"Ok Thom, I'll have to trust you on this; you have a good track record, so have the judge give me a call. Meantime, I'll alert my most trusted medical professionals and check on the patient's progress."

"Thanks, Matt," the chief said. When this is all over, we'll have a long talk…"

"I look forward to that, Thom. I'll be waiting to hear from the judge."

Chapter 50

Rory and Blake sat morosely in her office, the euphoria of winning the case for DeSean having worn off. Both of them were getting edgy, since they'd heard nothing from Sam since he'd left the previous day. Rory prayed Sam hadn't 'gone rogue' again.

"I can't text him anymore," Blake said peevishly. "I guess we have to assume that he's too busy to get in touch with us. I hope that's a good thing," he added.

Rory sighed, "Waiting and not knowing is the worst!"

"Yeah, look, why don't I go feed Sam's cat..." Blake said, without enthusiasm.

"Thanks, Blake, I have to finish the paperwork from today, and then pick up the girls from field hockey. Why don't you come over for dinner, say sixish?"

"You don't have to do that, Rory..." Blake began to protest.

"Don't be silly, why be miserable alone, when we can all be miserable together?"

"Well, when you put it that way, sure, thanks!" Blake said.

After Blake left, Rory went back to completing the notes for DeSean's file. She was pleased at how the hearing had gone. She'd had a long and candid conversation with DeSean and his parents, as they waited to be called for his juvenile hearing, which followed the decertification hearing. His case in juvenile court had been continued and in the meantime, he'd been placed on an electronic home monitor. Rory hoped she'd gotten through to him how careful he'd have to be, not only while on the monitor, but in the conduct of his affairs going forward. She didn't like to lecture kids, but she felt he'd be more likely to hear her after his nightmarish stay in prison.

After closing up the office and walking to her car, Rory's phone trilled; she looked at the caller name. It was Roland. "Hey, Roland," Rory said breathlessly, "you got any news?"

***

Sam's head was overflowing with new information; he was having difficulty processing it all. And still, no word on where Sarah might be. There was something niggling at the back of his brain, and he couldn't access it. He asked the judge if he could go outside for a few minutes to clear his mind.

Carson answered, "Go out back, enjoy the view."

Sam gratefully made his way through the double doors that opened onto a patio overlooking Long Island sound. The view was breathtaking; it calmed him and slowed down his racing thoughts. He sat and just took it in, knowing it would soon be lost in the gathering twilight. Looking to his right, he noticed a heavy fog layer rolling in.

He realized he hadn't checked his cell phone since the morning, so he looked at it now.

There were several texts from Blake, each message more desperate. He owed him a call; he could at least fill him in on what they'd learned. It might help him sift through it all, too. In any case, Blake and Rory should know what was going on.

As expected, Blake picked up immediately. "Sam! Thank God, we've been worried…"

"I know, and I apologize. It's just that things have been moving so fast all day; I've hardly had a moment to myself. But the good news is we've learned a lot. I just need to try to get it into some kind of order that makes sense. A few more of the perps have been arrested, and one is actually talking. It seems like we're on the verge of a break through."

Sam tried to remember everything that had happened throughout the day, trying to tell what happened chronologically; it was difficult. Finally, he was ready to sign off. "Please say Hi to Rory and everyone; I'll call you there later if we get big news. Bye."

Sam looked out over the Sound, and was astonished to see the fog had completely obscured it, in just in the past few minutes. There was something about Long Island Sound he was trying to remember; it had been nagging him all day, since…that was it, since the Thimble Island tour! He'd seen a cabin cruiser anchored off the largest island; he couldn't remember the name of it. Someone was sure to know. He might be way off base, but he had to give it a shot. He raced back inside to tell the judge.

***

Carlos slid down in his seat as he saw the police cruiser coming his way. He held his breath and waited. When he thought it might be safe, he brought his head up enough to see out the window. He could see the taillights of the cruiser slowly receding in the distance. He waited a few more moments before sitting up fully. He was sweating bullets.

The police were gone for now, but he still had to figure out how to get Pedro back to the boat. He noticed headlights approaching from behind; again, he slid down and out of sight. He could see the reflection of red and blue lights flashing. He stayed put, but was panicking. That was the second police car in the last few minutes; that couldn't be good.

As soon as the cruiser disappeared around the corner, Carlos made his move. He slowly edged out from his spot and, without turning his lights on, drove down the street, turning in the opposite direction from where the police car turned.

He had no idea where he was, but there wasn't much in the way of traffic. A driver coming toward him flashed his brights to signal Carlos that his weren't on. He immediately turned them on, waving to the driver. He thanked God that it wasn't the cops.

Carlos didn't have the best sense of direction, but he noticed that the side streets seemed to be headed downhill. As he recalled, that meant they were going in the direction of the harbor. Then he saw signs for Rt.1 South, and seemed to remember coming in that way, so he got on. He would have to look for signs to the harbor.

Carlos saw a sign to Rt. 146 S, and that also rang a bell, so he got off Route 1 and followed it. He could see that he was driving parallel to the harbor, but how to get down to it? His memory failed him and now it was full dark and foggy to boot. He pulled off the road and tried to think.

He remembered coming into the harbor from the boat, and stashing the skiff in an industrial area, near a factory. They had pulled the boat up the slope and hidden it behind some trees. But he didn't know where it was; he hadn't been paying attention, because Pedro was in charge. Fuck! He couldn't remember the street where they had left the boat. He would have to find a safe place to park until Pedro woke up. And if the doc had been straight with him, that should be soon.

Carlos heard Pedro stirring in the back, and turned around. Pedro appeared semi-conscious; he was muttering and thrashing from side to side.

"Fuck!" Pedro yelled, "It fuckin' hurts!" He sat up, looking at Carlos strangely. "My leg is killing me! I need meds!" He started sobbing.

Carlos realized, belatedly, that he hadn't taken meds from the doctor's office, and he certainly couldn't go back there now. "It's ok, Pedro, I'll get your meds; just stay cool."

He remembered having passed a pharmacy not too far back; he'd have to get some pain killers the hard way, he had no choice.

Looking back at Pedro, Carlos saw that he had slumped back on the seat. He was still muttering, but seemed only half-awake. Carlos pulled back onto the road and headed back the way he'd just come. Before long, a pharmacy came into view through the fog. He slowed down and pulled into the lot. There were only a few cars there; it was a bad night to be out.

Parking as far from the store as possible, away from the bright lights, he left the car pointed out, for a quick get-away. Then, Carlos locked the car and made his way around the back of the store, praying that Pedro stayed asleep.

Pleasantly surprised that a back door was open, he looked around for cameras, kept his head down and went in. He was in a storage area, but he knew there would be no drugs here. He heard water running, and noticed a bathroom. Someone should be coming out, soon...

CHAPTER 51

At Southampton Hospital, the patient Geraldo Banda, was coming around. He'd been out of surgery for almost forty-five minutes, and was showing signs of waking up.

Hospital security had been beefed up since the attempted murder of Joe Hayes hours ago. Hayes had been released from the hospital and taken with his sister to an undisclosed location, where the chief thought he'd be out of harm's way.

The nurse-anesthesiologist, Kerry Brighton, called one of the security guards over. "Dan," she said, "he's waking up now, please let Dr. Thatcher know we'll be ready for the next procedure in about a half hour."

Dan left the room, replaced in a few moments by another security guard. There were four in the room and they instinctively moved toward the patient. Geraldo was thrashing and muttering angrily, but was obviously still groggy.

The nurse spoke soothingly to him, rubbing her hand over his arm. "That's ok, Geraldo, you're waking up now. Everything is fine; the operation went well…"

Unexpectedly, Geraldo sat bolt upright, yelling, "What the fuck is going on?"

The guards moved closer and prepared to put restraints on the patient. It proved easier than they'd expected, as Geraldo had collapsed back onto the gurney after his tirade.

Kerry noted, "Not the way patients usually come out of anesthesia. But then, judging from what happened earlier today, he's not your usual patient. We'll need to proceed with caution."

***

Chief Mayer hung up the phone after speaking with Dr. Thatcher. It had been a long day. And it was growing longer, but they seemed to be getting somewhere. The hospital administrator had received the legal papers and had run them by the chairman of the board. They were set to go.

Mayer called to Sharon and Brent, who were waiting in the outer office. They would be bringing a third officer, Angela Gordon, AKA 'Viv,' who was already familiar with the case.

The four got into the chief's cruiser and headed for Southampton. The officers were unusually quiet, Mayer thought. It was probably a lot for these 'youngsters' to take in. Hell, it was a lot for him to take in, come to think of it. He'd been on this case only since Saturday, five days! Now that was hard to believe; they'd seen lots of action and been pushed to the limit during this time. The chief was proud, though, that his officers had had the fortitude to deal with everything. What a learning curve; it rivaled the time he'd spent on the streets of New York City. He'd come to East Hampton thinking it would be a piece of cake; hah! His ruminations were cut short by Sharon, inevitably the most vocal.

"Chief, what do you think we should say to the guy? This will be very different from questioning the other guys. The last thing Ricardo said, was 'I speet on you.' I didn't stick around to see if he actually followed through. But before we left, I told him I was going to see Geraldo."

The chief shook his head, smiling at Sharon's comment. "I think we have to be prepped by the medical staff. Apparently there are nurses and doctors on staff who've worked with Sodium Pentothal. In fact, they may do the questioning; we may just be a support team."

"Well, however it goes, this is all new territory, like this case has been from the beginning," Angela weighed in.

"Isn't that the God's honest truth!" agreed Brent.

***

Captain Alex Grayson had been out on the water since the call earlier in the day from Coast Guard Headquarters, New Haven regarding a stolen boat in Southampton. The Coast Guard cutter, Ridley, was out of Montauk. Grayson had sailed out past Block Island and over to Orient Point trying unsuccessfully to locate the cabin cruiser. There was a lot of pressure from the higher-ups to find this boat, but he wasn't given any explanation.

Watching the fog roll in, Alex called to his first-mate, "Hey Jack, what do you think? Should we turn back before we get completely fogged in?"

"It's not my call. I'll see what Headquarters has to say. They were pretty intent on us finding the boat today, Lord knows why!"

"I felt pressured, too." Alex said.

Jack radioed HQ, then turned to Alex, "They said to come back; behind the fog there's a nor'easter coming in strong. First I've heard…"

"I wonder if we'll be able to get out tomorrow," Alex mused.

"New Haven's going to take over," Jack shrugged. "I guess we're out of it, which is fine with me. New Haven's got those new 45-foot response boats; should be a piece of cake for them."

"Roger that," the captain said, as he prepared to turn the cutter around and head back.

CHAPTER 52

The pharmacist closed the door behind her and turned to go back into the main store. She had hardly taken a step, when a hand pressed over her mouth and a gun was put to her head.

Carlos hissed in her ear, "You need to get me Oxy Contin, 100 tabs, now! You go, I wait here. Remember, there's a gun on you so don't talk to no one. Now go!"

The trembling pharmacist, turned to speak to the intruder. Covering his face, he spat out, "Now!"

He watched from the shadows of the store room. Someone was at the counter asking for a prescription. The pharmacist told her, "I'll be with you in just a moment," and walked to an area out of Carlos's sight. He panicked; he couldn't go out into the store, with the customer standing there.

Soon she was back. He saw her slip a bag into her pocket and then she waited on the customer. Handing the woman her prescription, she said, "Thank you Mrs. Mooney, have a good evening."

Carlos noticed the woman give the pharmacist a strange look before she left.

When the pharmacist, Jeanine O'Hara, he saw her name tag, came back to the store room, she held a bag in front of her, offering it to Carlos. "Why'd that woman give you a funny look?" he asked, still holding his sweatshirt in front of his face.

"I don't know what you mean," she said. "Maybe she could see I was flustered, I mean it's not every day you have a gun pulled on you. Here, this is what you asked for."

Carlos looked in the bag; there were two prescription bottles labeled 'Oxy Contin' holding fifty tablets each. He took the bag and said, "Now, Jeanine, you go lock up the store."

She looked at him in disbelief, "I can't, the store's open until midnight!"

"Not tonight, now go lock up! And bring me a bottle of water," Carlos added.

Jeanine was clearly unhappy about this, but stalked off to do as she was told.

She walked back to him, handed him the water. "Now what?" she asked, "You going to kill me?" She stared boldly, as if daring him.

"Sassy bitch, ain't you?" Carlos said, pulling her by her hair and shoving her into the bathroom. He found a chair and propped it against the doorknob, then ran out the back door at top speed.

***

"Harry, Harry! I'm in the bathroom, come get me out!" Jeanine was yelling at the top of her voice.

Harry had been watching the thief make his getaway, after leaving his hiding place under the counter. He was a pharmacy aid, and was just a kid. He ran to the bathroom and easily slid the chair out from under the knob. "You okay?" he asked, with concern.

"I'm fine, just another damn druggie, let's call the police. We really need a security guard here; God knows, we've asked!" Jeanine was more angry than scared; this was not the first hold-up she'd encountered.

"He didn't really look like the usual strung-out junkies," Harry said. "He really looked hard-core."

"How'd you see him?" Jeanine asked.

"I poked my head out after he left; he had to run right under the lights to get to his car. Man, he took off in a hurry," Harry added.

"Maybe we got something on video," Jeanine said, as she picked up the phone to call the police. "You're right, though, he wasn't all shaky and scared like most junkies. I guess I got lucky he didn't do more than lock me in." A chill went up her spine.

She hadn't even dialed, when a police car, followed closely by a second, roared into the lot.

"Oh, I guess Mrs. Morris got my little note," Jeanine chuckled, as she went to unlock the door for the police. "I wrote '911' on the prescription, and called her by the wrong name." She smiled at Harry's look of admiration tinged with disbelief.

The officers came in, guns drawn and badges in sight. "You have a problem here?" Officer Taylor asked Jeanine.

"We did, but the armed robber left, maybe five minutes ago, Harry?" Jeanine asked.

"About five minutes ago, Officer. I saw him take off in that direction," Harry said, pointing toward the harbor. "And he was hauling ass…I mean, driving fast."

"Thanks, kid," Officer Taylor said. "Be right back," Taylor and the other officer walked out. Officer Taylor came back inside, while the other two drove off toward the harbor.

"He's got a bit of a head start on us, but we'll get him. Another druggie?" the officer asked.

"Harry got a better look at him than I did, and he didn't think so," Jeanine said.

The officer turned to Harry. "Can you describe him? And what sets him apart from the usual suspects?"

"He was dark, maybe Hispanic, pretty big. I didn't see him real good, only from the side when he ran under the lights. He didn't seem afraid at all, the way I heard him talking to Jeanine. Maybe we got him on one of the cameras…Oh, and the car looked to be blue, an older Honda; didn't catch the license."

"I'll radio my men with the car description and we'll look at the video." Officer Taylor said. "Hmm, similar car reported in another case," Taylor muttered to himself.

"Now, Ms. O'Hara, can you tell me exactly what happened?"

***

Carlos was running scared; he knew the police would be on him soon. Pedro was beginning to stir and moan in the back seat. "Hang on, I gotta' find a place for us to hide; the police gonna' be after me!"

"Que paso?" Pedro asked. Carlos knew Pedro was still out of it; he rarely spoke to him in Spanish.

"Callate! Poli!" he shouted. He wouldn't normally tell Pedro to 'shut up,' but he was past his limit, and figured Pedro was out of it anyway.

That shut him up for the moment, but soon Pedro began to moan again, "Owww, my leg fuckin' hurts! Gimme some meds!"

Carlos tossed the bag and water bottle to the back seat. "There you go, now let me drive in peace."

Carlos accelerated, giving his full attention to the road, which was dark, foggy and winding. He was looking for a secluded spot where they could lay low.

Before he knew it, he'd turned onto a street with huge, expensive homes, brightly lit. Oh, God, we don't want to be here, he thought with dread. Then, at the end of the street, he noticed a house under construction; there were no lights there, and the driveway wasn't paved. Looking around, he saw nothing to stop him, so he pulled into the drive and up next to the house, hidden from the street and cut the engine. By now, fog obscured everything.

He turned his attention to Pedro, as he heard him fumbling with the lid on the pill bottle.

"I need my fuckin' meds!" he spat out.

Carlos put his hand out, "Give it to me," he said. Unfastening the lid, he looked at the dosage instructions, which said, '1-2 capsules every 6 hrs.' He gave Pedro one pill, and opened the water for him. "Take this," he said.

"I need more than one, man," he whined, "this fuckin' hurts!"

Carlos bit his tongue and said simply, "The cops are after us. I had to strong arm the pharmacy bitch to get these."

"You, what?" Pedro came to life. "You fuckin' robbed a pharmacy?"

"Yeah, man, I did! The doc was about to call the police, so I got you outta' there and took off. No, I didn't stop to get meds; I saved your ass!"

"What'd you do to the doc?" Pedro asked, as he swallowed his pill down.

"I locked him and his secretary in his closet. I've been on the run ever since. Then you woke up and started moanin' for drugs, so I went and got 'em!" Carlos was getting angry as he thought about it.

"OK, I get it, thanks, man. I was really out of it," Pedro said.

Carlos knew this was as much of an apology as he would get. "I know you was, man. But now I need you awake. I don' know where the fuckin' dinghy is, the fog is like, everywhere, and the cops are after us. I need to you stay with me; we gotta' get back to the boat."

"What time is it?" Pedro asked.

"It's 7 p.m.," Carlos answered.

"How long was I out? I don't remember anything!" Pedro sounded frightened.

"I dunno,' man, we got there maybe two- something? Then the doc, he take a while before he come to me. Then he says 'another hour.' I don't trust him, so I go back into the office and he's got the phone in his hand, about to make a call. I didn't wait to find out who he's callin,' I tell him and the woman to take you to the car. I had to help; you were so out of it!"

"So, I've been out for what? Five hours? Shit, man! What day is today? I'm all fucked up!"

"Same day, Wednesday. Yeah, you been fucked up for a long time. Now, you see, I need you to be here. I don't even know where the boat is!"

"Can't see anything in the fog, but neither can the police. You think it's time to get another car?" Pedro asked.

"Shit no, man! I'm done for tonight; can't take no more!"

CHAPTER 53

Chief Mayer and his officers were in Dr. Thatcher's office, getting briefed by the medical team. It had been decided that the trained staff would do the questioning of the patient; they just needed to know what information was being sought.

The chief and his team would remain in the room, to suggest any questions they might have. They understood there were certain protocols to be followed when questioning a patient under the influence of this drug. They would be observers, albeit with some influence. The chief could sense some disappointment from his subordinates, but he understood how crucial it was for experienced staff to lead this questioning.

Dr. Thatcher escorted them to the OR, where the procedure would take place.

Meanwhile, the patient, who'd become obstreperous, had a valium drip going to keep him under until the Sodium Pentothal could be administered. It was obvious he wouldn't cooperate voluntarily, and the chief worried how his predisposition to be uncooperative might affect his reaction to the drug.

Chief Mayer asked the question, "Banda seems like a hard case, how much will that affect his responses?"

Kerry Brighton answered his question. "Every patient has a different reaction; it's all over the board. Basically, this drug has an anesthetic effect and frees the patient of inhibitions. So we're likely to get reactions atypical of the patient's usual behavior. Sometimes, it's the ones most tightly controlled that are freed up to give a lot of information, or to express emotions they are unaccustomed to. It can be like a dam bursting. As I said, it's not always predictable. And we need to stay flexible with our questioning as we notice what direction the patient is headed. You develop a sort of intuition after you've done this for a while. Does that answer your question, Chief?"

"Yes, thank you, it does. It's quite different from our approach." He'd asked the question as much for the benefit of his officers as for his own information.

"So," Dr. Thatcher said, "Are we ready to proceed, or are there more questions?"

Everyone was in favor of going forward.

***

Andrew Milano was speaking with the judge. Juan Gonzales and his mother had just had dinner. His mother had been taken under guard to a safe house, where Juan could join her when they had Sarah back.

"I don't know Carson, he's given us a lot on the workings of the cartel, including who the head honchos are; the FBI can't wait to get their hands on it. It seems he's given up some very damaging Intel. We'll have the bureau check it out, of course. Bottom line, I don't think he knows where they're holding Sarah, that's my gut feeling."

The judge sighed, "Well, let's hope Geraldo gives up something; he's sure to know. We just have to see if this 'truth serum' works to our advantage."

Just then, Sam hurried back into the room. "Sorry to interrupt, but when I was out looking at the Sound, I remembered something that's been nagging me all day. When I was on the boat tour this morning, I saw a cabin cruiser docked at the biggest island. At first I thought I saw a person on the boat, but when I looked back, the deck was empty. There weren't many other boats out there, so I asked the captain if there were usually boats there. He said something like, 'it belongs to Yale and they do what they want.' It may be a long shot, but do you think maybe…"

"I'll try anything to find Sarah! It's as good a lead as we've had…that's Horse Island, there's a dock to the side, sort of hidden," the judge said.

"That's right, it was almost out of sight." Sam affirmed.

"It makes perfect sense, Carson," Andrew said, "Sarah could be stashed on the boat, with a guard, while the others go ashore to do their damage. We know he was here, earlier in the day, but is he back on the boat, I wonder."

"Enough conjecture!" Carson grabbed the phone, "I'll call the Coast Guard and see what they know. They haven't reported back."

"Well, it's fogged in now," Sam said, "and it seems there's a strong wind blowing."

"That works both ways; the boat won't be going anywhere, either," the judge said as he dialed the Coast Guard. He waited for the call to be answered, then said, "Commander Truax, Carson Justice, any progress finding the boat?" He listened intently, frowning. "Yes, I'm sure the weather is a huge factor. I just wanted to say that I have information about a possible location; Horse Island, at the dock. A cabin cruiser was spotted there this morning…let me check."

"Sam, did you happen to notice the name on the boat?"

Sam thought, then said, "There was a blanket or something hung out over the back where the name would be."

"That makes sense," he muttered. Then he told the commander. After listening to his response, Carson said, "Thanks, I'll call them; thanks for your help."

Looking at the others, he said, "Well, the Coast Guard out of Montauk had a cutter out all afternoon; they went up as far as Orient Point, but were advised to turn back when the fog came in, and now a Nor'easter is predicted! Anyway, they've turned it over to New Haven Coast Guard." He thought for a moment. "Actually,

New Haven has those new response boats made especially to withstand foul weather and high seas, so it's a good thing."

Carla, who'd been listening, said, "I've heard the latest weather report, and it's not good, but it might buy us some time. If the storm hits as expected, there won't be any small craft out there."

"I know, but I hate sitting here when we could be out there trying to find Sarah!" The judge seemed at a loss. "I'll call New Haven, see what they think. I mean, since we have a possible location…" He picked up the phone to call.

CHAPTER 54

Six people squeezed into the breakfast alcove at Rory's. Blake and Roland had joined the family for dinner. There was excitement in the air as they'd discussed the information they'd received from Sam. It was mind-boggling. Rory wished she'd been on the scene as bit by bit the mystery of Sarah's disappearance unfolded. They were close, very close, she knew.

"Looks like so much hinges on that guy Banda giving answers while under Sodium Pentothal; hope that's not a long shot," Blake said.

"Well, they have the Coast Guard out looking for the boat that was stolen out of Southampton," Roland said. "At least that's something already underway."

"And the main information source, Gonzales, has given up everything but Sarah's location," Marc put in. "Just doesn't make sense he'd give up much more sensitive information, but not Sarah's whereabouts, if he knew. I wonder about him."

"So many pieces coming together, but where is Sarah?" Blake wondered.

"It's got to gel soon, we have to be patient." Rory said.

Blake's cell buzzed. He grabbed it out of his pocket and looked at the name. "It's Sam!" Blake said, putting it on speaker.

Sam's voice filled the room, "We're almost there; if anyone wants to be in on the action, you'd better get up here, like now!"

***

Carlos woke with a start; he'd had a bad dream. It probably had to do with his feeling the police weren't far from catching up with them. Looking out the window, he noticed the fog was lifting; it was being driven by a fierce wind. He looked at Pedro in the back seat, sleeping peacefully. He'd had enough rest, Carlos thought resentfully. "Hey man, time to get up! We need to get outta here!" Carlos said with urgency.

"Huh? What?" Pedro was not quite with it.

"We gotta get you coffee or somethin' and get back to the boat."

Pedro sat up, suddenly alert, "Don't need coffee, man; we got Coke in the trunk, remember? Get it out, I'll be fine."

Carlos got out and opened the trunk, bringing a six-pack into the car. He handed a can to Pedro and took one for himself. "Man, it's blowing out there! We better make tracks to the boat before it gets any worse. You know where the dinghy is?"

Pedro thought for a moment, got out of the car, wincing as he put weight on his bum leg. He looked around, then got back into the car.

Pedro was chuckling, "Man, you said you didn't know where you were, but we ended up very close to where the dinghy is stashed; it's within walking distance. We're better off on foot anyway, since the cops are probably looking for a car." He pointed to an area that was still surrounded by fog. "When we left the boat, I remember looking over here and seeing these big-assed houses, and hoping they couldn't see the boat. But, we hid it well."

That's why he's in charge, thought Carlos, with a mixture of admiration and annoyance. "So, what? We just leave the car here?"

"Sure, why not? By the time it's found we'll be gone. Take what you need and leave the rest," Pedro said. He made sure that he had his pills, and he took a can of Coke.

"Ok," Carlos answered, "let's get out of here!"

***

The persistent sound of the phone next to Captain Rogers' bed finally woke him. He wasn't happy, but since he was on call, he had to answer. It was Commander Hastings, as he'd feared. He sat up straight, "Yes, Sir!" The captain listened as the commander told him there was an urgent case, and despite the weather, they needed a response boat in the water ASAP. He would brief him when Rogers got to headquarters. "I'm leaving now," he told the commander.

The call had woken his wife, Katie, and he looked at her with regret. "Sorry Kate, that was the commander; I have to go out."

Kate looked frightened. "But, Honey, it's been blowing hard all night; I can't believe you have to go out in this!"

"Sorry Babe, duty calls. Besides, these new boats are meant for really bad weather; we'll be fine." He bent over to kiss her and she clung to him.

"Be careful, I love you!" Kate said.

"Love you back!" he said as he left the room. He hurried, because he didn't want to hear Kate sobbing, and because the commander had given him orders.

As he drove to headquarters, thankfully not far, he noticed the fog was lifting as the nor'easter moved in. He didn't want to think about that. He'd been out in nor'easters before, and it wasn't easy. He'd had some pretty close calls, but had made it back safely. And he had captained one of the new forty-five foot response boats in good weather. They were designed to withstand eight-foot seas; this would be his chance to personally check it out in a nor'easter. Horse Island wasn't far; the only 'unknown' was the danger that might await them once they located the cabin cruiser.

CHAPTER 55

The patient, Geraldo Banda, had been injected with the Sodium Pentothal. Dr. Thatcher, along with four other medical personnel, stood around the gurney, waiting for the drug to take effect. The chief and his three officers were seated behind the medical staff. An interpreter stood to the side, in case Banda spoke entirely in Spanish.

All were watching intently. After a few moments, the chief noticed that Banda was drumming his fingers on the side of the gurney. He was afraid that a more violent outburst was soon to come. But, he was wrong. Banda was apparently drumming the beat to a song. He sang lustily and off-key, "La cucaracha, la cucaracha, bueno, bueno, bueno, blah, blah, blah," then he began laughing hysterically. "Can never remember the fuckin' words!" He continued to laugh, but soon the laughing tapered off.

Kerry Brighton led the questioning. "How are you feeling Geraldo?" she asked.

"Me? I'm good, light as a feather, never felt so good!"

"I'm glad to hear that," she said soothingly. "We'd like to ask you some questions, would that be ok?"

"Yeah, sure, verde." Kerry glanced at the interpreter, who gave the "go ahead" sign.

"How old are you, Geraldo?" Kerry continued.

"Ah, treinta y tres, Julio." Kerry looked towards the interpreter, who held up three fingers twice.

"And where do you live?" she inquired.

"Mexico," Banda replied.

The chief listened as more banal questions ensued. He understood that a baseline of neutral questions had to be established. So far, it seemed Banda was being truthful; he seemed relaxed. The chief looked at his watch, wondering how long it would take before they got to the answers they needed. He tried to keep his impatience at bay.

Dr. Baylor now introduced herself and asked if she could ask some questions.

Banda nodded, then said, "I'm getting thirsty…"

The doctor was handed a glass of water with a straw; she said to Banda, "Here's some water," and guided the straw to his mouth. He drank thirstily.

"Better?" the doctor asked.

"Yes, gracias!" he replied.

"You're welcome," the doctor said. "Now some questions?"

"Yes, I'm better," he answered.

"Who do you work for?" Dr. Baylor asked.

Banda winced, as if uncomfortable, then he relaxed and said, "Numero Uno."

"I see," the doctor answered neutrally, "and is he a good boss?"

Banda paused, then said, "He good if you do just what he say. If not…" Banda made a distasteful face.

"Not so good if you don't do as you're told." Dr. Baylor said.

"Cierto!" Banda answered with feeling. The translator mouthed "true."

"Do you like working for Numero Uno? And, by the way, what did you say his name was?"

"Numero Uno, all I know…" Banda answered.

"So, what are you doing here, in the United States?" she asked.

"Big job, here. If I do good, I go high up!" Banda smiled.

"So, you must be doing good," the doctor said.

He frowned, "Maybe, I don't remember what happened. I think not so good."

"Are you afraid of Numero Uno? Because you don't need to be; we won't tell him."

"Gracias, gracias!" he said earnestly.

"So, what did he want you to do?" The doctor persisted with her questioning.

"I'm tired, very tired..." His words trailed off as his eyes closed.

Kerry, the anesthesiologist, cut back on the SP drip. She turned to the chief and his team. "This is not unusual; we have to find out how high his tolerance is for the drug."

The level was adjusted and Geraldo's eyes fluttered open. The doctor asked, "Better now?"

"Yes, better, feeling good." He smiled at the doctor.

"Ok, so I asked you what you're doing in the US; why did Numero Uno send you here?"

"He trust me to watch Pedro and Carlos, make sure they do it right."

"And are they doing it right?" Dr. Baylor asked.

"They don't call me, I'm afraid..."

Chef Mayer and his team sat up interested in the new line of questioning. Maybe we're finally getting somewhere the chief thought.

"Afraid of what, Geraldo?" the doctor persisted.

"They don't do their job, I get in trouble." Banda sounded frightened.

"They botched something? What did they do wrong?" Dr. Baylor asked calmly.

"They didn't get Juan, big trouble! And the girl..."

"You mean the judge's daughter, Sarah?"

"Yeah..."

"Do you know where she is?" Dr. Baylor asked.

Finally, the chief thought, as he and his team sat virtually on the edge of their seats.

"She in the boat, with Jesus; Carlos and Pedro go to get Juan. They don' know for sure if he dead. If he not dead, then we all in beeeg trouble!"

"Where's the boat, Geraldo?" Dr. Baylor asked calmly.

"In the water, by the island…"

"What island, Geraldo?" she asked.

"I dun' know, big one, some animal…"

Chief Mayer looked at his staff, and whispered, "Horse Island." He was familiar with the Thimbles. He mouthed to Dr. Thatcher, "We need to go…"

The chief and his team got up quietly and Dr. Thatcher walked them out. "Thank you so much; this may have saved Sarah's life!"

CHAPTER 56

Rory and Marc were on the Jersey Turnpike, headed for Branford, and hopefully, a long-awaited reunion with Sarah. They were nearing New York City and had made good time so far. Marc was driving and staying at what he considered a safe speed, not too far over the speed limit.

"Not much traffic for NYC," Rory noted, making conversation.

"Well, that's good for us, but probably has to do with the predicted nor'easter, which is not so good for us. But, one step at a time," Marc said taking a deep breath. "Glad you thought to throw the slickers in the back, I'm thinking we'll need them," Marc added.

"It sounds like they have things under control, I mean, they know where Sarah probably is." She tried to sound hopeful, but her heart was racing and her stomach felt leaden.

"It's all in the details," Marc said cryptically.

"Meaning?" Rory asked.

"It ain't over 'til the fat lady sings. You know, Rory, we're very close and things could go wrong. I'm not sure I really trust that Gonzales, but I hope I'm wrong,"

"I know what you mean," Rory said. "They are putting a lot of hope in his information. But, Jeez, look at where we were three or four days ago! And let's not forget Sarah in this equation; she's smart and tough, and you know she's working to find a way out."

"You're right, Rory, Sarah's not a person to take this without a fight." Marc smiled.

"How about I turn on the radio?" Rory asked Marc. "I'd like to hear the latest on the weather." She found an all-weather station and didn't learn anything new. So she switched to classical music, which was relaxing.

***

Carlos and Pedro had managed to get to the dinghy without being seen. It hurt to walk, but Pedro had toughed it out, and his leg actually felt better. The walk had loosened it up.

Pedro looked out over the sound with fear in his gut. The fog was lessening, but a strong wind had moved in. Carlos had told him a nor'easter was predicted. The water was very choppy, with large swells Pedro figured were at least six-feet high. But they had no choice, they had to get back to the boat.

Pedro and Carlos hauled the boat down the slope from where it had been hidden. They'd just begun to shove off when they saw a cop car coming in their direction. They were far enough down the slope to be out of his sight, but instinctively, they ducked and hid in the reeds, holding onto the rope attached to the boat.

Pedro sank down even lower when he heard a car door slam, and heard pebbles crunching underfoot as someone walked toward them. They both froze.

"Alpha 2, this is Officer Phelps. No boats on the Sound; nothing going on around here. Surf is up, and I don't think a small boat could make it. I'll keep patrolling, and get back. Over and out."

The crunching resumed and then the car door shut. They heard the car drive off; it took a few moments until they were ready to try again.

Pedro said, "Good, they don't expect us to go out, so we'd better get underway now!" The cop's dismissive words made Pedro more driven to get back to the cabin cruiser off Horse.

Holding the skiff steady enough to get in wasn't easy, and both were drenched by the time they sat in the small boat. They used the oars until they were far enough from shore to start the engine. The roar of the wind and crashing of the sea also muffled the sound of the boat.

Out in the open water, the swells were enormous. Pedro decided to take a course down the middle of two parallel groups of islands, using the islands for cover and shelter from the driving winds. They weren't making much headway against the huge swells, but the sea between the islands was a bit calmer.

Pedro handed binoculars to Carlos, and said, "Keep an eye on the shore and let me know as soon as you see anything!"

Carlos took the glasses with a shaking hand. He stared into them and trained his gaze on the shoreline, which was slowly but steadily receding from sight.

Pedro continued on his course, staying close to the islands. He'd had some experience as a sailor, but never in seas like this. There wasn't much boat between him and the deep water of the Sound. Belatedly, he wondered if there were life vests in the boat, but he didn't have time to look now.

"See anything?" Pedro asked.

"Naw, just some cars pulling into the lot where we were; looks like they're going out to look at the barges docked by that factory. But no cops!"

"Good!" Pedro shouted to be heard over the wind. A giant wave splashed up and over the bow, drenching Pedro, who was already shivering. He used his shirt sleeve to wipe the salt water out of his eyes, which were stinging. He could hardly bear to open them, but he had to keep them on course. They were in danger of being flung about with no way to direct their course.

Pedro made a command decision, and let the current take them close enough to an island to pull up onto land. "I can't do this no more, man. We gotta' leave the boat and stay on the islands; they're close enough. We can swim between them."

"Swim? I can't swim, for fuck's sake! What am I gonna' do?"

"Fuck yourself for all I care! Did you notice that last wave just about took us under? It's not working, man! You don' wanna' go? So stay here, like the fuckin' pussy you are. I don't give a shit, I'm going!"

Carlos began frantically searching the boat for anything that could help him and finally seized upon a life-saving ring hanging on the side of the boat.

Pedro was far ahead of him on foot, when Carlos caught up, out of breath. He didn't speak, just walked a few steps behind.

***

Just as the chief and his team were leaving the hospital, he heard his cell buzz; it was the judge. "Yes, Sir, Mayer here." He listened to the judge. "He's right, you know; our guy said she was in a boat off a big island in the sound; I figured it was Horse."

The judge informed him: "Thank God you can confirm it! I've alerted the New Haven Coast Guard; it's in their jurisdiction now." The judge rang off.

"Well, our job here is done, for now," the chief told his officers.

"So now what?" Sharon asked.

"Well, call me crazy, but I think we've all earned a good night's sleep! I don't expect much to happen in this storm, and we can't get to Connecticut tonight in any case!"

CHAPTER 57

Chaos reigned in the judge's house, but it was good chaos. All of his staff were gathered, with the exception of the two guards on Gonzales, in the courthouse basement. He was a few hours away from freedom, if all went as planned.

Sam was tired, but the euphoria and adrenaline rush were keeping him going double-time. He couldn't wait for Rory and Marc to arrive and hoped the storm wouldn't affect their trip. His heart was full to bursting, thinking about having Sarah in his arms, soon.

He ticked off in his mind all of the things that were happening. He was pleased that his hunch about Horse Island gave credence to the information given by Banda under Sodium Pentothal. And the New Haven Coast Guard had been dispatched immediately. They didn't have far to go, and he figured they'd navigated through a nor'easter before, not that the storm should be minimized.

Sam wandered out to the patio. The wind was so strong it took his breath away. The patchy fog was dissipating with the wind, but the pre-dawn darkness obliterated the Sound. He said a small prayer the Coast Guard would get through safely. Then, he hurried back inside, shivering. The fire in the living room grate calmed Sam and he headed for it.

The front door opened and Nate walked in. The judge welcomed him warmly, then said to Sam, "Come meet Nathan!"

Sam went over to shake Nate's hand, but instead gave him a bear hug. "Well, you started this dialogue, so hopefully you'll get to see the conclusion, and soon!"

***

Sarah and Jesus had found some canned goods and eating utensils, so had pulled together a semblance of dinner. More importantly, they'd also found bottled water. The house was a bit eerie as darkness fell, but they'd found a flashlight and some candles; lighting them made it feel cozy. She'd decided against building a fire in the fireplace; the gale-force winds could sweep down the chimney. So, they made do with blankets that were draped over the couches.

Before dark, Sarah and Jesus had explored the house from top to bottom; it was in decent shape and obviously was used, but probably not on a regular basis. It was her understanding that Yale used the land around the house—where birds and other wildlife flourished—as an outdoor classroom.

The cupola, at the very top of the house had given a breathtaking panorama of the surrounding area in daylight, before the fog had rolled in. Jesus was up there now, hoping to be able to see any approaching water craft. The pea-soup fog had hampered their view a few hours ago and the darkness now made it virtually impossible to see anything.

The wind was howling and the waves were crashing. Sarah had lived in this area long enough to know the signs of a nor'easter. But she hadn't told Jesus; he had enough to worry about. Sarah was tamping down her fear, but just being in this familiar place, gave her the courage she needed. She could visualize the way home. The almost overwhelming anxiety she'd endured since her capture had faded since Pedro and Carlos had left the boat. Funny, she thought, it had been only a few days since their departure. She wondered now what had happened to them. Had they been caught? Were the on the way back here to kill her? She wouldn't let that happen to her or to Jesus; he had saved her and she would repay the debt.

Sarah could hear Jesus coming down the steps. He came into the candlelit kitchen and sat down next to her at the table.

"Can't see nothing," he said, "too dark, and the wind, she blow hard!"

Sarah smiled at Jesus; he'd come so far with his English, and her Spanish was getting better. They'd found a way to communicate with each other. Jesus was a very sensitive young man. She wondered how a man like him survived in the soulless jungle that was the cartel. Maybe many young people felt that was the only way to make a living; it was part of the Mexican culture. Of course, Jesus had a personal reason for joining; he was biding his time until he could carry out a vendetta against Pedro.

"So, do you think they will come back?" Sarah asked Jesus.

"They will, Pedro fuerte." Jesus flexed his muscles to illustrate.

"He may be physically strong," Sarah muttered, almost to herself, "but he's morally bankrupt."

Jesus looked confused. Sarah clarified, "Pedro not a good man!"

Jesus readily agreed, "El diablo!" He pulled the pistol from his belt and said, "Jesus ready for Pedro. He very bad man."

Sarah put her hand on Jesus's arm. "If he does come, you be careful, cuidado!"

Jesus shook his head, "He must not hurt you!"

***

Captain Rogers was in his 45-foot response boat with his first mate, James Hunter. He'd requested James because he was solid, had experience and would stay strong. They'd just been cleared to shove off and the boat nosed out into Long Island Sound. The waters were choppy, but Joe Rogers had been in worse, and in lesser crafts than this one, which was state-of-the-art. "Not so bad," Rogers said to Hunter.

"Right, I've seen it rougher. Fog is clearing, I guess that's good, and we don't have far to go. So, what are we looking for at Horse?" James asked.

"Looking for a stolen cabin cruiser, anchored off Horse Island, at the dock on the north side," Joe answered.

"But, hey, there's got to be more to it than that for Hastings to send us and the sharpshooters out in a nor'easter!" James protested.

"Of course," Joe agreed. "But I had to press the issue with Hastings, you know what a tight-ass he is! We're out here in the storm, we have a right to know what we're getting into. So, he told me there was a girl kidnapped off the beach out in Gardiner's Bay, last week. A boat was reported stolen some days later, and the assumption is the girl is being held on the stolen boat. And just such a boat was reported out by Horse. The perps, as many as three, should be considered armed and dangerous."

"Sorry, but this can't be just any girl!" James sputtered.

"No shit! But we're left to piece it together. Ok, she was taken out in East Hampton; that tells us she's either rich or a celebrity."

"Haven't heard anything about a kidnapping..." James said.

"Which tells us, it's been hushed-up, I mean my imagination could go wild with that!"

"What orders did Hastings give you?" James asked.

"To take prisoners, and free the girl, oh, and to call him and report our progress." Rogers frowned. "What an asshole he is! Whoever the perps are, might be more of a threat than the weather, to be honest."

James smiled at that, "Yeah, you're right, these new boats sure make it's easier to take on a nor'easter!"

A huge wave crashed over the bow, and conversation stopped; James went to see if there was any damage. "She's ok, Captain, you might want to slow her down a bit..."

Rogers pulled back on the throttle, let the response boat go with the waves for a bit. This would be slow going, but they would get there, he was sure. It was the reception they might get that worried him.

***

Pedro and Carlos were fighting to stay upright with every ounce of strength they had. The swells had nearly knocked them down on a few occasions, but they were staying as close to the ground as they could, hoping for shelter from the winds and cover from any other boats.

Looking through the driving rain was damn-near impossible, but Pedro knew he had no choice but to move on. If he didn't finish this job, the cartel would finish him. It had already slipped almost beyond his reach. But they were slowly gaining ground, and soon Horse Island would be in view. The water was choppy at best and the slanting rain cut like hundreds of tiny knives. Pedro had forgotten the pain in his leg. Visibility was so poor they'd been running on guess work; that, and his memory. He'd been counting the islands as they passed, and if he was right, they would go by two more before they arrived at Horse. He was visualizing the trip over from Horse Island a few days ago. True, it appeared different with the raging storm. But the weather, as awful as it was, had its advantages; they would be more difficult to make out.

CHAPTER 58

Captain Newsome, of the New Haven Police force, had been awakened from a deep sleep by Commander Hastings, not one of his favorite people. Giving Newsome only a thimble full of information, he'd ordered him to bring at least two cars to the Coast Guard Station. They were to provide back-up to the Coast Guard, in the event some prisoners needed to be processed. He didn't awaken his wife; he knew better after all these years of midnight phone calls and hasty exits.

Leaving a note for her on the kitchen table, he exited the house, his mood as foul as the weather that awaited him. He cursed as he made his way through the stinging rain, driven by a fierce wind. He was going out in a nor'easter, at the behest of that fuckin' Hastings, whose ass would be warm and dry in his office.

Arriving at police headquarters, he was surprised to find it a beehive of activity. He grabbed some coffee and asked his lieutenant, "What the fuck is going on? Did Hastings call everyone?"

"It's bigger than that; we've got a Federal judge coming over here!"

***

Pedro was almost certain the island ahead was Horse. It was big and heavily forested, as he remembered it. He was afraid he was seeing a mirage, that the pelting rain had skewed his perception. He blinked and looked hard; it had to be Horse Island. He motioned for Carlos to look ahead.

Thank God, Pedro thought; he didn't know how they'd made it. Limping to the edge, Pedro prepared for the short swim to Horse. He heard Carlos splashing behind him. Adrenaline took over as he neared his goal. Through the rain and surf, Pedro could make out the shape of the cabin cruiser; it was still there.

Pedro pulled himself up onto the dock and just sat, head in hands catching his breath. Carlos was still splashing in the water. He soon joined Pedro and the two of them made their way carefully to the boat.

***

Rory and Marc were relieved to be off I-95, and heading for the judge's house in Branford.

The wind-driven rain had been dogging them for the past half-hour. There was no doubt the nor'easter was coming through. The weather reports were somewhat conflicting, as usual. Some stations forecasted a low-grade storm, while others predicted it to be 'moderate,' with winds of 30 knots. Whatever that all meant, Rory thought, she just knew they were in for nasty weather She prayed it would all be over soon; Sarah's rescue was paramount. The storm she could deal with.

Rory looked at the map, and the written instructions. "We're about twenty minutes out. Once you get off Rt.1, I'll direct you. The judge lives on the Sound," she told Marc.

"Good, good," he said tersely, focusing on the road ahead.

CHAPTER 59

Among the many details Carson needed to take care of, one was to call the bureau chief at the FBI. He'd known Bill Sayres for years and they were colleagues, if not fast friends. The hour being late, Carson called Sayres's cell.

A very sleepy Sayres answered the phone with a wariness no doubt learned from experience. "Sorry to awaken you Bill, Carson here." He waited for recognition to take place, and it did, quickly.

"No problem, Carson; the cartel case heating up?" he asked, sounding suddenly alert.

"It is, and I'm afraid if we don't give you all the Intel now, your kingpins in Mexico might just disappear. So far, it's been under wraps, but it may blow open tonight."

"Thanks, thanks for keeping me current. What do you have?" Sayres asked.

"I think you'll need to write this down," Carson replied. "It's quite a lot; in fact, I think we've hit the mother lode!"

"Ok, then, I'm ready!" Sayres was all business and enthusiastic about the news.

Carson gave out a dozen or so names of men at the top of the Corizon Cartel. Then he added, "These were all from one source, Juan Gonzales, who himself was close to the top. Your people on the ground should know if there's a credibility issue. He's still in our custody, until we've gotten Sarah back safely," he couldn't control the hitch in his voice, "and verified his information. Only then will we place him and his mother into the WPP."

"All right, Carson, I think I need to get on this right away. I hope your daughter is found soon," he added before he hung up.

That brought a tear to Carson's eye, recognition from this tough-as-nails man that Sarah's abduction had taken a toll on him. He was being silly, he thought to himself. But then he had to acknowledge that it had indeed taken a huge toll on him. And, God willing, Sarah would be returned to him. He vowed to do his best to make up for lost time.

Shaking his head, he moved on to the next item on his list. It was difficult to concentrate, with the loud conversation in the room. He looked over at Sam, and noticed he had a look of apprehension on his face that matched his own feelings.

***

Outside of the judge's home, Rory and Marc had been stopped at the gate. Two armed officers, a man and a woman, came to either side of the car, asking what their business was and wanting proof of identity.

As Marc complied, he was struck with the gravity of the situation and by the power the judge wielded. He looked up at the large, old stone house, surrounded by a luxurious lawn with very large trees. Around the perimeter of the entire property was a high, wrought-iron fence, now locked.

The officers radioed the judge to inform him of his visitors, then the gate swung open and they were ushered through.

As they drove up the long driveway, Rory glanced at Marc, saying, "It's pretty secure, isn't it?"

"It's good to know the judge is so well protected."

At that moment, Sam rushed out of the front door, making a beeline for the car. He opened Marc's door and gave him a bear hug. "We're almost there, my friend, so glad you made it ok."

Then, Sam went around to Rory's door and helped her out, catching her in a hug. "I'm so glad you're both here! Let's get you in, out of this miserable weather!"

Sam escorted them into the large, open foyer, filled with tapestries and antiques.

The judge, Marc assumed it was he, came towards them, first offering his hand to Rory, and then to Marc. "Thanks for all your support. With your help, we're very close to finding her; we have all of the information we need. The Coast Guard and local authorities are on it. Now we wait for it to happen."

"It will, Judge, I have a very strong feeling about this," Rory said.

"I understand you are like a mother to Sarah," Carson said, turning to Rory with a smile.

"I think that's true; I wasn't really aware of it until this happened…" Rory answered.

"Funny how that works; I wasn't aware of how important Sarah is to me, and I am sure she doesn't know," he said, tearing up.

Rory bit her lip, to keep tears at bay, and nodded.

"Come," Carson said, pulling himself together, "meet some of the people who have been working this case since the beginning."

***

Later, after everyone else had left to go to the Coast Guard station, Carson and Sam sat chatting. The judge had a few loose ends to tie up before he joined the others and, eager as he was to see Sarah, Sam had offered to stay with him.

It pleased Carson that Sam had stayed; he had been impressed so far with Sam and understood what Sarah saw in him.

After a few minutes of talk, Sam said, "I should let you get back to your work. And I need to use the bathroom." He left the room to go to the powder-room.

"Sam," Carson called, "the mud room is next to the powder room; why don't you grab yourself a slicker? I think you'll need it."

"Thanks, Carson, I'll do that."

Carson went back to his work, checking things off his list. The phone rang. It was Sayres, from the Bureau.

"Carson," the judge thought Sayres's voice sounded strained. "I hate to tell you this, but the only Intel that was accurate involved the men in the kidnap operation; not a shred of the info on the kingpins was accurate. I don't know what kind of game Juan is playing, but I'm sorry…"

"I see," said the judge as he hung up. He put his head in his hands. He didn't look up when he heard someone enter the room, assuming it was Sam.

CHAPTER 60

Rogers was at the wheel as the response boat made its way east across Long Island Sound towards the Thimble Islands. An identical craft was not far behind.

"This boat really rules the waves," Rogers said to his first-mate, Hunter. Noticing that Hunter was looking at the control board, he asked, "What course are we taking to Horse?"

Hunter studied the sophisticated control board, talking out loud as he plotted the course. "I think we need to go in south of the Thimbles… then, let's see. We have a choice of getting to Horse either from its East or West end. I think we have more protection from the West, and Cooper's boat can come around East. That way, when we go in, the second boat will stay to the East and out of sight, until and unless we need them."

"Sounds like a good plan. Why don't you radio Coop, and make sure he's 'on board,' pun intended," Rogers said.

Hunter smiled at the joke, and then radioed Greg Cooper's craft. He got Coop's first mate and told him the plan.

"We were just talking about it and that seems good to us. So, we just wait between Horse and Pot Islands, while you guys go in? Should we begin to close in, as you approach?" the first-mate asked.

"What do you think, Joe?" James asked.

"Rogers here," the captain said, as he took the radio. "Let's decide that as we begin our approach; we'll stay in radio contact, and in fact, we'll leave the radio on. But it's not a bad idea to slowly move in the direction of the dock."

Hunter took back the radio, and said, "That's the plan; over and out."

***

Carlos and Pedro just sat on the deck, exhausted, while they surveyed the damage the storm had done already. Everything that had been on deck was either drenched or had washed over. Pedro took a swig of Coke with one of his pain pills. He was too tired to go below deck, so he pushed the door open and called, "Jesus, get up here!"

There was no response from below, so he yelled louder, but still got no answer. Alarmed, he said to Carlos, "Go get Jesus and bring him up here!"

"Just give me a minute, for fuck sake! We just about got killed out there."

He sounded resentful, Pedro thought. "Get your ass up and get Jesus; I did most of the work out there, you fuckin' whiney bitch!" Pedro lashed out.

Carlos said nothing, but got up slowly and took his time getting below deck.

Pedro listened as he heard Carlos throwing things and slamming doors. He yelled down to Carlos, "What the fuck you doin'? Just bring Jesus up here, now!"

There was silence below. Pedro moved, with less pain now, to the steps and looked down into the darkness. He saw Carlos emerge and walk slowly up the steps.

The look on his face was unreadable. "What the fuck?" Pedro said.

"Gone, nobody here…" Carlos said.

"What do you mean?" Pedro asked. Pushing past him, he went down the steps. He looked for himself, in every possible hiding place. Then he bellowed, "That fuckin' pussy Jesus jumped ship!"

As he rejoined Carlos on deck, he said, "They can't have gone far, we gotta' go find them!"

The words were hardly out of his mouth, when a large boat emerged from the gloom, headed straight for them, foghorn blaring.

***

Looking up, Carson was appalled, but not really surprised, to see Gonzales, with one of the marshals, Corey Davis. His arms were around Davis's neck and a gun was at his head. Davis was handcuffed, no doubt with his own cuffs.

It came to Carson in a flash, how naive they'd all been to believe that a cartel boss would crack for any reason. Carson felt foolish, and despondent. How would they get Sarah back now?

Juan Gonzales was grinning widely. "You really didn't think I'd give up mes amigos; they're my life. I cannot live in USA. Now we do things my way; you do as I say, exactly, or you will not see your precious Sarah, again!"

The judge managed not to glance towards him, but he saw Sam in the hallway behind Gonzales, wearing a bright yellow slicker. Then Sam receded from sight, making no sound. Carson was sure Sam would do the right thing. He gave his full attention to Juan, hoping to keep him talking as long as possible, playing to his considerable ego.

"What happened to Taylor?" the judge asked, referencing the other guard.

"I only needed one guy, so this one got lucky!" Juan answered.

"You didn't answer my question," the judge answered calmly.

"No, and I ain't gonna'! Don't you get it yet? You not in charge; I got this," he waved his gun. "And him," Juan said, pushing the gun into the side of Davis' face. "Like I just tell you, we doin' it my way!"

***

Sam reacted quickly, but carefully, to the scene he'd witnessed. He had to do something and it had to be now. He found his way outside and ran towards the front of the house to where the guards were supposed to be. Looking around frantically, he noticed the gate was wide open, but he didn't see the guards anywhere. The wind had picked up and the rain was hitting his face like tiny knives.

Seeing something that looked like a mound, he ran to the hedges, walking quickly along the inside perimeter. He saw a heap on the ground. Looking closer, he could tell it was two bodies, one on top of the other, a man and a woman. They were the marshals who had guarded the gate. He checked the woman for a pulse, and found a slight one. The other marshal's pulse was stronger. They were handcuffed together. Sam tried to revive them, speaking to them quietly, but urgently. "The judge is being held captive in the house; you need to wake up!" He slapped their faces and shook them.

He spoke to the marshal with the stronger pulse; Sam could see his name tag: Walter Aldridge. "Walter, wake up! We need to save the judge."

Walter's eyes fluttered open, but were unfocused. Then they fluttered closed. He was unresponsive.

Sam looked for a gun, but found none in their holsters. Frantic, he checked around the area, looking under the hedges. Then something caught his eye, metal flashing in the light of the street lamps. He looked closer and found that a gun was caught in the hedge, and he grabbed it. Checking for ammunition, he found the chamber empty. "Fuck!" he muttered to himself. He decided to check the marshals for ammo, and found clips on Walter's belt. He took two clips, placing one in the gun and shoved the second clip into his pocket. Before leaving the guards, he checked to see if either was coming around. Both were still out. At least they had rain gear on to protect them.

His thoughts went to Sarah; it was only because of her that he knew anything about guns. He smiled and vowed to himself that he would find a way to get her back.

Checking his cell to dial 911, Sam saw no bars; he had no cell service in this area.

He crept back towards the house, out of options. Sam decided he had to let Gonzales believe he was in charge, and wait patiently for him to make a mistake.

CHAPTER 61

In the basement of the courthouse, inside the cell, Alfred Taylor was coming around. His mind was fuzzy. He tried to remember what had happened and why he was locked in the cell. He hurt all over, his lip was split and bleeding; he felt like shit. But what had happened? He focused on trying to remember. It took a few minutes for the events to replay in his mind.

Davis had gone to the bathroom. While he was out, Gonzales had started coughing, then appeared to be gagging. When he'd asked him if he was ok, Juan looked at Taylor, red-faced, and gasped, "Water!"

Without thinking, Taylor had reacted quickly, gotten water, and handed it through the opening in the cell door. In a flash, Juan had Taylor's arm in a vice grip, pulling him close. He put a shank up against Taylor's neck until he drew blood, then said, "Gimme' the keys!"

Taylor held on, trying to buy time. Juan increased the pressure on his neck until it became unbearable; he dropped the keys and fell to the floor, holding his bloody neck.

Like lightning, Juan grabbed the keys, opened the cell, stepped out and dragged Taylor inside. He punched and kicked him, took the bottle of pain pills out of Taylor's pocket, then shoved some pills in Taylor's mouth. Juan held Taylor's mouth closed until he had to swallow.

It was all too clear now. That fucker, Gonzales; he'd demanded the pain medication, noticed who kept the pills and then lulled them into complacency, pretending to be cooperative and doling out what must've been misinformation.

Taylor got slowly to his feet, found the alarm button and pressed it. Then he sat down to wait.

***

Pedro was in the shelter of the doorway when he spotted the large boat; he wasted no time reacting, despite his wounded leg. He ducked back inside the cabin, closing and locking the door, even as he heard the booming voice through the megaphone. "This is the Coast Guard. Put your hands up, drop your weapons!"

Pedro figured he had seconds to get away. He punched out a window, slid out and onto the dock. Staying in the shadows, he hunched down and scrambled over the rocks until he reached the forest, then he ran as fast as his leg would allow, ducking behind trees, going in a zig-zag pattern. He had to find Jesus and Sarah; he needed hostages; they were his only hope.

***

Sam was preternaturally calm as he walked toward the house. The gun was in his right hand, against his leg. He knew he had to prevail if he wanted to save Sarah and her father.

Entering the house quietly, Sam stopped to listen. He could hear Juan talking. The judge was no doubt trying to stall him, and Juan seemed more than happy to boast of his exploits.

Sam crept down the hall to the edge of the doorway. From where he stood, he could see the judge's reflection in the mirror. Juan was standing close to the judge, still holding the guard in a headlock. He was showing Carson a tattoo on his hand, saying "See this CC3; you know what that means? Of course you don't! I'm numero tres in the Corizon Cartel, they need me!"

"And the others on this mission, the ones whose names you gave us?" Carson asked calmly.

"They are nothing, nada. It is what you Americanos call 'collateral damage,' I believe. They are used to get me free; that is all."

"What will happen to your mother?" the judge asked.

"She will come with me to Mexico, or not. Where is she?" he asked.

"I don't know where she is," the judge said evenly, "that's why they call it a 'safe house.'"

"But you know who knows and you will find out!"

"That depends on getting Sarah back. Surely you see that's a fair trade; my daughter for your mother. I won't do a thing, until I know Sarah is safe."

"But, you see who has the gun!" Juan reminded him loudly.

"You heard my terms; I could care less about your gun. You can kill me; without Sarah, I have no life, no reason to live. But then, you have no way of getting your mother."

"You do not tell me what to do!" Juan bellowed as he lunged towards the judge.

***

Alfred Taylor was relieved when he saw the face of one of the night security officers. Alfred gave him a weak smile. "Thanks for coming quick," he said.

"Man, what happened to you? Where's Davis?" the guard asked, looking around.

"Juan got the drop on me while Davis was in the bathroom; I got knocked out. When I woke up, they were both gone. I assume he took Corey with him. But I have no idea what his plan is."

"But, how'd he get out? I was watching the cameras, didn't see or hear anything.

"Well, assuming he took Davis, that's how he got out; he used his security card. And he probably took Corey's gun to use as leverage. Let's have a look around and see what we can find out. You got a phone on you? We gotta' call the chief."

***

Captain Rogers stood on the deck of the response boat with his first mate who had a gun trained on the suspect. The sharpshooters were already in the water, the pontoon boat headed to the dock. Carlos was standing on the deck of the cabin cruiser with his arms raised. He wore a defiant look, but said nothing.

The captain asked, through the megaphone, "Where is the other man? There were two of you."

Carlos said nothing, his facial expression and body language telling the story of his hatred and rage.

When the gunmen had climbed onto the cabin cruiser, Rogers said, "Search below decks." One man trained his rifle on Carlos, while the other broke open the door and went down to the cabin.

A few minutes later, the man came up, "No one there!" he shouted over the howling wind to the captain.

"You'll have to go into the woods. He spoke into the radio, saying, "Coop, send your men into the woods to back up my guys. One bad guy on foot, one female victim, and maybe another perp."

Captain Rogers turned his attention back to Carlos. "If you tell us nothing, we have no reason to go easy on you. If you cooperate...Do you understand English?" Rogers asked.

"I tell you nothing!" Carlos spat out.

"OK, your choice," Rogers said. Addressing the gunman, Rogers said, "Cuff him and bring him over."

CHAPTER 62

Rory was standing with the others inside the Coast Guard station. The New Haven police were outside in three squad cars. The CG commander, Hastings—in radio contact with the lead boat—was aware of what was going on in real time. He was, of course, inside a glassed-in office, so none of the information he received was passed on.

Perhaps if the judge were here, Rory thought, they would have more access. Looking at her watch, Rory grew alarmed; it had been nearly an hour since they'd left the judge's house. He and Sam were planning to join up shortly.

Rory grabbed Marc, standing beside her, and whispered, "It's been an hour since we left the judge; don't you think he should be here by now? Why don't you call Sam?"

"Already did," Marc said; "I've tried him twice and got no answer; I've been concerned, too. Should we call the judge's house?" He asked. "On second thought, we should check with Milano first."

"Good call," Rory answered. They went outside to find the marshals. The wind and rain took her breath away, but she was at least protected by her rain gear.

As Rory and Marc walked towards Carla and Andrew, they noticed the marshals speaking with each other, urgently, Rory thought.

The marshals looked up as the two approached. Marc said, "We're concerned that the judge isn't here yet…"

"So are we," Milano answered. "We're headed back, shouldn't have left him…"

***

Sarah and Jesus were up in the cupola again. The flashlight they'd found had been helpful, especially as they navigated the winding staircase. As dawn was approaching, they turned the flashlight off. They could see the islands more clearly, despite the driving rain and dark skies. There had been movement out on the sound, and lights flashing. They had also heard what sounded like a fog horn, and other, muffled, unclear voices. They looked at each other in alarm.

"Something's happening," Sarah said. "I just hope it's the good guys in charge. We need to be ready for anything!"

Jesus held up his gun, "I'm ready," he said. "And so are you," he said, handing her a revolver.

Sarah thanked him and hoped it would really be that simple. She knew she had to stay alert. If Pedro were on the loose, there was no telling what could happen. If he'd arrived back at the boat and found them gone, he would be enraged. She knew to expect the worst.

"I'm going down to check the doors and windows," Sarah said to Jesus. "You stay here and watch. I'll call you if I need you."

Sarah went slowly down the curved stairway. Once in the living room, she grabbed one of the lit candles and blew the others out. Walking from room to room with the candle, she checked the windows and then pulled the curtains tightly closed.

She and Jesus had wedged a piece of old wood over the window they'd broken to get in. It wouldn't take much to get in that way, Sarah thought belatedly. Still, she pulled the curtains closed. Then she wrapped a blanket around her and settled anxiously on the living room couch to wait.

As soon as Juan lunged at the judge, Sam made his move. In two swift strides, he reached Gonzales and his hostage. He pulled Davis free, pushing him to the floor. Juan, surprised, wheeled on Sam and fired. Sam ducked in time, going for Juan's legs.

Gonzales went down and Sam was on him, trying to shake his gun loose. Juan fired his gun wildly. Sam shouted, "Carson, get down!" He continued to struggle with Juan, noticing the older man was incredibly strong, and feeling his own energy flag.

Davis came to his senses, moved the judge out of the room to safety, then came back to help Sam. Just as Davis reached Sam, Juan freed himself from Sam's grip, stumbled, and then took off running, gun in hand. Sam got off a few shots, then went after Juan.

"I'll stay with the judge, keep him safe!" Davis called to Sam.

"And call 911; the guards outside need help," Sam called back as he ran full out, trying to keep up with the fading figure in front of him. Thinking as he ran, Sam assumed Juan must have the car he came in, probably an official car, stashed somewhere. And maybe even an accomplice. He had to keep Juan from reaching anything or anyone who could help him escape.

Reaching the front lawn, Sam looked around, seeing no movement, trying to focus through the driving rain and howling wind. He didn't have time to check on the marshals, still in a mound under the hedges. For a moment, he considered that Gonzales might take them as hostages, but with the two cuffed together, it would be unwieldy, he thought.

Sam caught his breath as he waited, watching for movement. He must be out here, Sam thought, Juan hadn't been that far ahead of him; but he was very cunning, and capable of anything.

***

Out on the first response boat, Captain Rogers directed his armed colleague to take the captive, Carlos, below deck and keep him under guard. James Hunter accompanied the man, Skipper, because he had a gut feeling that Carlos was about to blow.

Hunter frisked Carlos from top to bottom, finding a switchblade shoved into his boot. He'd expected as much, and thought there might be more weapons, so he strip-searched him; the ultimate humiliation for a man like Carlos. And Carlos fought back, impeding Hunter's efforts at every turn.

James refused to take the bait and strong arm the man, so he stepped back until Carlos settled himself. Truth was, he hated doing these searches; they were so invasive. He did them only when he believed they were absolutely necessary. And this was one such time. He would do it thoroughly.

"Ok, Carlos, we're almost done here. Bend over and spread em."

Finding nothing, he returned him to Skipper's custody. "He's all yours."

"Thanks!" Skipper replied.

"He's one who needs watching." Hunter said. "I have to talk to the captain, be right back."

Speaking briefly with the captain, Hunter was half-way down the ladder when he saw Carlos attempt to head butt Skipper, knocking him off balance.

Hunter came up quickly behind Carlos and put him in a headlock, while Skip got himself back up. "Thanks, man, didn't see that coming…"

"Ok, Carlos, you've about used up our good will for the day, so we need to get you into the hold." Hunter marched him, with a gun at his back, to the holding area, which was a small room. As Hunter was pushing him through the door, Carlos turned around and begged, "Please, they will kill me in jail!"

"Sorry, pal, you might want to think about cooperating with the authorities. Your choice," he said as he closed the door.

CHAPTER 63

Andrew and Carla were speeding back to the judge's house, Carla at the wheel. "We really let our guard down," Carla said. "I guess we got caught up in the moment, figured the danger was over, and got complacent. Damn!"

"Yeah," Milano agreed, "we fucked up. Let's hope Carson is ok; I can't even begin to imagine what has gone wrong, but I feel it in my gut. I know it's something bad."

Andrew pulled out his cell phone, saying to Carla, "I'm gonna' call Walter first." The phone rang until it went to the recorded message. "This can't be good," he said quietly. "The gate is probably not guarded."

"We're almost there; think we should use the siren?" Carla asked Andrew.

"No, we should go in quietly, and try to assess what we can first." Andrew advised.

As Carla turned the corner to the judge's house, the first thing she noticed was the front gate hanging open, with no guards in sight. "Fuck, this is so not good! What should I do?"

"Slow down and pull over, we can get a better look on foot. Ok, let's go in!" Andrew got out of the car, closing the door quietly.

Carla did the same, and walked behind Andrew, slowing creeping towards the house.

As they went through the open gate, Carla looked to her left, hearing a small sound. She touched Andrew's shoulder, and pointed to what looked like a large mound, near the hedges.

After a whispered discussion, Andrew went towards the hedges, while Carla scanned the area.

Soon, Andrew motioned for Carla to come over. With one last glance around, she ran to join Andrew. When she reached him, she saw Walter, one of the guards, sit up, rubbing his head.

"Man, I dunno' what hit me! My mind is all fuzzy. Is Ellie ok?" Walter asked.

Carla went to the other marshal, Ellen, rubbing her arms, and feeling for a pulse. "She's still out, but she's got a pulse. Let's get you guys inside. Lucky you had on rain gear, with this storm cranking up."

Carla assisted Walter, as Andrew carried Ellen.

As they were approaching the house, the blare of sirens sounded close-by. An ambulance soon pulled up in the driveway.

Carla and Andrew took the injured guards to the ambulance and told them what they knew. Carla gave the medics her card and asked they call her with information.

Andrew gave a sigh of relief, "Well, someone had the sense to call the ambulance; let's go inside and see what we can find out."

They decided to go around the back of the house to make a less conspicuous entry. The side door was ajar, so they went in, looking at each other in alarm.

They were checking each room, finding no sign of anyone, when, suddenly the door to the library opened, and Corey Davis walked out.

"Thank God you're here!" Davis said.

"What the fuck, man? Where's the judge?" Milano exclaimed.

***

Sam had seen movement at the far corner of the gate. He watched as a figure darted through what must have been an opening in the gate. Of course, Sam thought, with a sinking feeling; Gonzales had gotten lucky.

Sam wasted no time running to the opening in the gate. While keeping an eye on the retreating figure of Gonzales, Sam was barely able to squeeze through the opening left by a rusting piece of metal.

He still had Juan in his sights and was closing in. He heard sirens not far behind, and prayed help would come soon.

Juan had obviously heard the sirens; he moved into the shadows and kept himself low.

Sam continued to run in Juan's direction, hoping he wouldn't be seen. He slipped on the rain-slick pavement, and fell to his knees. Just that quickly, Juan was out of sight.

Sam couldn't stop now, not with that maniac loose, and so close! He got up, and limping a bit, went to the area where he'd last seen Juan. This was obviously a wealthy area; there were many huge houses, with large, manicured yards. Where to start looking?

Scanning the area, he tried to think like Juan, although it was a stretch. Juan obviously needed transportation. He was unlikely to steal a car from one of these big houses, houses that were bound to have cameras.

At that moment, a motion detector light went on, three houses from where Sam stood. Bathed in bright light and standing like a deer in headlights stood Juan Gonzales.

CHAPTER *64*

Sarah heard a noise in the back of the house; it sounded like someone was trying to break in. She walked to the stairwell leading to the cupola, meeting Jesus, on his way down. She said quietly, "I think someone's trying to break in; stay hidden until I need you, please!"

Jesus nodded and stayed in the recesses of the stairwell.

As Sarah had expected, a loud crash exploded from the back. She looked at Jesus and put her finger to her lips.

She took her seat on the couch and waited for the inevitable. She was as ready as she could be.

Soon, she saw Pedro—she was sure it was him—creeping in the shadows, looking around the room, waving his gun at objects. It would've been amusing if this were not a life and death situation. But, for some reason, Sarah felt calm. She was ready to confront her abductor.

Pedro continued to walk around; now she could see clearly that it was him. And soon, his eyes would adjust to the darkness and he would see her. But that was part of the plan. She held the gun Jesus had given her tightly to her side.

She could kill him now; it would be so easy. But, no, Sarah did not want her hatred for this man to push her into acting prematurely, or worse yet, stooping to his level.

When Pedro finally spotted her, he was right in front of her. He flinched in surprise.

"Hello, Pedro, I've been waiting for you," Sarah said calmly.

Pedro gasped as if he'd seen a ghost, then he tried to grab her. Sarah ducked under his arm and scuttled across the floor. She was behind him now, and gave a sharp elbow to the back of his leg.

Pedro howled in pain, as she hit his wounded leg, and he went down hard. Sarah was on him in an instant, putting the gun to his head. "Drop it," she ordered.

"I like it when you're on top," Pedro said suggestively, thrusting his pelvis.

"Drop it now, you disgusting pig!" Sarah yelled, feeling sick.

Pedro sat up quickly, batting the gun out of Sarah's hand. Laughing, he said, "Is that the best you can do?" He grabbed her arm, twisting it behind her until she grimaced in pain. She would not give him the satisfaction of hearing her scream.

"Once more, for old time's sake?" Pedro said as he flipped her on her back. Putting his gun on the floor beside her, he unzipped his pants.

As Sarah struggled, a bright light flashed on Pedro.

"Let her go, NOW!" boomed the voice of an enraged Jesus.

Sarah took advantage of Pedro's surprise to push his gun out of reach.

Pedro pulled Sarah up and put her in a headlock, trying to see who his opponent was.

"Let her go!" Jesus said calmly. "What kind of man hides behind a helpless woman? That is not the Corizon way," Jesus taunted Pedro.

"Jesus, is that you? You bitch! You let Sarah escape!"

"No, Pedro, I helped Sarah escape," he corrected. "I have the gun; last time, let Sarah go!"

"Make me!" Pedro snorted derisively.

Jesus shined the flashlight directly into Pedro's eyes, momentarily blinding him. He pulled Pedro up by the front of his shirt. Sarah quickly rolled out of Pedro's grasp to free herself, as Jesus fought the larger Pedro.

Though slight, Jesus seemed to have the upper hand. They tumbled around the floor, Pedro trying to feel for his gun on the floor. Sarah saw it and kicked it out of his reach. In the midst of the struggle a gun went off.

In the same instant, the front door was broken down and four heavily armed men wearing flak jackets entered. "Drop your weapons; raise your arms!"

CHAPTER 65

Andrew and Carla were relieved to see the judge walk out of the library behind Corey Davis. Carla went over to embrace Carson, saying, "I'm so sorry we left you behind; we just assumed you'd be safe. Thank God you're ok!" She hugged him again.

"I am fine, my dear, and who could've guessed Gonzales would break out. No need to stress yourself." Carson patted her arm.

"But I am worried about Sam," the judge said. "He freed Davis from Juan's grasp and ran off after him. That was, what, ten minutes ago, Corey?"

"About that; he ran out and told me to call 911. He had a gun, probably got it from the guards who were knocked out on the lawn. We can talk later about how Juan pulled it off, but I sure feel like a first class chump!"

"Don't," Carson said to Davis, "that cunning bastard had us all fooled!"

Andrew broke in, "The guards are on the way to Yale-New Haven hospital and we'd best get going if we hope to find Sam and track down Juan. I don't like the idea of Sam out there going it alone."

"Right! Let's go. Call us if you need us." Carla said.

"Do you want police back-up?" Davis asked.

"We'll call them if we have any action," Andrew said as they turned to leave. "Why don't you two head down to the Coast Guard station? Lock the house up tight and call us if anything else goes down."

***

Rogers was radioed by one of the sharpshooters. He was told, "Mission accomplished, Captain. We have two suspects, one with a serious gunshot wound, and we have the victim, Sarah. We are on the way to the ship as we speak."

The captain breathed a sigh of relief. Then he said to Hunter, "Radio Coop and instruct him to take the injured prisoner directly to the CG station. Make sure there's at least one ambulance there."

"And the other?" Hunter inquired.

"We'll put him in the hold with Carlos. We should probably think about getting blankets out for Sarah; she may be in shock."

Rogers soon heard a commotion coming in his direction. He looked through his binoculars and despite the hindrance of driving rain, he could see a small, blonde woman walking in step with one of the sharpshooters and apparently arguing with him.

Rogers commented, "Well, the victim seems fine."

Putting the binoculars away, Rogers watched as all seven arrived on the dock. The captain called orders through the megaphone. "Bring the girl and the uninjured suspect to the boat. The injured prisoner can go back in Coop's boat. The ambulance is on its way."

The guards did as they were instructed, and in a few moments, Sarah climbed onto the response boat. The captain was surprised she didn't seem relieved; instead she appeared to be combative. And despite the fact that she was draped in a soaking wet blanket, with strings of her wet blonde hair plastered to her forehead, she was beautiful.

Sarah held out her hand to the captain, saying, "I'm so appreciative for the rescue; thank you so much." She paused, "But the man you have in handcuffs, getting on the boat now, is not a villain; he saved me, and I intend to do the same for him."

"Sarah, you're welcome; I'm so glad we got to you in time. And I'm sure you have a story to tell. We're just following orders; we can get this straightened out once we reach shore. We'll be headed out now," Rogers informed her.

Jesus was brought on board, and taken below deck. Sarah tried to follow, but the first mate restrained her.

"I'm telling you, Jesus is my friend; he saved me!" Sarah said, trying to push by.

James calmly took Sarah's arm and said, "Look, I know you're upset, but we will get this sorted out. So please, be seated. Would you like a blanket?" Hunter asked.

"Yes, thank you," Sarah replied, dropping the wet cover and accepting a dry blanket. "I got a bit wet out there". Then she yelled down the stairs to Jesus, "I won't forget you, Jesus! I'll get you released, I promise."

She turned to see a skeptical look on Hunter's face. "My father is a federal judge; I think he will help to get this sorted."

***

Carla and Andrew were on the road, looking for Sam and Juan, hoping they were in the same general area. The judge had left for the Coast Guard station with Davis as they were leaving the house. They were both armed with guns from Carson's collection.

This time, Andrew drove while Carla kept up a vigilant lookout. They drove slowly through the streets surrounding the judge's house. They knew Gonzales had a head start, with Sam in hot pursuit.

As dawn crept in, the rain and wind continued, but now with less force. Carla had listened to a recent weather report that predicted the storm would move out of the area by day's end. Though still dark and cloudy, the early morning light gave them better visibility. Carla worried that Gonzales would now be more likely to hide out somewhere.

She voiced her concerns to Andrew, "I don't know where we can go with this; Juan's certain to be hiding, now that daylight is here. You don't suppose he'd double back to the judge's house, do you? At least it's all locked up now."

"But he already knows his way around there," Andrew said.

"Hmm, now that I think about it that may be exactly where he's going. These big houses around here are sure to have alarm systems and cameras…"

"So, we go back?" Andrew asked.

"Why not?" Carla answered. "It's better than no plan."

CHAPTER 66

Sam stayed in the shadows when the motion sensor light had gone on, illuminating Gonzales. His bright yellow slicker made him quite hard to miss, so he was forced to stay back.

He watched as Juan hurried towards the tree line that separated houses from one another.

Keeping in shadow, Sam was able to follow Gonzales; he had to follow from a distance or the street smart Juan would disappear in a flash. If only he could get close enough to get off a shot, to wound him.

Sam continued to follow. He'd thought Gonzales had a plan as he retreated, but now it appeared he was headed back to the judge's house. This alarmed Sam, but he was sure the judge would be safe this time.

***

At the Coast Guard station, Rory watched and waited anxiously, grasping Marc's arm tightly as the first response boat came toward shore. She could see, barely, that another boat was following it. The first boat was definitely going faster. Rory prayed Sarah was safely on that boat.

The scream of a siren filled the air and Rory turned to see an ambulance race toward the dock. Oh God, did that mean someone was hurt? Rory and Marc traded looks of alarm. A police squad car pulled up behind the ambulance and two officers got out to converse with the medics.

Rory watched as the lead response boat docked. Two men dressed in flak jackets carried a stretcher to the waiting ambulance. The man on the stretcher was put into the back of the ambulance and two officers got in with him. The ambulance took off, sirens blaring.

There were no more passengers departing the ship. Rory looked at Marc and said, "Well, I hope that means Sarah isn't hurt, and since the police went with the ambulance, it must be one of the bad guys."

"We should know soon," Marc answered. "The next boat is coming in."

Rory looked around anxiously, "And the judge isn't here yet! Oh Jeez, what can we tell Sarah?"

"We'll deal with it when it happens," Marc answered. "First order of business is getting Sarah here safe!"

The second boat pulled slowly into the dock; there seemed to be no urgency this time and it took a while for the passengers to disembark. Rory noticed that another squad car had pulled up next to the dock.

Two men, appearing to be Hispanic, Rory thought, were escorted by armed men wearing flak jackets. The two prisoners were delivered to the police and put in the cruiser.

Rory watched, breathless, as she waited for a sign of Sarah.

She didn't have long to wait. Sarah emerged from the boat and ran down to shore. Then she walked up to the police cruiser and banged on the driver-side window. Rory could hear her yelling, but couldn't understand what she was saying. She smiled at Marc, saying, "Well, it looks like Sarah's just fine." Still, tears began to form in Rory's eyes.

Rory turned at the sound of a vehicle close by, and was stunned to see the judge emerge from his Lexus, driven by one of his marshals. She ran to Carson, pointing at Sarah, "She just got in!"

Carson Justice took off like a bolt running towards his daughter, arms outstretched. When she saw him, she closed the gap between them and rushed into his arms. "Daddy, Daddy! I love you!"

The judge hugged her so tightly it seemed he would never let go. He whispered something in her ear, and both of them were crying. They seemed oblivious to the rain and wind.

Sarah then turned back to the police car, pulling her father with her. There was a long discussion, which Rory couldn't hear, but it appeared to mollify Sarah.

Arms around each other, Sarah and her father made their way to Rory and Marc.

"Thank God!" Rory said, as she pulled Sarah into an embrace, "My God, you're really here! Our prayers were answered."

"I'll say," said Marc, giving Sarah a hug.

"Oh my God! You guys are a sight for sore eyes; I knew I could count on you to find me!" Sarah was smiling, but began to look around anxiously. "Where's Sam?" she asked.

Her father answered, "Your fine young man is out looking for a fugitive. He ran off before I could thank him for saving my life."

CHAPTER 67

It seemed pretty clear to Sam that Gonzales was headed back to the judge's house, so he slowed his pace; no need to be caught-out by Juan at this point. He kept back further and stayed in the shelter of trees.

Closing in on the judge's house, Sam saw Juan disappear around a corner, and then he didn't see him at all. He ran to where he'd last seen Juan and looked around in all directions; no Gonzales.

Fuck, he knew I was behind him the whole time! And that was the last thought he had before he felt a vicious blow to the back of his head.

***

Juan smiled as he walked away from where he'd stashed Sam under some bushes. He was home free, well, almost. He just needed to get a car, any car would do…but he couldn't take the official federal car he'd arrived in. And he couldn't steal one from this neighborhood. Or could he? That was an idea so bizarre, so unlikely, that it just might work. The last place they would look would be the judge's house.

Before coming in to the Judge's house, Gonzales had hidden in the bushes, watching several cars leave. He'd heard them talking about reuniting with Sarah at the dock. He assumed that by now, the Judge had joined that group and no one was home.

He went back into the judge's yard the same way he'd come out, through the opening left by rusted metal. As for his mother, the feds had been fooled into believing he cared; well, he did care, after all she was his Madre. But all she did was harp on him about the evils of the cartel, and she prayed for him. He had to make a choice. He cared about power and money, the two went together. He'd paid his dues in jail, it was time he enjoyed what he'd worked so hard for. And he had given his mother the freedom of leaving Mexico. He felt that was sufficient.

Gonzales was behind the judge's house now and all was quiet. The detached garage sat out back. One of the doors to the garage was gaping open; he approached with caution. Moving slowly closer, he peered through a window and saw that one space was empty, but two other cars remained.

He chose the older Camry, because there were so many on the road. The Jaguar, which he'd have loved to take, was too risky. Besides, he'd have one of his own once this was over.

Checking in every direction and seeing nothing, Juan went into the garage and got into the driver's seat, preparing to hot-wire the car.

***

Carla and Andrew had been sitting out in front of the judge's house. They were beginning to wonder if they'd made the right call, or if they were just wasting time.

Andrew was getting antsy, he needed to move. He said to Carla, "You stay here, while I go back around the house again; maybe we missed something. I just need to check before we move on."

"Ok, be careful! You know who we're dealing with," Carla warned. "Are you sure you don't want me to back you up?"

"Stay here and keep your eyes open. If I'm not back in five minutes, then you can come, quietly, ok?" Andrew asked.

"Yes, check your watch; I have seven a.m. on the dot," Carla reported.

"Me, too," Andrew said as he left, moving slowly towards the back of the house. As before, he saw no sign of the house having been entered. So much for that, he thought. Then he heard a small sound. He listened intently; it seemed to be coming from the garage. His antennae were up as he approached the building. He could see one of the doors stood open, as it had before. He still heard a sound, a quiet, scraping sort of sound, and now he was sure it was coming from the garage.

Andrew stood, rooted to the spot, trying to figure out what to do next. He took a chance and looked through a window; he could see someone sitting in the driver's seat of one of the cars, leaning over, intent on his task.

It had to be Gonzales, and it didn't take much imagination to figure he was hot-wiring the car, something every teen-aged gang banger knew how to do. But it seemed to be taking him more time than it should have. Now Milano could see he was banging on the steering wheel, and it was Juan. He had to make a move now!

Standing behind the open door, Andrew took a stone and threw it in the direction of the car. As expected, Juan got out of the car and, gun in hand, looked around in every direction. Andrew could feel him coming to look behind the door, and he was ready. Andrew kicked at the door, hitting Juan, but failing to knock his gun loose.

"You're done, Gonzales, drop it!" Milano commanded.

Juan appeared to be complying, but ducked and went for Andrew's legs, knocking him down. Both men still had their guns, and began rolling on the ground, trying to gain the advantage. Milano was big and strong, but was barely holding on...

Just then, a gunshot rang out.

CHAPTER 68

Back at the Coast Guard station, Sarah and her father had reached a compromise. The New Haven police would take Jesus to the station, as they'd been instructed. He and Sarah would meet them there, after she'd been checked out by Carson's physician. Sarah had agreed to give the police a full account of the kidnapping. The FBI would be there as well, and would no doubt take over the case.

Marc and Rory decided to follow them to the station. There was nothing they could do at this point. She called the twins and spoke with Kate, told her the good news and said they'd be staying in Branford for a few days.

Then she called Blake and told him all that had happened.

"Sounds like you've been up all night; you must be exhausted," Blake said.

"I am, but in a good way. Call you later, Bye."

***

Chief Mayer awoke early, after a fitful night. The case that had consumed him was still on his mind. He wondered if it was too early to call the judge. Oh well, the worst he could do was not answer. So he punched in the number and waited.

The judge answered immediately. "Good morning, Chief Mayer; what can I do for you?"

He sounded chipper, so it must be good news. "I just wanted to know how it's going. Did you find Sarah?"

"Yes I did!" he said. "I can't believe my good fortune, but she's sitting next to me right now!"

"Thank God! I'm so happy for you. We need to talk business at some point, but now is probably not the time. Maybe you can call me later?" Mayer asked.

"I'll do that, for sure," Carson said. "I really appreciate all your hard work."

"Really glad things worked out," the chief answered. "By the way, how is Sarah?"

"She just passed her physical; my own doctor saw her, and apart from being a bit dehydrated, she's doing very well. Thanks for asking. We'll talk later."

When he got off the phone, Carson looked at Sarah. "Are you feeling ok?"

"I'm feeling fine, just tired and stinky; I'm looking forward to going home."

"Good, I'm glad, we'll head home as soon as you've given your statement," Carson replied. "I need to make some calls now."

"Sure, Dad," Sarah said, leaning her head on his shoulder.

Carson called headquarters, and was put through to the director. "Howard, good morning, Carson here." The judge listened as the director congratulated him on Sarah's safe return. Then he said, "Pedro Lopez, one of the main actors in this kidnapping, is on his way to Yale-New Haven Hospital. I'm asking that you send three of your best to the hospital at once. This man cannot be underestimated, please make sure they understand that. Thanks, bye." Carson looked down at Sarah, sleeping against his shoulder. He was overcome by a deep feeling of love and contentment.

CHAPTER 69

Juan grabbed the back of his leg, where Carla's bullet had hit; it was oozing blood.

Milano rolled out of Gonzales's reach, kicking away the gun Juan had dropped.

"Good work, Carla!" Andrew shouted, as he trained his gun on the wounded man. "Cuff him, quick and then get an ambulance."

Carla moved swiftly to Juan's side and pulled his arm away from the wound, then took the other arm and pulled them behind his back, cuffing him.

Juan winced, and complained, "They're too tight! Gimme' a break!"

Carla ignored him and called 911. Within minutes, they heard the wail of a siren. The ambulance arrived, along with two New Haven squad cars.

Walking around to the front to meet them, Carla opened the gate and directed them to where Gonzales lay. She spoke with the police as the medics loaded Juan into the ambulance. "Can you please escort the ambulance to the hospital; we'll ride with the suspect. This is a Federal case, but we'd welcome your help."

"OK, you got it," Officer Anderson said. "See you at the hospital."

Inside the ambulance Carla and Andrew sat uncomfortably, while the medics worked to stabilize the combative patient.

Carla said, "I'll call the judge, oh, wait! We don't know where Sam is! And I'm damn sure Gonzales isn't talking."

"You got that right!" Gonzales laughed.

Carla moved closer to Andrew and whispered, "He's a little too damn cocky for a man in his position; I think there's still someone out there. We need to look in his pockets."

Milano took one of the EMT's aside and said, "We need those pants you just cut off him and when you're done with him, we need to go through everything."

The EMT picked up the pants from the floor and handed them to Andrew. He went through the pockets and found a cell phone, which he handed to Carla. The first thing Carla did was to remove the battery. "Mind if I put this in your fridge until we get there?" Carla asked the EMT. He nodded and she handed it to him to deposit in the small refrigerated unit.

She watched Gonzales closely as the phone was deactivated. He had tensed up considerably, and did not take his eyes off the phone. Carla felt sure her hunch had been correct. She wondered, where did he get the cell phone? And were there others waiting for him? She knew there was more going on than met the eye. Even with all the suspects they'd taken into custody, there could still be more out there.

Milano looked at Carla, as if reading her mind, and mouthed, "We need to keep alert."

Carla nodded and then remembered that she'd planned to call the judge. She did so now, turning her back from Juan and speaking quietly into the phone.

She learned that Carson and Sarah had just arrived at the New Haven police station, where they'd be occupied for a while. Carson, too, was concerned about Sam, but didn't want to alarm Sarah. He told her he would take Marc and Rory aside and ask them to look for Sam.

"In the meantime," the judge told Carla, "do not, under any circumstances, let that man out of your sight. I've already sent over some marshals to guard Pedro, and I'll send more to relieve you. I'm calling the hospital director and asking for an isolated room where we can put both Pedro and Juan under guard, away from the rest of the patients."

***

Marc and Rory were relieved to be out looking for Sam, they were very concerned for his welfare. They'd been told to search the area near the judge's house, but had no more to go on.

"I just hope we're not too late," Marc said, gripping the steering wheel.

"Me, too, especially since Carla is worried about there being other perps on the loose!

Christ, how big is this operation?" Rory asked.

"Well," Marc answered, "I think we agreed from the beginning that a larger than average force had to be behind it. And with several suspects in custody, it's possible the cartel sent in replacements."

"That's if the original perps were willing to admit defeat. I'm just not sure they would let the kingpins know they failed, for fear of retribution. They all seem to be in fear of 'Numero Uno.'"

Marc had been driving slowly down the side streets near the judge's house. Rory resumed looking intently out the window.

When they'd driven about a half mile from the judge's house, Rory suggested, "Maybe we should go in the other direction for a while."

"Just what I was thinking," Marc said. "Now, if you were Sam, and able to move around, where would you go?"

"Probably back to the judge's house," Rory reasoned. "So?"

"So, why don't we restrict our search to streets closest to the judge's house?"

"Do you think we should go on foot?" Rory asked. "Then we can look around better."

"Good idea," Marc agreed, as he pulled over and parked not far from the house.

***

Carson was sitting in an office at the police station with Sarah. At his suggestion, the FBI had been called in. They were now questioning Sarah, while in a holding cell, Jesus, separated from Carlos, was speaking with another FBI agent.

Carson had asked that any Intel Jesus gave be immediately sent to the FBI bureau chief, Sayres, for verification. Sayres had passed this directive on to the agents. If Jesus's Intel was corroborated, he could be taken to the safe house, where Gonzales's mother was. The FBI would gladly give him immunity for any legit information.

Now, that was a can of worms, thought Carson. How would Gonzales's mother react to her son's escape and recapture, he wondered. Obviously, Juan was no longer eligible for the WPP, but he'd been very close to freedom. Why had he jeopardized it? Carson was left to conclude there must be others, 'out there' ready to spirit him away. And did they have Sam? The thought made the judge's blood run cold.

Just then, Carson's cell phone buzzed; he left the office to take the call.

"Marc! What do you have?" Carson waited anxiously for the answer. Then he tapped on the window to get Sarah's attention, a wide smile on his face.

CHAPTER 70

Rory and Marc dropped Sam off at the New Haven police station, after they'd had him checked out in the ER. Rory was overcome with fatigue. Sam's head had been bandaged, but miraculously, he didn't sustain a concussion.

She asked Marc to drive to the inn where Sam was staying, where she planned to sleep for the rest of the day.

As Marc drove, Rory thought over the unsettling, but ultimately rewarding night. Finally, she could let her guard down. It had been an incredibly touching scene when Sarah and Sam first laid eyes on each other. They'd hugged and cried and kissed, with expressions of euphoria on their faces.

Arriving at Kelsey House, the inn on the sound where Sam was staying, Rory wearily tumbled out of the car.

Marc and Rory introduced themselves to the owners, Sue and Ken. They confirmed there was an open room, and it would be ready in a matter of minutes. Sue offered them breakfast.

"That sounds wonderful!" Rory said. "But hold the coffee."

***

Carla and Andrew arrived at the Yale-New Haven hospital, just as four other marshals were entering the building. Andrew went to speak to them. The marshals informed him the hospital was setting the two suspects up in the "penthouse," usually reserved for their famous patients. In this case, it was their infamous patients, Andrew thought with wry humor.

He came back to tell Carla. While the EMT's removed Juan from the ambulance, they walked with them. Before leaving the ambulance, Juan had been secured to the gurney. Nevertheless, both Carla and Andrew had their guns at the ready.

They got into the elevator and went up to the top floor. Andrew noticed that the floor number was not listed, and a key was required to get to that floor. As the doors opened, two marshals met them and escorted the entourage to Juan's room. He did not need major surgery, as the bullet had passed cleanly through his leg, but would be examined soon.

Before he was released from the gurney, his hands were cuffed in front. Once in the bed, his body was again secured to the bed. He was administered a morphine drip for pain. It also helped to keep the patient sedated.

Carla and Andrew sat in the spacious room. Juan's belongings, including the phone—which was in a cold pack to prevent it sending signals—were in front of them. They found a wad of cash stashed in his underwear. They counted over two-thousand American dollars.

Andrew left the room to phone the judge for further instructions. He found Carson in a state of excitement. His relief at finding Sarah was evident. And, Andrew was happy to hear, Sam had been found by Rory and Marc and was with Sarah now. Though he hated to, Andrew had to break the mood to discuss business.

"I'm so happy things have worked out, Carson, and I'm sorry, but we still have some other concerns. We have Gonzales at the hospital now and the place seems secure. We've searched his belongings, and in addition to a cell phone, which has been deactivated, he had cash. We think the FBI might want to talk with him; there may be others in the area who he was planning to meet up with."

"Ok, that all seems probable; I'll have Sayres send over some agents, then maybe you and Carla want to take a break? Get some rest? And thank you so much for your loyalty; I couldn't have gotten through these past several days without you," the judge's voice trembled.

Before returning to Carla, Andrew looked into the other designated room. Two marshals he knew were sitting in chairs. "Hi guys!" Andrew said. "Where's Pedro?"

"He's still in the OR," Lew answered. "He's in pretty bad shape; he was shot by the guy who supposedly saved Sarah, one of his own."

"Hmm, anyone on guard outside the OR?" Andrew asked.

"Yeah, FBI, we're cooperating with them on this," the other marshal answered, a frown creasing his brow.

"I know how you feel," Andrew sympathized. "But look at it this way; these are very bad dudes we're guarding. Isn't it good to be able to share the blame if anything goes wrong?"

Both marshals chuckled, "When you put it that way…" Lew said.

"Ok, got to get back to my partner; we'll be gone as soon as the feebs get here. See ya'!"

When he went into the room, it appeared that Juan was sleeping, and Carla had a speculative look on her face.

"What's up?" Andrew asked. "I can always tell when you're in deep thought."

She walked out of the room and motioned for him to follow. "Perhaps I'm being paranoid, but I don't want to talk in earshot of that man. So, I've been pondering the cell phone, and wondering how it might be helpful in nabbing whoever it is waiting to help Juan escape."

"Oh, Jeez, really?" Andrew was surprised. "What are you thinking?"

"That maybe we should reactivate it and drive around to a new location. Or maybe look through the numbers in it. I don't know, but it could be useful." Carla said.

"I'm impressed!" Andrew said. "I can hardly put two thoughts together, given the hours we've been keeping. Why don't we dump this in the FBI's lap when they arrive? Carson said he's having more agents sent over. There are already two outside the OR where Pedro is being operated on."

"How do you know that?" Carla asked.

"Just talked to the two marshals down the hall. Apparently, Pedro's in bad shape."

"Can't say that I'm sorry to hear that. But, yeah, ok, I'll give it over to the agents when they arrive. Now that you mention it, I'm dog-tired; what day is it?" Carla joked.

***

At the New Haven police station, things were hopping. Sam sat next to Sarah, holding her hand as if he'd never let go. She was on a break from speaking to the agents.

Jesus had given an incredible amount of information to the agents he'd spoken with. One of them was on the phone with Sayres now. It might take some time before the director could verify the information. Jesus had been on a lie detector as he'd given his testimony, and he'd passed that test.

"So now we just have to wait," Sarah said, sighing. "They just have to let him go," Sarah said passionately. "Jesus was kind, and he helped me escape; he didn't lay a hand on me..." Sarah stopped suddenly.

Sam noticed and inferred the implication, but he didn't think this was the time to bring it up. Just thinking about what might have happened to Sarah made him crazy, but right now he just needed to be here with her. He squeezed her hand.

Sarah looked up at him, and he said, "I love you so much; I couldn't imagine life without you." He buried his face in her hair, just taking in the scent of her.

"Sorry, but I don't smell so good right now," Sarah tried for a joke, but there were tears in Sam's eyes.

"You always smell good to me; I can still smell Sarah," Sam said, smiling.

Carson came into the room. "It's a waiting game now, but the FBI gets quick results." He sat down next to Sarah, and took her other hand. They sat quietly for a moment; one of the officers called to Carson, "Phone call for you." Carson left to take the call.

***

Three FBI agents showed up at Juan's room. Prominently displaying their badges, they introduced themselves to Carla and Andrew.

They talked outside the door. The agents were young, wore their hair closely cropped and were business-like. They were, in Carla's mind, the quintessential stereotype of what the title 'FBI agent' called forth. But, she knew better than to think of people in stereotypes.

She told agents Lawrence and Rizzo her idea of using the cell phone to flush out any other perps who might still be out there. Rizzo seized on it first, "We do that often in our investigations," he said. "The phone can be very useful; we might be able to find the location of any others by using the numbers in the cell. We can do more than most people are aware of, but we like to keep it quiet."

Lawrence weighed in, "I'll call the bureau and ask them to send over one of our experts. We can assign it to him and he'll run with it."

"That sounds great," Carla said. "Now, we just have to make sure we have coverage before we leave." Looking at Andrew, she asked, "How many marshals do we have, total?"

"We're waiting for two to arrive and replace us, then, after we hand over the cell phone, we can leave." Andrew answered.

"Thank God!" Carla replied. "I think I could use a little shut-eye about now."

Chapter 71

She knew immediately from his expression the phone call had brought good news; he looked years younger.

"Spill it quick, Dad!" Sarah got straight to the point.

"Well," he took in a long breath, "there's so much! It's all good," he hastened to add. "Jesus's information was verified, in spades; he even gave out names of prominent business men, operating under the radar. He named two others who may still be in the area, waiting to spring Gonzales."

"So, I guess Jesus has earned the safe house and immunity?" Sarah asked.

"Absolutely, in fact the agents are eager to get him there soon; word travels fast!" Carson replied.

"I want to ride there with him," Sarah said adamantly.

"Well, you can't," Carson said with finality. "For your safety and his. The agents will be very cautious with him in their custody and the fewer people who know where the safe house is, the better for all concerned."

"Can I go and say goodbye to him? And I want Sam to meet him. Is that ok?" Sarah asked.

"Yes, but make it quick; they have to move fast." Carson answered. He led the way to the office where Jesus waited.

Sarah went straight to Jesus and hugged him. "Jesus, I will never, ever forget what you sacrificed for me, and I will see you whenever I can." She remembered Sam was with her and added, "This is my best friend, Sam."

Sam smiled and shook his hand, "You can't imagine what your courage means to me; I wish you the very best."

Jesus seemed overwhelmed, but managed to say, "I thank you, too. Sarah is wonderful girl!"

And then it was time for him to leave; three agents accompanied him out the back way.

Sarah stood, watching until he was out of sight. She took a deep breath and said to her father, "Let's go home, Daddy."

Taking Sam's hand and linking arms with her father, the three left, followed by Marshal Corey Davis and two FBI agents. Sarah guessed she'd have to get used to the entourage.

***

Sarah had taken a long, soaking bath, washed and dried her hair and had gone straight to bed. Luxuriating in lavender-scented sheets, she drifted off quickly.

Doreen, the judge's house keeper was back in charge, making sure everything was up to the judge's high standards. She had missed her week away. She'd been shocked to hear about the kidnapping but was so relieved it had all worked out.

After Sam left to go back to the inn, Carson went upstairs to take a nap. He had given Doreen orders to wake him by six p.m. As it turned out, he was awake by five; his nap had energized him. He still had work to do.

Showering and dressing quickly, he surprised Doreen by walking down the steps early

"Well Sir, I guess you don't need me to wake you up. You don't need to worry, everything's been seen to. Is there anything special Miss Sarah would like for dinner?"

"Oh, you know her, Doreen, she'll eat anything you make. But don't go to a lot of trouble; she may sleep through dinner and she may not have an appetite." He paused, then said, "I think I'd like to

284

have a dinner party Saturday night, to invite the many people who've helped with Sarah's rescue. Maybe twenty or so guests?"

"That's not a problem, Sir, just let me think on it and I'll work up some menus; you can choose what you like best."

"That sounds good, thanks Doreen. Of course, I'll have to run it by Sarah, see if she's up to it. She'll have the final say," the judge added.

He went to the desk in his library and looked at the list he'd made. He checked his cell to see if there were any messages. Surprisingly, there were none.

Carson called Sayres at FBI Headquarters. He learned they had a special agent tracking numbers that were in Gonzales's cell phone; Sayres thought they may be onto something. "You know, it was your marshal, Carla? I think it was she who made the suggestion to use the cell phone. She's pretty sharp!" Sayres added.

"Oh, she's plenty sharp; I'm very fortunate to have her as my marshal," the judge said, then added, "She likes her job, don't get any ideas!" He hung up, smiling.

CHAPTER 72

By eight p.m., Saturday, the dinner celebration was in full-swing. Carson marveled at the number of people who'd come. Of course, all of the FBI agents mingling in the crowd increased the number.

Sarah looked radiant. No one would've guessed the ordeal she'd been through in the last week. Had it been just a week? He couldn't fathom how much his life had changed in that short amount of time. He thought of his wife, Sondra, and how happy she would be that their Sarah was safe and Carson could now appreciate his daughter. Sarah was, he realized with surprise, very much like her mother. She had a will of steel; her ordeal had made her even stronger.

Rory and Marc broke into the judge's thoughts as they came to greet him warmly and thank him for inviting them. He chatted with them for a few minutes before deciding to circulate.

Carson noticed officers from different branches of law conferring with each other, and he joined them to see what he could find out. Apparently they had nabbed one possible suspect involved with Gonzales. They'd found him by using Gonzales's cell phone.

When Carson spotted Geneva, the forensics expert who'd been so kind to him after he'd seen the horrific picture of Sarah, he had to talk to her. "Geneva, so glad you could come."

"I'm so glad this turned out for the best, I'm very happy for you." Geneva smiled. "Although the evidence left behind will keep me busy for several weeks! It's all good, though."

"Come meet my daughter," Carson said to Geneva, and led her over to Sam and Sarah.

"I was wondering when you'd get around to us," Sarah said, joking. She extended her hand to Geneva, and said, "I'm Sarah, and this is my boyfriend, Sam."

"So nice to meet you," Geneva said. "It's good to have you safe!"

"Carson, I'll leave now, I don't want to monopolize you. Wonderful to meet you Sarah and Sam." And Geneva turned to go.

"Doreen did a great job on dinner," Sarah said.

"Yes, I've really missed her this past week; since the marshals were at the house, I told her I'd been called away on business. We couldn't let too many people in on what was going on."

"You should eat, Dad," Sarah said. "You've lost considerable weight since I last saw you."

"Didn't have much of an appetite," he mused. "But, now that you mention it, I am hungry."

Before he could get to the food, his cell phone buzzed. "Excuse me," Carson said to Sarah and Sam, turning away to take the call.

When he turned back, the two were looking at him expectantly.

"Dad, you look like you've seen a ghost, what happened?" Sarah asked, alarmed.

There was nothing but the truth to tell. Carson told them, "That was Sayres, FBI director. Pedro Lopez didn't make it; he never regained consciousness after surgery and died today."

Sarah closed her eyes, while a hint of sadness, followed by a look of supreme relief washed over her face like a tsunami.

EPILOGUE

Gardiners Bay, East Hampton
Early November

Sarah wasn't sure how she'd feel, coming back to the scene of the crime. Rob and Lisa had opened their cottage to the East Hampton crew who'd been involved in finding Sarah. It seemed like a cast of thousands, but Sarah knew there were probably under a hundred people.

Sarah had begun healing during the past several weeks, and Sam had been incredibly sweet and sensitive. He'd never asked her what Pedro had done to her. She would tell him, in time. Surprisingly, her father had taken her aside and told her about the photograph he'd received. He sobbed when he told her, and that act in itself, was a balm to Sarah.

She'd heard Jesus and Mrs. Gonzales were in the same safe house and got along very well. Juan's mother was appalled at what her son had done and wanted to be allowed to stay in The Witness Protection Program. Both Jesus and Maria Gonzales had lost people they loved and took refuge in each other.

Sam was driving, and Sarah looked over at him, aware of how just being in his presence calmed her. He'd been to East Hampton only once, when he mostly tried to avoid the police. He asked, "How much longer do you think?"

"What, are you a little kid?" she asked, teasing him.

"No, I'm just anxious to get there. You couldn't ask for a nicer day in November; it's perfect!"

Then, Sam asked, "Sarah, are you ok coming here?" He had a worried frown.

"I'm not sure…but I think I'll be ok with you along. Now, three streets up on your left, last turn," Sarah said.

Soon, they were turning into the crushed shell driveway next to the cottage. There were several cars already parked, and people were walking on the beach, and sitting out on the deck.

Sarah was scanning the crowd, looking for someone she knew, getting panicky. Then, she spotted Rory and Marc and breathed a sigh of relief.

Lisa came running out of the cottage, straight to Sarah, opening her car door and giving her a bear hug. She had tears in her eyes. "It's so good to see you, I'm sorry we couldn't come to Connecticut when your Dad had your homecoming dinner. You look wonderful!" Lisa said, holding her at arm's length.

"Thanks for having us all here, Lisa." Sarah said quietly, "It means a lot to me. Lisa, this is Sam," Sarah said, "He and my dad have helped me get through the aftermath. My dad is incredible; he's not the man I've told you about, not any more. As for Sam, he's still the wonderful man I've described."

Sam and Lisa hugged; they'd spoken to each other during the ordeal, but had never met.

Rob came out of the cottage, and joined the group, shaking hands with Sam and giving Sarah a hug. "I'm so glad you came," Rob said sincerely, "I'm happy you gave us another chance!"

After a pause, they all laughed and Sarah noticed some of the anxiety slip away.

"Come, get some food," Rob urged, "I'm manning the grill, and I'm good!"

Sarah noticed, suddenly, that she was hungry. She and Lisa walked into the cottage, arms around each other. Sam and Rob trailed behind, talking sports. Sarah smiled, knowing that Sam didn't know squat about sports, but he was a good bull-shitter, she thought.

They had lunch on the crowded deck. It was beautiful out here, Sarah thought. And the day couldn't be more perfect.

After lunch Sarah and Sam went to mingle with other guests who were walking and talking in groups on the beach.

Rory came over to give Sarah a hug. She sat and talked with her for a while. "I've met the most incredible people here; I had no idea how many people were involved. That's the chief over there, talking to the guy who sort of looks like Rob? Well, he played the part of Rob, as an undercover cop."

"I heard about him; the likeness is uncanny," Sarah said. "And there was a female cop who was supposed to be Lisa, is she here?" Sarah asked.

"Yep, she's the blond standing next to Brent," Rory informed her.

"But, she doesn't look like Lisa," Sarah said.

"She did, with a black wig on," Rory smiled. "You should ask her about that wig; much as she hated it, it saved her life."

"Wow! I bet that's a story," Sarah said.

Sarah and Sam made the rounds together, trying to talk with everyone. They approached the chief and his officers. Sam, a little embarrassed, apologized to the chief for his interference.

The chief replied, "You were quite a pain in the ass, but we survived." Holding his hand out to Sarah, the chief said, "We're delighted to have you safe!"

Sarah hugged him and thanked him, before they moved on to talk with others.

"So, I heard you were quite the bad boy! But, I understand, and I love you for trying."

Sarah noticed suddenly that everyone seemed to be drifting back to the deck. She said to Sam, "You think dessert is out?"

"Yeah, probably, let's go see," Sam agreed. "You know I can't miss that!"

Sarah thought she was mistaken when she saw her father on the deck; he'd said he couldn't come. She ran to him, "Dad, I thought you couldn't come," Sarah said hugging him.

"Really?" The judge said, "I wouldn't miss this for the world!" He looked at Sam and winked.

Sarah looked around for Sam, and found him, on one knee, holding a small box.

He didn't need to ask and she didn't need to answer, the smiles on their faces said it all.

About the Author

Jacquelyn Bishop lives in Media, a charming small town, not far from Philadelphia.

Though her formal training, at the bachelor and masters levels was in social services, her life-long dream was to write. And, having written her first novel, Death Sentence, she continued with this, her second.

Writing is a full-time job, she's discovered, but she finds time for walking, yoga, Zumba, and quality time with her grand-daughter, Lilia, who, at six, is a very wise little person.

Travel also takes up a good deal of time, especially visiting with friends and family in California.

ORDERING INFORMATION

Death Sentence by Jacki Bishop is available now at online booksellers.

To order additional copies of this and future books by Jacki Bishop, please use the contact information below:

Early Riser Publishing
P.O. Box 711
101 E. Baltimore Ave.
Media, PA 19063
www.JackiBishop.com
jaxstir@gmail.com

Thank you for reading this book. I would appreciate any and all reviews online. ~Jacki

www.ingramcontent.com/pod-product-compliance
Lightning Source LLC
Chambersburg PA
CBHW021328250626
47155CB00002B/634